A Merry Little
CHRISTMAS

Center Point
Large Print

**This Large Print Book carries the
Seal of Approval of N.A.V.H.**

A MERRY LITTLE
CHRISTMAS

Anita Higman

CENTER POINT LARGE PRINT
THORNDIKE, MAINE

This Center Point Large Print edition is published
in the year 2014 by arrangement with Summerside Press,
an imprint of Guideposts.

The text of this Large Print edition is unabridged.
In other aspects, this book may vary from the original edition.
Printed in the United States of America on permanent paper.
Set in 16-point Times New Roman type.

ISBN: 978-1-62899-337-0

Library of Congress Cataloging-in-Publication Data

Higman, Anita.
A merry little Christmas / Anita Higman. —
    Center Point Large Print edition.
    pages ; cm
Summary: "City meets country when Charlie offers to buy Franny's
Oklahoma farm on the condition that she stay long enough to teach him
the farming business. In the process, they discover what is truly
important"—Provided by publisher.
    ISBN 978-1-62899-337-0 (library binding : alk. paper)
    1. Single women—Fiction. 2. Large type books. 3. Christmas stories.
    I. Title.
PS3558.I374M47 2014
813'.54—dc23
                                                        2014030524

DEDICATION

To my beautiful daughter-in-law, Danielle.
You add such joy to our lives!
Always know that you are greatly loved.

ACKNOWLEDGMENTS

Much praise goes to Susan Downs for her wise editorial input, her encouragement, and her friendship, and to Connie Troyer for her editing expertise in making this novel a better read. Also many thanks to the other fine folks at Summerside Press who help to make my life wonderful, such as Rachel Meisel and Jason Rovenstine.

I'm indebted to my agent, Sandra Bishop, at MacGregor Literary Agency, for her solid advice and tireless support.

Gratitude goes to my brother, Jerry Breitling, for his help in checking my farm scenes for accuracy. Also, I want to thank Andrew Bland for his valuable assistance.

Any errors in the text are solely the fault of the author.

CHAPTER ONE

The Martin farm, Oklahoma, 1961

Franny's mother always said that if humans ever landed on the moon, the first thing they'd need was music. It was the one essential that made a place inhabitable—you know, to get through all those dark and lonely—not to mention unmarried and dateless—nights.

Franny sighed and turned up the dial on her transistor radio. Frank Sinatra's version of "Have Yourself a Merry Little Christmas" wooed its way over the airwaves like a slow kiss under the mistletoe. She swayed and sang along as she dumped the last of the slop into the troughs of her forty rambunctious hogs. Then she climbed up on the fence for a little swine soiree.

"You know, I can't wait to see who Dick Clark features next on *American Bandstand*, but now that I'm thirty-three, I guess I should be watching *The Lawrence Welk Show*. Right?" The hogs grunted their replies, but it wasn't anything worth repeating. "Honestly, you guys can be such boars." She chuckled to herself at her bad pun.

The fact was, Franny had a soft spot for her hogs, and with each season it was getting harder to sell off her herd. She felt like Fern in *Charlotte's*

9

Web. "Well, gotta go, little loves. You'll miss me wildly. But I have to attend to the cows and see about the eggs. Any more activities, and I'm gonna need a social secretary."

As the last musical ribbons of "Have Yourself a Merry Little Christmas" tied up like a bow, Franny hopped down on the other side of the pig fence, picked up her radio and slop bucket, and heaved a sigh. Christmas was coming, and it looked like she was going to spend the holidays alone. Again.

With that piteous little thought bobby-pinned to her mind, she turned around and came face-to-face with a man. A stranger! She let out a yelp loud enough to startle the man and arouse the poor hogs into a frothing frenzy. The bucket and radio went flying as Franny went slip-sliding onto the muddy ground.

The man reached out and caught the radio before it landed in the muck. He looked at her and winced. "I'm really sorry. I could only catch one of you." He stretched out his hand to lift her out of the mud.

"That's okay. I'm glad you caught the radio instead of me."

The stranger got her upright and steady again. Franny looked at her overalls and wool coat, which were covered in mud. She tried to brush off her clothes, but the thick sludge sort of fell in hunks like flattened Milk Duds.

"It was my fault," the man said. "You wouldn't have lost your footing if I hadn't scared you. I'm sorry."

The stranger offered her a little-boy shrug—even though he looked thirtyish—but Franny couldn't tell if it was an act of contrition or just an act. "Who are you, anyway?" She'd never been afraid of strangers before—never even locked her doors at night. Who did? But she wasn't accustomed to strangers appearing out of nowhere.

"I'm Charles . . . Charlie Landau."

Charlie. Good name. Even better brown eyes. He didn't quite have that James Dean look to make a woman lose all her senses, but it was close enough. "I'm Franny Martin. And how long have you been standing there watching me, Charlie Landau?"

"Long enough to know that you love music. *And* you talk to your pigs like they're family." His grin lifted one side of his mouth, but it was a guileless smirk, so she let him off the hook. For now.

Franny rested her mitten-covered hand over her heart. "Well, who doesn't love music? I mean, it's the artistic glue that holds the corners of the world together. It's our porch view of heaven. Without music, we'd be wallowing in the mire like these hogs." She glanced at her pigs. "Sorry, boys." Then she turned back to Charlie and added, "Without music we'd be less inspired, less human. Wouldn't we?" She stared at him, wondering if he thought she was crazy.

"Pretty impassioned speech." He grinned. "Like a politician . . . only believable."

Franny fiddled with the ends of her woolen head scarf, a little embarrassed that she'd gotten so carried away with a stranger. "I don't get many visitors out this way."

"I came to buy your farm." Charlie straightened his shoulders. "I have plenty of money, and I'll pay cash. I'm determined to be a farmer, you see."

Franny lifted her chin, studying him. "It's been for sale for almost twelve years. You *really* want this old ramshackle dirt farm with a hundred-year-old house? Just you and the coyotes, scraping along, trying to make a living?"

"Yes, I really do want to buy your farm. That's it."

"How did you find out about it?"

"Your Realtor had a small ad in one of the papers."

"Oh. Well, are you willing to pay me what I'm asking?" *Hmm.* Maybe Charlie would mention whether he had a wife.

"I saw the asking price." Charlie raised his chin a mite. "And I'm willing to pay you every penny. More if I have to."

More? Franny wondered if *he* were the crazy one. It was a lot of money, but then he looked well-off, dressed as he was in his tailored trousers and leather jacket. Certainly not country-boy clothes. She paused to take a peek at the dreams she'd folded away in the hope chest of her heart, remembering how she'd always longed to move to the city. It didn't take but a few seconds to pull them out, give them a good shake in the fresh air, and try them on again—only this time for real. The dream fit just fine.

"Well, then, Mr. Charlie Landau . . ." Franny's smile widened with every word. "I have to congratulate you on investing in a one-of-a-kind charming farmhouse, which sits on two-hundred-and-fifty acres of the finest Oklahoma farmland in the state . . . where the wheat crops rise to meet you, the sun shines always on your back, and the fatted cows just get fatter." Franny grimaced. "I think I just made a mess of an Irish blessing."

"I think you did." Charlie chuckled. And then he smiled at her—a devastating smile.

"All right." Franny pulled off her head scarf. She no longer needed it anyway. Charlie had made her forget all about the autumn chill. "How about a tour of the property and then a cup of coffee? I have the best: instant Folgers." She fluffed her hairdo.

"Do you have any Ovaltine?"

"No, but I can make you homemade hot chocolate." The deejay, fuzzing in and out on the radio, said something about Christmas and Brenda Lee, but Franny didn't absorb the

13

announcement. She'd gotten lost in the eyes of a man who'd just made the most romantic offer she'd ever heard—a way out of farming, a way to fulfill her ultimate dream to be closer to the music. The transistor whirred to life again like a tiny alien spacecraft, this time playing Brenda Lee's "Rockin' Around the Christmas Tree."

Charlie took a purposeful step toward her. "We can't miss this. It's got a great tempo. Know how to do the Swing?"

Franny cocked her head at him. "You're kidding. I'm covered in mud."

He shrugged and held out his arms. "Shall we?"

His spontaneity and smile were too charming to dismiss, so she latched onto Charlie's hands and they danced the Swing. As he spun her back and forth, their laughter rose up as bubbly as a freshly shaken bottle of soda pop. When the tune closed, another melody took its place. This time the deejay played Elvis Presley's "Blue Christmas." Franny stepped away from him, a little embarrassed that she'd gotten so carried away—after all, they'd only just met.

But Charlie held up his hands and said, "Who can say no to an Elvis classic?"

Franny moved toward him again and replied softly, "Well, that's what I've always said."

Then they melted into a slow dance to the smooth serenade of Elvis.

"Seems a mite early for holiday tunes. It's not even Thanksgiving yet."

She gazed up at him. "This deejay says it's never too early for a little Christmas music."

"Well, that's what I've always said." His grin warmed her all the way to her toes.

Along with the music and mirth, Franny wondered why, after all her lonely years on the farm, God would finally send a pleasant man with possibilities to her door just to have her life go full speed in the opposite direction.

CHAPTER TWO

Once their dancing wound down to a mutual gazing session, Franny broke away from Charlie's scrutiny. "How about a grand tour of the farm?"

"I'm more than ready."

"All right." Franny led Charlie toward the fields of winter wheat. She wished she'd taken the time over the years to paint and repair some of the older buildings, but it was too late for that now. Charlie would have to love the farm just as it was.

Franny showed him the creek, the barn, the chicken house, the windmill, a working outhouse for emergencies—which came with its own tarantula under the toilet-seat rim and was said to cure anyone of a sluggish constitution—a herd of beef cattle, two gardens, the brooder house, the orchard, and the farmhouse. Whew! No wonder she wanted to flee to the city!

About a hundred questions and answers later, they both settled in the kitchen with some hot chocolate. "So, what do you think? About the farm and the house?" Franny blew on her beverage but watched Charlie over her mug to get his immediate reaction.

"I think it's a one-of-a-kind, charming farmhouse, which sits on two-hundred-and-fifty acres of the finest Oklahoma farmland in the state."

Franny grinned.

"It's just what I need, actually. As I mentioned earlier, if I can make a profit, hopefully my father will see that I'm capable of running his enterprises."

She bobbed her marshmallows up and down with her spoon. "What enterprises?"

"Oh, scintillating businesses such as construction, pipeline operations, and oil-field equipment. That sort of thing." He looked bored with what he'd just said, but his eyes lit up when he added, "But ever since I was a kid I've been intrigued with farm life. You know . . . growing things for a living." His gaze darted around the kitchen and landed on a cluster of photographs of her parents. "Is this your mother and father?"

"Yes."

"They look happy." Charlie pointed to the

photograph at the end. "And I assume that's you next to them."

"That's me with pigtails and two of my Christmas presents, a Slinky and my first bicycle."

"Pretty adorable. And who's the colored gentleman standing next to you?"

"That's George Hughes. We called him Uncle George." Franny paused. "He was our farmhand, but after a few years he became like family to us. At Christmastime he used to dress up like Santa Claus and give us all homemade gifts." She waited for Charlie to disapprove, like so many people had in the past, but he merely nodded.

"I hope you don't miss this place too much," he said. "It seems like a wonderful home."

"I grew up in this house. It was always full of laughter." Franny ran her finger around the rim of her mug. "But my parents died in an accident over a decade ago." She looked at him. "Now I'm surrounded by faded memories and yellowed photographs on the wall. But after all these years there are traces here and there of love. I can still feel it."

"Sounds like a sweet and sad love song."

"Yeah? Maybe I should write it down." Franny smiled, feeling a wistful tug at her heart. "Sometimes I think in lyrics."

Charlie leaned toward her. "So how did your father and mother pass away?"

Franny took a sip of her cocoa, but it was still

too hot. With very little encouragement, the scene of her parents' death played in her mind. "We were having stormy weather that day, and we'd gone down into the cellar. But the door kept banging open, so Daddy went up to secure it. And Momma followed behind him—to help him, I guess. Anyway, in that brief moment, an elm tree crashed through our enclosed porch. The tree fell on the cellar door and killed them instantly."

Charlie reached out to her but didn't touch her hand. "I'm so sorry, Franny."

"It was a long time ago."

"But it must have been hard on you. How did you ever get over it?"

"Some part of me recovered, but I'm convinced there's another part of me that will never mend. Anyway, I've never been back in that cellar since that day. I always use the hall closet when there's a storm."

"It's pretty heavy. And you must have been very young at the time."

"I was eighteen."

Charlie blew on his cocoa and took a cautious sip. "So you stayed. But I'm curious. How did you run a farm all by yourself? You were just a kid."

"Well, the neighbors all knew what had happened. And even though it was unusual for a girl to run a farm, I didn't want to leave my home. So, some of the neighbors said they'd give me a hand with the work for a while until I could do for myself. I never did plant and harvest the wheat, though. I've always leased the land out to my closest neighbor, and we share the profits from the harvest. But after a few years, I realized that I didn't want to do this for the rest of my life. So that's when I put the farm up for sale."

Charlie's gaze lowered to her left hand. "And you didn't get married? At least a man could have helped you with the chores."

"Yes, a husband would have come in handy, since I've had backaches for a decade." Franny grinned. "But I have this little problem."

"And what is that?"

"I want to marry for love." It wasn't necessary to look at Charlie's empty ring finger. It was the first thing Franny had looked for when they were dancing. "I see you never married?"

"Never found it . . . love, that is. I'm thirty-five, and nothing's ever happened. Nothing real, that is."

"Real?"

"I've met lots of women, but I'm beginning to think it's impossible to find love. But then, who really knows the interworkings of romantic love except God, who invented it?"

Charlie's comment surprised her. He wasn't at all shallow. But for someone as appealing as Charlie, she could easily imagine love arriving at his door in a golden coach. "You'll find out soon enough that most men around here don't have many romantic notions about love. They think of women in practical terms. They're valuable for four things: cooking, cleaning, keeping the house . . ." She held up her fingers, counting. "Well, and for making lots of babies, especially boys to help with the farming." Heat rose in Franny's face, and she chuckled at herself. *Nonsense.* It was the 1960s, not the '30s. "So, I'm assuming you'll want to farm your own land and not lease it out as I do. Do you know about plowing and planting and harvesting wheat?"

"No."

"Do you know how to operate machinery?"

Charlie shifted in his chair. "Uh, no."

"Or about animal husbandry?"

He looked bemused. "That doesn't sound quite right."

Franny chuckled. "Guess you weren't in FFA."

"I don't think so." Charlie rested his thumb on his chin. "But I was a scout leader one time. Does that count?"

"I don't think so." Franny grinned.

"So what's FFA?"

Oh dear. "It's Future Farmers of America." Franny wondered if it were ethical to sell the farm to Charlie. He was likely to perish in an accident on his first day on the job. Or he could be injured. Fortunately, the local doctor only charged a dollar for house calls. "I must warn you, there's a lot to know about farming. What you don't know can kill you . . . or, at the very least, put you in the poorhouse."

"I'm not scared of dying, and I'm not worried about the poorhouse."

"But there's a lot to know. You'll need to keep records on the hogs—when they're bred and when they'll give birth. That way you'll be ready and the sows won't have their babies in the field. There are recipes for their various feeds, depending on how old they are. You'll need to know—"

"Doesn't sound *too* impossible. Does it?"

"Yes, but there are hundreds of things like this to know."

"I'll just hire a farmhand." Charlie shrugged. "Once I get into town, I'm sure I can find some-one—pay somebody to help me out."

"Honestly, I've never heard of anybody wanting to call himself a farmer that badly. You know, to hire someone else to do the work." Franny hated to be a dream killer, but the more she talked to Charlie, the more he didn't sound like farmer material.

Charlie looked at her as if he were peering over reading glasses. "You know, you're not like other women I know."

What did that have to do with anything? "True. Other women don't have pig manure under their fingernails."

Charlie chuckled. "I mean that you're different in the way you express yourself. And you have a

21

boy's haircut, kind of like Audrey Hepburn in . . . what's the movie?"

"*Roman Holiday*?"

"Yeah. I like it. Unfortunately, most of the women I know are somehow convinced they've got to look just like Jacqueline Kennedy. They all look the same to me . . . carbon copies."

"A fancy bouffant just doesn't work out here. All that ratting and spraying and primping—*oof!*" Franny blew her bangs off her forehead. "The pigs wouldn't appreciate it anyway." She shook her finger. "But now that you'll be buying the farm and I'll finally move to the city, maybe I'll change my style. Pluck my eyebrows and grow out my hair." She raised her shoulder in a shrug, hoping it came off as feminine. Working on the farm all day didn't give her much time to practice her flirting skills.

"I like your style—just the way it is."

His words seemed cozy and familiar, and the sound of his voice made Franny feel as though she'd eaten a red-hot chili pepper.

Charlie played with the cloth napkin. "You mentioned moving to the city, but what are you looking for?"

"A life." She took a swig of her cocoa and then wiped off her marshmallow mustache with the back of her hand.

"Oh? Are you sure about that?"

She puckered her face. "Well, I'm surer of

making it in the city than *you* are in farming."

He laughed. "All right. That's funny. *You're funny.*"

Franny relaxed her expression. She hoped he meant that she was funny in an adorable way and not a clownish sort of way. His brown eyes offered a mellow gaze. She broke the connection by looking down into her brew.

Even though they'd just met, she knew Charlie had the power to make her forget about leaving. But Oklahoma City would have plenty of fine Christian men to choose from. And most of all, there'd be lots of radio stations where she could be close to the magic—close to the music. She would apply at every radio station there. Beg if she had to. And if there weren't any openings for a deejay, she'd be a receptionist until something opened up. God would make a way. After all, He was the one who'd put the music in her soul.

Charlie's mug struck the table, which startled her back to the present. "By the way, my father has an attorney. They'll take care of the transaction right away. That is, if it's all right with you."

"Sure," Franny said, "that's fine." Charlie sounded so formal all of a sudden. So detached and businesslike.

He laced his fingers together as if he were trying to hold onto something. "By the way, you'll know soon enough, I guess. My father is

Albert . . . Landau." He looked uncomfortable, as if he were sitting on a prickly pear.

Oh my. Charlie had mentioned his last name, but Franny never suspected he was from *the* Landau family of Oklahoma City. "Surely you don't mean . . ." She knew her mouth was open, so she made a conscious effort to close it.

"I do. It's him. I'm sorry." Charlie shot down the last of his cocoa and moved the mug across the table.

"You don't have to apologize." No wonder Charlie wore such luxurious clothes. And that explained why there was a Rolls-Royce motorcar parked in the yard. And why he didn't care about how much the farm cost. Charlie could easily buy a vocation. From what the newspapers wrote, he came from one of the richest families in Oklahoma.

"Franny, are you still with me?"

She nodded. That was about all she could manage at the moment.

CHAPTER THREE

Charlie slid his hands toward hers, which were now bonded to the dinette table, but he stopped just shy of touching her fingers. "Please don't let this news change anything between us."

Franny's skin felt as if it were covered in

24

ants. "You don't have to worry about anything changing, Charlie, since there's nothing between us." Immediately after the words flowed out of her mouth, she regretted them. She was far too impulsive sometimes, and what she'd said wasn't true anyway.

Charlie pulled back. "Well, I thought we were sort of becoming friends."

"I don't know why I said that. Please know that we can always be friends."

"Thank you."

"But I'm sure you have plenty of friends, especially lady friends. I mean, you must be used to a huge social circle. You know, dinners and fancy parties." What must he think of her humble abode? And that huge pile of S&H Green Stamps on the table? Bet the Landaus didn't sit around getting their tongues gummy from licking hundreds of Green Stamps. Did her surroundings look like the city dump to him? He surely wasn't used to cracked wallpaper, yellowed linoleum, or rusty metal kitchen cabinetry. How would he live in such a crude farmhouse with these plain furnishings after a life of luxury?

Charlie fingered his gold watch. "Looking from the outside in, I appear to have it all. But mostly my life's been as hard as iron and just as cold."

"When you have everything, it's hard to imagine how life can be the way you describe it." Franny shook her head, touching her fingers to her forehead. "What's the matter with me? That sounded so—"

"It's all right." He put up his hands. "I've heard that before. What people don't realize is . . . well, money doesn't come without strings, even for the children in the family. *Especially* for the children in the family. Lots of pressure. Lots of eyes on me, watching my every move."

Franny glanced out the kitchen window. "Is someone watching us now?"

Charlie chuckled. "No. I just mean in general. But I get inspected often enough that it makes good clean living as you know it almost impossible."

"Well, looking from the outside, my life may *look* good and clean until I start scooping manure out of the chicken house, dehorning the cattle, and giving cows their medicine in unmentionable places."

"Yeah." Charlie smiled. "But I'd rather do all that than give my father updates on my failures. You see, he wants me to run his company someday, but he won't let me do that until I make a go of an enterprise on my own. He won't trust me otherwise. Every young man wants to please his father, no matter how difficult it might be."

Charlie leaned back in his chair. "The rest of the story is . . . over the years my father has set me up in a variety of businesses. I've been unsuccessful at every one of them. Because of all my past failings, I also see this as a personal challenge."

"It's hard to imagine you failing at anything. You seem so with-it to me."

He folded his arms against his chest. "I put on a quite a show, don't I?"

"But I'm certain God has given you a talent." Franny leaned on the table, her palm cupping her cheek. "Perhaps you just haven't found it yet."

"Well, like you, I've always loved music."

"Really?"

"I play the guitar and piano some, but I always wish I could do better."

Franny tugged on a strand of her hair. "How marvelous, to play."

"Unfortunately, my father doesn't see it that way." Charlie looked as though he wanted to say more but stared at his hands instead.

Franny had intended to ask him why he wanted a farm that was a two-hour drive from Oklahoma City, but maybe he'd just answered her question. "In the papers, I read that your father is a philanthropist, a good man. I just assumed he had a happy family."

"Assumptions can be such runaway fantasies."

"What is it like to live inside the Landau family—you know, with that kind of burden of expectation?"

"It isn't a storybook life," Charlie said. "I can tell you that."

"I'm sorry."

"I've survived it so far, but thanks. Sympathy isn't something many people feel toward the Landaus."

Franny had only known a small version of that kind of family pressure, but in the end, she knew her parents would want her to be happy, even if it meant selling the farm. She had to admit, though, now that she really was leaving, she felt some anxiety along with the excitement. Maybe that's why she'd kept the sale price high all those years—she was a little afraid of the bigger life that lay beyond her small world.

Charlie dipped his head and caught her gaze. "You seem to be in outer space with your thoughts."

"I was. Funny how new people can sometimes make a person see what was there all along, even if she couldn't see it before. Does that make sense?" Franny asked.

"Yes, it does."

While Franny absorbed the revelations, her dog, Henry, lumbered over to them. "Hey there, boy. Where have you been?" She ruffled his ears with affection and then looked at Charlie. "Henry's been my best chum for a long time. He's not moving as fast these days. He's got arthritis, and he mostly stays in the house, but he's still my Henry. Aren't you, boy?"

The dog wagged his tail and then ambled over to Charlie to give him a sniff or two.

Charlie reached down and scratched him behind the ears. Henry nudged his pocket. "Sorry, boy. Are you looking for a treat?"

"Sometimes my father would put a small rawhide chew in his pocket and Henry would try to nudge it out. Ever since then, he's always enjoyed the game as much as the treat."

Henry curled up on the rope rug next to Charlie and looked up at him through shaggy tufts of gray hair. His black eyes seemed a little forlorn, but then Henry lived with sad eyes most of the time. It was as if he too hadn't fully recovered from the storm that had changed their lives. "He must like you, to sit next to you."

"It's nice to be liked." Charlie turned his focus from the dog back to Franny. "I need to ask you something."

"Henry doesn't come with the farm, if that's what you're wanting."

Charlie grinned. "No. I was going to ask you something else."

"What is it?"

"Stay with me."

"What?" At first Franny thought he was joking, and when she realized he was serious, she rose from the table, nearly knocking over her chair. "I hope you mean something else by your remark, because your proposal is indecent!"

CHAPTER FOUR

Charlie suddenly realized he'd been paying more attention to Franny's pretty gray eyes than to what he'd been saying. "Wait a minute. No, that's not what I meant. What *did* I say?"

Franny picked up the mugs from the table and headed to the sink. "I'd heard folks in the city did that sometimes . . . you know, live together in sin and all . . . but—"

Charlie bolted from his chair. "I didn't mean what you think you meant. Or *I* meant."

Franny scoured the mugs with a vengeance, as if she could scrub the words from her memory.

"Look, if you have a pastor, even the good reverend would endorse what I was so clumsily trying to offer. I promise you it was as innocent as snow on Christmas morning."

"What did you mean, then?" She turned around, her face red enough to look sunburned.

"I meant that you could teach this city boy how to farm and I would pay you. We'd both benefit. Well, me more than you, but I'd learn how to farm and you'd have some extra money to live on in the city. That way you wouldn't have to live off the money from the sale of the farm. You could put it away as a nest egg for your retirement."

Franny seemed to mull it over. "We couldn't

possibly stay under the same roof." She puffed out some air, making her bangs fly. "It wouldn't be—"

"Of course not." He slowly returned to his seat. "I would stay at a hotel in town and drive out every day. You could live in the house."

"All right. You've redeemed yourself." Franny grinned. "A little." She went to the water bucket on the counter, lifted the metal dipper, and took a sip.

"I'm sorry I didn't make myself clear earlier."

She sat back down at the table. "You're forgiven."

"But you do appear to have quite a fervency about you."

Franny crossed her arms—tightly. "Only when absolutely necessary."

Charlie grinned. Fact was, he liked her fire. She had morals and grit and loved music as much as he did. But also, he liked the way her cheeks lit up when she got riled. Most of the women he knew were pale, pampered imitations of what an authentic woman should be. Since he'd never met a *real* woman before, he found himself mesmerized by the sight of one. In fact, he couldn't stop staring at her.

"By the way, there isn't a hotel in town. Used to be, but it closed down about ten years ago. But my father fixed up a tiny apartment over the toolshed. I could stay there while you live in the house. After the papers are signed, you'll own all of it anyway."

"No, *I* could stay in the apartment. I insist."

"Well, I'm not sure you'll be able to handle the rustic surroundings. The mattress is lumpy, there's no room service, and I think a squirrel has taken up residence in the tiny bathroom attic."

He rested his hands on the table and leaned toward her. "I can handle it." Charlie wasn't about to tell her about his fear of squirrels. "Money hasn't made me *that* soft." She looked uncertain, but her doubt-filled expression also made him want to prove her wrong.

Franny shook her finger. "But only for three weeks. I want you to succeed for your father. I do. I'll help you as best I can. But I'll only stay for three weeks." She splayed her hands on the table. "I'll leave right after Thanksgiving."

"More than fair." Franny slid her hand over to his sleeve and grasped a tiny bit of the material between her fingers. The simple gesture became surprisingly intimate, or maybe he just wanted to take it that way. She really did resemble Audrey Hepburn. Only with soft gray eyes.

"Because, you see," Franny went on to say, "if I don't leave now, I might not ever have the courage again. I have to know whether I can do something besides tend animals. I have to find this dream. Somewhere out there, it has my name written on it."

"I'll learn fast. I promise. And then you'll be on your way. I can already see myself milking all your cows."

"Well, that sounds good except that I have beef cattle, so milking could get pretty awkward." She lit up. "But I appreciate your enthusiasm."

"I really do want us *both* to have our dreams." He leaned toward her. "I won't hold you back, Franny Martin." *And God help the man who ever tries.*

Franny licked her lips. "Well, I'd like to visit more, but I haven't finished the chores."

"I should help you."

"All right. I still have some of my father's overalls and boots in the attic. They'll probably fit you. You'll need them. You wouldn't want to ruin all your fine clothes."

"I'm ready." Charlie scooted back his chair. "As they say in the city, 'Let's book it.' "

Many hours later, accompanied by screaming muscles, Charlie flopped down on the scruffy mattress in Franny's makeshift apartment. The bed exhaled, making plumes of dirty smoke with a smell he couldn't quite place. But then, he was content not to know its origin. What an apartment. Franny hadn't exaggerated. At all. The three tiny rooms *were* rustic—so primitive, in fact, that he could see right through the floorboards offering a lovely view of the farm tools . . . which were

33

more like instruments of torture than equipment.

He felt keenly annoyed with himself. He'd been caught whimpering like a pup, at least in his thoughts. Had wealth indeed made him go soft?

Charlie undid the hooks or fasteners or whatever they were that held up his overalls. The clothes were too big, but they would work. And he would do the job. He'd never been afraid of hard work, at least not the kind that required his brain. The only thing he truly was afraid of was failure. Oh, and squirrels. Ever since he'd been bitten by one of the varmints when he was six, he'd been afraid of the things. Charlie broke out in a cold sweat just thinking about the various ways those razor-sharp teeth could gnaw off his foot during the night.

He crept over to the bathroom, flipped on the bare bulb, and looked at the holes and loose boards in the ceiling. Hmm. There was no running or scratching, but he shut the door anyway. Showers weren't going to be a picnic. But then, one didn't die of being dirty. Maybe he'd forgo showers for a while.

Charlie sat down on the bed again and picked up his guitar from the stand. He'd made certain Franny hadn't seen the instrument when he pulled it out of his trunk. Knowing her love for music, she would have wanted a performance right away, and he still wasn't satisfied with his playing. It was an art he'd kept to himself mostly out of necessity and from a reticence to perform.

He popped a Life Saver into his mouth and began picking and strumming, humming his way through one of the Christmas songs he'd written. If only music were something his father loved too. If only he considered music a worthwhile endeavor, an inspired pursuit and not a thorough waste of time. Perhaps if his father had given him even a word of support, he wouldn't have been so tentative about his music. But how long was he going to blame his father for his own hesitations in life? His own ineptitude?

Charlie stopped playing when he heard a faint noise. What was that? Didn't sound anything like a squirrel. He set down his guitar and listened again. It was some kind of howling. Had to be coyotes. What else could it be? A few more of the beasts joined the first one until there was a whole chorus of yelps and howls. Kind of a surreal and lonely sound . . . but peaceful too.

He walked over to a window and pulled back the curtains, but the glass was so dirty he couldn't see outside. After undoing the two latches and pounding on the frame with the heels of his hands, the window budged a little. He slid it open, leaned outside, and looked up at the starry night.

Thousands of uncountable, dazzling stars filled the sky. It made him think of the night when the shepherds were watching their flocks and a host of angels appeared in the heavens—on a clear bright night just like this one—and made the most important announcement ever made.

He continued staring, captivated by the sight. The stars couldn't show off in the city. Too many artificial lights. Charlie took in a deep breath of the brisk air as his musings drifted right back to Franny. None of the women he'd dated in the past could have managed what she'd done. She'd dealt with a tragedy and taken on the burden of a family business even at a young age. And, amazingly, she had done it with an upbeat attitude.

Charlie memorized the details of the night sky and then shut the window. Maybe he'd practice his tune some more. There was still plenty of time, and he would be able to sleep late in the morning anyway. They'd both worked so hard all day; surely Franny would want an extra hour or two of rest. He gave the ancient radiator a kick to get it started again and then went back to his guitar. But the moment he started strumming, he heard another noise. This time it was a scratching sound, like an animal trying to get in out of the cold.

The squirrel.

Or maybe a whole nest of them.

In spite of the chilled air in the room, perspiration beaded on his scalp, ran down his forehead, and dripped onto his guitar.

It was going to be a long night.

CHAPTER FIVE

Franny sat on her twin canopy bed and swung her legs like she had when she was three. The gentle squeak of the bedsprings comforted her as she absorbed the day's events. She was used to hard work, bad weather, and rough times, but she'd never had a day so full of hope and possibility. Or a day so full of anyone like Charlie Landau. He was unique and funny, not altogether unattractive, and he stood out like a harp in a field of banjos.

She liked him. And she'd liked him even before he'd mentioned his family name.

The only male she'd really gotten to know, for recent comparison, was Derek Mauler, the local vet. She could safely say that it hadn't worked out well. He'd asked her out on six dates. Each time, he'd taken her to the drive-in for a movie, which was fine, but later, at the drugstore, over her favorite meal of ham-salad sandwiches, chips, and an icy-cold Coca-Cola, Derek had mostly talked about the maladroitness of the local stockyards. Somehow Derek had become enamored with that word in high school, and the two of them—he and that word—had built quite a relationship over the years. So, Derek spent his days ingenuously trying to figure out how to work *maladroitness* into ordinary conversation so that it came off as natural as wheat in a silo. But no one in the town or the county, including herself, was brave-hearted enough to tell Derek that he had never once used the word correctly.

Of course, Derek wasn't a man of only one word. He also had a surplus of commentary on every subject, including his remedy for purging the land of root rot. Not the creamiest way to top the parfait on a romantic evening. But even if Derek had talked about music and city life, he still wasn't the one for her. Not even close.

"What a day. What a day." Franny couldn't stop saying it, thinking it. She'd prayed for change and it had come. Guess she should have prayed about it a long time ago. Maybe she was too afraid for an answer. "I'm sure there's a country song in there somewhere."

Franny sent a smile up to the Almighty on that one. She thought for sure He smiled back. "Lord, the only thing I can't figure out is . . . well, Charlie seems like somebody I'd like to get to know better. Someone I already feel a fondness toward." In fact, she was feeling so fondly, she almost needed to turn on the watercooler. "So, Lord, why did *he* have to be the one to give me my freedom?" Franny felt sure God was up to something wonderful. His ways were still quite the mystery to her. But she trusted Him enough to leave it in His hands.

Franny smooshed her lips between her fingers

as if they were bread dough—a habit she found strangely comforting. Hmm. Something Charlie had said, though, niggled its way into her thoughts. He'd mentioned trying to make a profit over the next year. Did that mean he would sell the old place just as soon as he could make a quick buck? Seemed kind of sad to hold onto her family's land for so long just to sell it to someone who didn't really care about it.

Even though she didn't love the farm as her parents had, she did have an attachment to it, and she would hate to see the farm change hands every year or so. She'd always imagined a small family buying the land—a father and mother who wanted to raise their children here. A family that would want to drop their fishing hooks into the creek together, lean into the ebb and flow of seasons, and choose to stay for a lifetime.

It's 1961, Franny. The world is changing. People are changing. She would need to make the mental adjustments or be left behind.

Franny scrubbed her face clean in the bathroom, slipped on her flannel pajamas, and burrowed under her Eight Maids a-Milking quilt. Back to business. She would need a plan for teaching a city boy how to run a farm. Seemed like Don Quixote's impossible dream to teach someone in three weeks what it had taken her a decade to learn.

What to tutor him in first? She started to hum,

since it helped her to think. One of the sows was about to have her little ones. Franny would have to ease the mommy-to-be into the farrowing pen. It could be Charlie's first lesson. Yes. Perfect. That settled it. In the morning, early, before the chickens were up or the roosters were crowing, Charlie could help her deliver the piglets. And maybe she'd remember to take her Brownie camera and shoot photos of it all.

CHAPTER SIX

Charlie roused for a moment when he heard a sound. What was that noise? *Probably just my imagination.* He rolled over and smiled. Amazingly, despite the yammering coyotes, the mattress with lumps the size of grenades, and the threat of being dismembered by a pack of wild squirrels, he'd floated off into a long autumn nap. Franny had given him several hundred blankets since the radiator was on the clunky side, and under those covers, he'd slept like a newborn infant. *Guess I'd better be careful who I tell that one to.* He tucked the blanket under his chin and moaned softly. The sun hadn't come up yet, so there was still plenty of time for more slumber. Was that a rooster crowing? Too early.

Just as he sailed away again on the sleigh ride of snoring bliss, there came a rapping at the door. But coyotes didn't knock. Was he dreaming?

Then he heard the tap again. And this time it was accompanied by a voice that sounded faintly like Franny. Surely not. No human creature was up at such an unearthly hour. No rational person did farm chores in the dark.

"Charlieee." He heard a voice like a cherub's whisper through the crevice in the door. "It's time."

Time for what? To get up? She had to be kidding. Charlie tried to shake off the haze of sleep but left the blankets just under his nose. Was Franny humming "Good King Wenceslas" this early in the morning? "Yes? What is it?"

"It's the sow, Tutti. She needs a midwife," Franny said. "And you're *it*."

Charlie's chuckle got muffled under the covers. "That's a good one."

A chasm of quiet filled the space between them.

"Franny?"

"Yeah?"

"You're not joking, are you?"

"I always get up this early. Most of the farmers do. It's the only way you can get all the work done before nightfall."

Charlie had to admit that until that very moment he'd harbored a more gentlemanly vision of farming, but Franny was determined to dislodge that refined illusion with a good swift kick out of bed. His plan would not be thwarted by laziness, however, so he threw off his covers, hooked up his overalls, tied up his work boots, and opened the door.

Franny looked him over and chuckled.

"What is it now?"

"You look like you've had a squirrel wriggling in your hair all night."

Not a good word to wake up to. Maybe he'd used too much Brylcreem. Charlie ran his fingers through his hair and shrugged. "I'm ready. Let's birth some babies." It would be the first time in his life he'd gone to work without taking a shower beforehand, but he didn't think the pigs were going to be concerned about body odor. They had plenty of their own to manage.

"Well, first you look like you could use some breakfast and coffee. I've made eggs and biscuits and gravy."

"You did that all this morning?"

"Always do."

While I slept.

Franny looked chipper and rosy-cheeked and ready to attack the day.

Charlie grabbed a coat from a box of old clothes and followed her to the farmhouse. He felt ravenous. He had no right to be, since he hadn't hefted anything this morning, but he knew he could eat everything in sight. She'd already proven herself to be a good cook from the previous evening. Not the gourmet fare he'd grown up with, but hearty and appetizing nevertheless.

As a matter of fact, what would he do for food when she left? Frozen dinners came to mind, and he shuddered. He could always hire a chef, but where would he or she live? Certainly not in the apartment. He'd have to build a house for his cook. But somewhere in all the expenditures, he was bound to end up in the red. And the whole point of the venture was to make money, not spend it.

"Are you still cold?" Franny walked so quickly, he nearly had to run to keep up with her.

"No, I was just wondering what I'd do for food when you're gone. You're a good cook, Franny."

"Thanks, but you'll do fine. I had to learn too. My mother taught me some of it, but I'm afraid that when I was younger I wasn't always paying attention to what she told me. So I made a lot of mistakes. You will too." Franny turned around and smiled at him.

It looked as if the sun had already come up in her smile. Charlie loved her face that way.

Minutes later, they arrived in the kitchen to mounds of steaming food. Charlie pulled out a chair for Franny and encouraged her to sit down. He heaped her plate full of eggs and biscuits and gravy and handed it to her.

"Thanks." She accepted the plate. "I'm not used to anyone serving me."

Wish you could get used to it. Wish you could stay a little longer. A lot longer. If she stayed, he would devote his time to finding ways to please her, just to get her face to light up as it had now.

Charlie sat down but nearly missed the seat.

They both laughed.

"You sure I can birth pigs? I can't even sit down."

"You'll be great." Franny took a big forkful of eggs. "The babies usually come all by themselves, but sometimes they need a little help. So we're there in case Mom needs us."

Charlie sat so close to Franny that he wished he'd showered. Hopefully he'd have plenty of time later in the morning. Farmers surely took coffee breaks.

After Charlie scarfed down a second helping of breakfast, they headed to the farrowing house. The morning was so hushed, he could hear his breathing. See it too. His boots crunched on the mud-spackled ground. Although he still felt tired and the hour seemed unnaturally early, the moment was agreeable. The stars were still out, full of audacious glory, the air as crisp as fall apples, and the smell of—his reverie halted at the pungent, stinging odor of hog manure. "That scent. Ohh, that is profane."

"My father always said it was the smell of money."

Charlie laughed. Sounded like something *his*

father would say, only it would have been accompanied by a colorful expletive.

The farrowing house turned out to be a small redbrick structure, which held several pen-like metal apparatuses with places for the sows to rest on their sides to birth and feed their young without concern of accidentally stepping on them. The contraption, which appeared to be home-made, looked ingenious. "Did you make these?"

"My daddy did. He kept experimenting until he figured out this design. He made them himself with his welding machine and metal scraps from around the farm." Franny showed him the gate and the levers.

"Looks like an engineering marvel." Charlie looked down at Tutti, who seemed happy to be there.

"Daddy would have appreciated hearing that from someone who must be very used to hearing brilliant ideas."

"Well, some of the people my father invites to the house are better at being slick than smart." Charlie grasped the metal railing. "Did your father ever try to get a patent on this device?"

"No, but it's a thought." Franny turned on a heat lamp and angled it toward the sow.

"At least it's warmer in here." Charlie opened his coat. "So what can I do to help? Looks like the work is done. How did Tutti get in this thing, anyway?"

Franny shrugged, tossing a sheepish grin at him. "I wanted to let you sleep in a bit, so I got up early enough to make sure Tutti was ready to go."

Sleep in a bit? He almost laughed. He'd never been up this early in his life. "Next time, though, no matter how sissified I act, get me up to help you. All right?"

"All right."

"Now that I'm here, what can I do?"

"Well, you can help Tutti by keeping her calm. Scratch her behind the ears and talk to her like you're her friend. This is her first litter, so she might be a little skittish."

Charlie knelt down next to the sow's head, reached over the railing, and stroked her behind the ears. He felt awkward, but he'd get over it soon enough. He didn't think he'd ever met a pig before—at least not of the hooved variety.

Tutti seemed to give him an appraisal. She looked dubious of his abilities. *You're not alone with that sentiment.*

Franny added some hay here and there and then knelt down on the other side of the pen. "Why don't you try whispering to her?"

Ah yes, sweet nothings. "All right. Let's see." He had no idea what he could say to calm a sow during labor, but he'd give it a try. "Tutti, you're probably thinking this could be the worst of times. But then again, you might be thinking it's the best of times. Or maybe it's what you've waited a lifetime for. Still. You're bound to be scared. You might even doubt that you can do this thing."

He raised his hands for effect. "Yes, you might even be dealing with a whole slop bucket full of misgivings and insecurities." *Like me.* "Trepidation and shilly-shallying." He rolled his eyes. He was making a mess of things, but Franny urged him on with a nod. "You're probably even wondering how you got into such a predicament. But there's good news, Tutti. Yes, good news. Franny's here. That's right. She's here, keeping watch, and I promise, everything's going to be just fine."

Tutti grunted contentedly and then rested her head on the floor.

When Charlie looked into Franny's eyes, they were misty.

"Charlie? That was so . . ."

"Yes?"

CHAPTER SEVEN

Franny reined in her emotions. "I'm sure *Tutti* thought that was beautiful, Charlie. Thank you."

"Anytime." Charlie's face shadowed with what looked like disappointment.

Perhaps he'd wanted her to say how much she'd loved his tender sow soliloquy, but there was no reason to get overly sentimental. She would be leaving for the city in three weeks—the day after Thanksgiving. "I was thinking of the upcoming holiday. I assume you'll be going home for Thanksgiving. Do you all have a big dinner in the city?"

Charlie paused and then said, "My father doesn't really celebrate the day. As far as home goes, I'm wanting to make this farm my new home." Franny had never heard of anyone not celebrating Thanksgiving. She had a hundred more questions about his family life but thought it best to leave the subject alone for now. "Well, then, I'll make us a turkey dinner you won't soon forget."

"Only if you'll let me help."

Franny nodded, gripped the metal railing, and told herself to get back to business. "By the way, it's good you're getting the hang of this."

"Why's that?"

"Because just about the time I'm gone, there'll be another sow ready to have her babies."

"Oh?" His smile warped into a grimace.

Franny grinned.

"The other sow is also a Yorkshire breed, and she's an even-tempered animal. You shouldn't have any problems with her. No misgivings or insecurities. No trepidation or shilly-shallying." Franny hoped Charlie didn't mind a bit of teasing. "But you need to know that the other sow loves Chuck Berry music."

"So what's the other hog's name? Frutti?"

"You guessed it." Franny clapped her hands in the air.

Tutti let out a squeal, and the cry startled them both into action.

Charlie went back to scratching Tutti behind her perky ears. "Now what do we do? Her breathing is pretty heavy. I don't think this is working anymore."

Franny repositioned the light. "The first baby is about to arrive."

"Really?"

"Maybe if we sing her favorite song, she'll settle down."

"What is it?"

"It's 'I Love You Truly.' Do you know it?" Franny pulled a couple of bobby pins out of her pocket and pinned back her bangs. She'd helped sows in the farrowing pens countless times, and yet it always made her a little anxious. Perhaps she could feel the moment more intensely because she was also female, and deep down she knew one day she might be the one struggling to have her child.

"I know the song a little," Charlie said. "I heard it on the radio when I was a kid."

"Good." Franny started the song.

Charlie sang along with her.

Then Franny broke into harmony while Tutti birthed the first of the litter.

Charlie came around to Franny's side and knelt beside her, and together they gazed down at the pink, wriggling newborn pig. Franny wiped the piglet with a cloth and then set it down to suckle. "Too much intervention isn't good, so remember to keep your handling of the babies to a minimum."

"Got it."

The piglet rooted around for a minute, almost seeming about to give up, and then, as if realizing how hungry it was, reached out and took its very first drink of nectar.

Charlie grasped the metal bars. "I'm speechless."

"That's the way I felt the first time I helped my father. It's one of the many miracles farmers are privileged to see." When Franny turned her face back toward Charlie, he was very near her. They gazed at each other, and the moment suddenly turned into a dreamy drive-in movie scene—when the guy gets so close and stays so close that there's no doubt what his starry-eyed stare is all about. In the movie, he searches the girl's eyes to make sure she's receptive and isn't planning to retaliate with a stinging wallop, and then the audience gets what they came for. The magic. Music builds as the amorous moment comes to fruition with a sweet-as-a-rosebud kiss.

Franny knew it as sure as she knew the *Farmers' Almanac*—Charlie was going to kiss her.

But.

They hadn't even been on a date yet. Charlie hadn't bought her a sandwich or a Coca-Cola. Even Derek Mauler—who was a royal clodhopper when it came to dating—had accomplished that much. Yes, if she were ever going to kiss Charlie Landau, it would have to be somewhere a little more romantic than a pigpen!

CHAPTER EIGHT

Just as Charlie leaned down to execute the oldest boy-girl tradition in the world, Franny turned her head toward Tutti. "I think we'd better get back to it, Charlie. We're about to have another baby."

Amusement lit Charlie's eyes, and then he chuckled.

Franny grinned at him as they both went back to their posts. *Is Charlie trying to be adorable, or did God just make him that way?* He was like some sort of angel. Wouldn't *that* make a dreamy song—Charlie Angel? It would be so easy, too easy, to find more things to teach Charlie just so she could stay around a little longer. He was, after all, a novice beyond anything she could have imagined. But he was an adorable novice. "*Have* to stop thinking that."

"What did you say?"

"Oh, just arguing with myself." Franny toweled

off another piglet and went through her usual routine.

"Yeah, I do that sometimes . . . argue with myself."

"And who wins?"

"It's usually a tie."

Franny laughed. They kept up the banter until all twelve Yorkshire piglets were eating and squirming and tumbling happily over themselves. When they were all finished eating, they piled up in the corner near the heat lamp and went to sleep.

"We should celebrate." Charlie stood and wiped his hands on his overalls. "This is a major life accomplishment. We've birthed 'The Twelve Days of Christmas.' "

"Well, I guess we could make merry by feeding the cattle." Franny grinned.

"Can't think of a better way to celebrate."

What a guy.

When lunchtime rolled around, Charlie seemed to have an appetite with no boundaries. Before long she might have to dig into the back of her pantry for more jars of her home-canned fruits and vegetables. She'd put up extra last season, so she hoped he'd have enough to last through the winter, even with his voluminous appetite. It felt good to cook for someone, though, especially for someone who enjoyed her food like he did. Charlie complimented her so often that it brought on a blush. But soon she'd have to say good-bye to that schoolgirl delight too.

Just as Charlie finished up the last bite of his lard-laced cinnamon pie, the telephone rang.

Franny answered it and listened as Eunice Raeburn gave her the extended version of the town's latest news. But right in the middle of her speech, Franny heard heavy breathing, and it wasn't Eunice. "Jinni Lynn, I can hear you listening in. Give us a minute, please." She heard a click. *Good.* Jinni—the youngest of the neighbor's daughters—hung up the telephone. The closer Jinni got to her teen years, the harder it was to endure a party line, since the girl lived most of her waking life on the telephone. Eunice went on to give Franny a few more distressing details surrounding the reason for her call and then hung up.

"Anything wrong?" Charlie picked up his dishes from the table. "Didn't look like good news."

"It isn't. I have something I need to do in town, if you want to help me." Franny pulled off her apron and grabbed their coats off the hook.

"Sure. What is it?"

"I'll explain on the way. We'll need the tractor, so let's head to the barn."

Minutes later Franny started the engine as Charlie hopped onboard the farm vehicle. The old Case tractor started up without a cough. "Good girl." She patted the wheel.

They took off with a slight jolt, and Charlie, who was standing right next to her, put one hand on the fender and one hand on the seat.

"Hold on." Franny jammed on the throttle as she let out the clutch.

With the smell of diesel fuel perfuming the air and the wind whipping their hair, they bounced along the dirt road toward Hesterville. The tractor hit a rut, which caused another joggle, but considering the goodly number of ruts in the road, Charlie had already learned how to balance himself.

"We'll be there soon," Franny yelled over the roar of the engine.

Charlie hollered back, "Why are we headed to town? Did I eat up all your groceries?"

"We have plenty of food."

"What is it, then? If I'm to be taken as a prisoner, I have a right to know where my kidnapper is taking me."

Franny looked up at him. Then she fixed her gaze right back on the road. "Well, Hesterville is a good town—a peaceful little town, mostly. But I'm afraid there's a dragon in their midst."

CHAPTER NINE

Franny appeared to be many wonderful things—but she was also a jigsaw puzzle with lots of intricate pieces. He would, however, enjoy seeing the picture come together.

He bounced along, wondering what kind of human dragon could be hiding in a small town. Or maybe Franny was joking and she was really headed to an annual tractor race.

Charlie suddenly got a vision of the female socialites who frequented his city home. If they could see him now, bobbing along the road on a tractor and dressed in overalls, the laughter and jabbering gossip would never cease to spew from their ruby-painted lips. Something about that sight thrilled him as much as it disgusted him.

He glanced around the countryside, taking in as many details as he could. The songwriter in him might say they were surrounded by autumn fields of russet soil plowed in endless arcs, but that was as much poetry as he could manage at the moment. Except for the green sprigs of winter wheat coming up—and except for Franny—there was little color all the way to the horizon. An early freeze and some good stiff winds had apparently taken all the pretty leaves.

Dreary or not, it was time to embrace the area as well as the town since this would be his new home for a while. He wasn't all that anxious to move back home anyway. There, he had his own wing of the house, which helped, but that wing was still connected to the mansion owned and lived in by his father. With each passing year, his father had become more like a pebble in his shoe than a real father. Only, lately, the stone felt more like a razor blade.

He leaned down to ask Franny a question, but she veered the tractor off the road. "I thought we were going into town."

"Hesterville is just ahead, but this is what we came for." Franny reduced her speed but didn't stop. She pushed a lever forward, and the bulldozer implement, which was hooked to the front of the tractor, slowly lowered. What was she going to do? Bulldoze the side of the road?

The tractor smacked into all sorts of tall, dead weeds until they approached something more immovable—a road sign. He felt certain Franny would turn to miss the sign, but instead she headed straight for it.

Charlie leaned down and hollered, "You're going to hit it!"

"I know. That's what we came for!"

Had Franny lost her mind? He steadied himself for the impact.

Within seconds, the tractor bashed into the

wooden sign and then steamrollered over it without a struggle.

Franny cut the engine and hopped to the ground. Charlie followed. "What's going on?"

She yanked the sign out from under the tractor and turned it over so the words faced up.

The sign read: *NO NEGROES ALLOWED IN TOWN AFTER SUNDOWN.* A bit of life drained out of him. He stuffed his hands into the pockets of his overalls. "Oh, I see."

Franny's breathing came hard and fast as she glared at the sign.

Over the years he had come across similar signs, but they were more about separating blacks from whites in cafés and theaters and hotels. He'd never seen a sign that banned a Negro from living or even sleeping overnight in a particular town. The longer he stared at the sign, the more disturbing it appeared. There was an ugliness to it, and no doubt it was planted there in a spirit of hostility. Maybe with a threat of violence. Had he ever been so close to such a warning? Why did it suddenly feel personal?

Without discussing the sign, Charlie helped Franny load it onto the tractor.

"I need a minute." She strolled over to a nearby pond—the silvery kind one might read about in a poem by Keats—and sat down on the edge of the bank.

Charlie gave Franny a moment to unwind. After

a minute or two he walked over to her and sat down.

Franny looked at him, her eyes pleading. "Please tell me. Does it make you crazy to see it too?"

"Yes. It's cruel and should not be tolerated." Charlie knew his answer was honest, and yet he couldn't say why he hadn't spent much time thinking about it before. Too wrapped up in his own world of trouble, he supposed, which now seemed minuscule compared to what some people endured. "Do you know who put it up? It doesn't look like an official government sign."

"Yes, I know who did it. Same person who always does it. Same person who runs this town, even though he's not the mayor or the sheriff. It's Payton Dunlap."

"Why doesn't somebody stop him?"

"Fear, I suppose . . . or apathy."

"So how come you're not scared of him?"

Franny looked at him as if assessing something important about his character. "It's a long story. Are you sure you want to hear it?"

He wrapped his arms around his legs and looked at her. "I have nowhere else to go."

She crossed her legs and turned back to face the water. A bird that had just steadied itself on a log seemed to change its mind and took off as if pursued. The water in front of them swirled with a turtle or fish or some such water beast. Their presence had no doubt stirred up the social life of the pond.

Franny hugged her arms around her middle.

"Are you cold?"

"No. Actually, it's almost warm for early November." Franny plucked a dried sunflower. "You know that family photo on the wall, the one with the man I called Uncle George?"

"Yes."

"Well, there's a story there."

"I thought there might be."

Franny twirled the lifeless blossom in her fingers. "As you know, George was our farmhand. He was a good Christian man. Worked hard. *And* he had a sense of humor like no one else." She chuckled. "Oh, he could really make me laugh sometimes. He could do magic tricks and create little homemade toys out of scraps my daddy had around the farm. Uncle George was so ingenious I always thought his cleverness was wasted on us. But he never thought so. Or never let on. I grew to love him like family. We all did. Anyway, one of my momma's friends, Lorene, came out to help us can a mess of beans we'd picked, and Lorene happened to see that family photo on the wall."

"The one with George in it." Charlie cringed, knowing the story was about to take a painful turn.

"Yes. Lorene asked about the photograph, since she'd never seen a white family posing with a Negro before, and Momma told her plainly how we all felt about George. Then Momma regretted telling her—not because she didn't mean it, but because she knew that Lorene was loose and sweeping with her tongue, like a frog going after a cricket. Anyway, Momma had been right. Lorene made a beeline into town and told all the ladies at the beauty shop. I can just hear her now: 'My stars and purple garters, you can't imagine what I saw out at the Martin farm.' Then those women from the shop blabbed the news to every living soul in town."

"So what came of all the gossip?"

Franny said nothing for a moment. "One week later, George died. The doctor who pronounced him dead said he'd passed away in his sleep from heart failure. But I knew what had happened." She crushed the dried sunflower in her hand. "He was murdered in his sleep . . . by Payton Dunlap."

CHAPTER TEN

"That's dreadful." Charlie could hardly believe what Franny had just said. "How do you know Payton did it?"

"I just know." Franny tore at clumps of grass beneath her fingers. "You see, Payton always had a peculiar smile when I saw him. Like he was trying to tell me something with that curl of his lip. I knew what he'd done, and he seemed glad for me to know. He was also certain that no one would believe me if I told people what he'd done. He meant it as a sick kind of torture. You know, that he'd gotten away with it and there was nothing I could do about it."

"Did you tell anyone?"

"I told the doctor my suspicions about Payton, but he disagreed. Besides, I was a kid, and no one would listen to me. He claimed there was no evidence."

"What about your parents?" He touched her arm. "Did they believe you?"

"They thought George's sudden death looked awfully suspicious, and they demanded that the sheriff look into it. He did—or I should say, he pretended to—because my parents were so respected in the community. But nothing came of it. And now a lot of years have gone by since that happened." She sighed. "Payton's much older, but he still goes on breathing and eating and living with that sin going unconfessed . . . the evil that went unpunished. But my father always believed it would be like the walls of Jericho."

"How do you mean?"

"That life and time and the silent burden of sin would march around Payton Dunlap until his walls, his facade, his deeds would come tumbling down."

"Have you seen any progress?"

Franny shook her head. "I've only seen

defiance, but then I shouldn't disregard the methods of the Almighty. He can bring down empires with one sweep of his hand. One word. It's just a matter of timing." She smiled. "I'd like to see it happen in my lifetime . . . justice for Uncle George."

Charlie longed to reassure Franny in some way, so he took a chance by reaching out and enfolding her hand in his. "People can be so wicked. I'm sorry for George and for your loss."

"For a long time I hated Payton. It took all of my Christian will and God's grace to help me forgive that man. I finally did, but it's impossible for me to forget."

"I'm sure it is. By the way, I want you to know . . . *I* believe you." Charlie gave her hand a squeeze and released it, even though he hated letting go of the warmth—the nearness. "And I hope you see justice served in your lifetime."

"Thanks, Charlie." She took in a deep breath. "Integrity and decency seem to be draining out of this country like rainwater through a sieve, and the holes just keep getting bigger. We've entered a new decade, and I do feel some hope. Yet I believe sometimes a lot must happen before things are made right."

Charlie looked at her. "You have my vote if you decide to run for office."

Franny chuckled. "Do I sound that canned?"

"No, you sound that *sincere*."

They sat for a moment with a comfortable silence between them. The quiet gave him time to ponder his own view of civil rights. Racism was an abomination in the sight of God—and yet he'd never done anything about it. Did he live a lie, since he loved justice in word but was deficient in deeds? He felt like less of a citizen next to Franny, less of a Christian, and it bothered him. He wanted to be more, a man of integrity in his heart *and* his actions.

"I miss them all so much," Franny whispered as if to the wind. As if he were no longer there. "I miss my parents and Uncle George, even after all these years. Perhaps it is a sign of a weak character."

How could Franny, of all people, think that of herself? "No, it's a sign of the best character. To grieve for those you lost, those you loved. It's okay to miss them."

"It's just harder right now because Thanksgiving and Christmas are coming. Makes me miss them all the more." Franny looked up at him and then rested her head against his shoulder. "I've always tried to hold back the tears. I was always afraid that if I started to cry, I might never stop."

"You may cry on my shoulder any time you want." Charlie wrapped his arm around her. In fact, he wouldn't mind staying that way for a long time to come. She felt sturdy next to him, which was an unusual sensation, but fascinating and appealing. Most of the women he'd held over the years were a bit too flimsy, in his opinion.

Charlie suddenly wondered if women were trained early in life to become helpless around men. Deep down, maybe some of those ladies wanted to play baseball or manage a company or run for president. Franny could be one of those women. "When I think about all you've done, I am amazed. To become a farmer at such a young age and after such a great loss . . . to succeed in a profession that hadn't previously been open to women . . . I think you are the bravest person I've ever met."

"Really?" Franny eased away and looked at him, her lovely eyes glistening with mist and joy.

"Yeah." He nodded. "That's what I think, for what it's worth."

"I've only known you for a day, but it's worth a lot."

A moment of quiet, of sweet tranquillity, settled between them.

Far above them, a bird's sharp call pierced the air. They both looked up and watched the hawk glide and swoop on unseen currents far above them as if no care or burden on earth could touch it.

"It's a red-tailed hawk," Franny whispered. "They say they're common in Oklahoma, but I don't think it looks common at all. It looks rare and splendid to me."

Charlie looked over at her and smiled. Then his thoughts drifted back to the sign and the reason for their presence by the pond. "By the way, we destroyed Payton's sign, and I get the impression he's not going to take this well. So is he going to force the sheriff to put us in jail?"

Franny shot him a surprised look. "You're not scared of Payton too, are you?"

"No." Charlie shrugged. "I just need to know if I'm going to miss my spring planting because I'll be in prison."

CHAPTER ELEVEN

Franny saw the twinkle in Charlie's eyes and gave him a good shove.

He put up his hands with pretended injury. "I surrender."

They laughed. What a relief to know he was joking. She would hate to think that there would be one more farmer around Hesterville who lived in fear of Payton Dunlap. "By the way, nobody's going to jail. It was the mayor's wife who called to tell me about Payton's sign."

"Well, the spring planting is safe, then." He grinned.

Franny rose from the ground and dusted herself off. "We did such a good job with the sow and her babies that I think we deserve a break. It's warmed up some, so maybe there's a slight chance the fish are biting. A mess of catfish would be nice for supper."

"You have some fishing equipment with you?"

"No farmer worth her salt goes anywhere without fishing gear." Franny ran back to the tractor and promptly returned with two cane fishing poles and a tackle box.

Charlie took one of the poles and helped her untangle the lines. "I can't believe you keep this with you."

"Something my daddy taught me. Love God, work hard, and always make time for fishing . . . even if it's more about the sittin' than the catchin'."

Charlie finished unraveling the lines and handed her a pole. "I would have liked your dad."

"He would have liked you too." Franny opened the tackle box.

"Yes, but from what you've told me, I think your dad must have liked everybody."

"He didn't like Payton Dunlap. But you? I know both my parents would have liked you. And Uncle George too." She wanted to say how much *she* liked him as well but thought that comment might still need some simmering.

Franny handed Charlie a red-and-white bobber, and with furtive glances, she watched him as he fumbled with his line, trying to figure out where the bobber should go. She smothered a grin. He surely didn't mean to, but with every smile and every heartfelt conversation he was making it harder to say good-bye. And when he put his arm around her, Franny felt as if she might not be able to move. Right there under the curve of his arm felt like home, and she couldn't imagine how the city with all its music and light and energy was going to compete with the pleasure and wonder of being with Charlie Landau.

How can this be? Lord, how can I feel these things in such a very short time? Have I been starved for male company? Am I that pathetic? All I know is, the next three weeks are going to vanish like dandelions in the wind.

Charlie looked into the tackle box. "You don't have any lures."

"I do. You'll find some worms in that can of dirt. Catfish are smart enough to know the difference between a real meal and a fake one. Or at least that's what my daddy always said when I was little." Franny grabbed a worm out of the can, jiggled off the dirt, put him on the hook, and swung the pole outward, making the worm fly toward the surface of the water.

Charlie glanced up from his work, smiling.

"What is it? Haven't you ever seen a woman bait a hook?"

Charlie laughed. "Not in my life." He swung his line into the water and eased down onto the grass.

Franny leaned back against a fallen log and

sighed. "There now. Doesn't this feel right?"

Charlie gave her a long and leisurely gaze. "It does indeed, Franny."

Any more double entendres or gazes like that and she would be in serious trouble. She tried to shake off the swoony feeling darting around her heart like a dragonfly. *Time to change the temperature.*

"And most women I know wouldn't sit in the grass either, because they're afraid of snakes."

"Actually, I had a pet snake when I was twelve. I used to bring him into the kitchen to let Momma have a look. It used to scare the woozoos out of her."

Charlie laughed. "Now, Franny, I'm surprised at you, tormenting your poor mother that way."

Franny sighed. "I have a lot of regrets."

"I do too."

"What do you regret?"

"Not meeting you sooner," Charlie murmured.

Oh my. Did he really say what she thought he said, or was he just being as smooth as a record needle gliding on vinyl? "I've told you about my parents. I'd love to know more about your people. Are you lucky enough to still have your grandparents with you?" Franny asked.

"I have one grandfather left on my mother's side," Charlie replied. "But he lives abroad. We've never been close. Do you have any grandparents still living?"

"No, I'm sorry to say, they've all passed on."

"That's too bad. I think you would have made an ideal granddaughter to spoil."

"Thanks," Franny said. "I noticed you haven't said anything about your mother."

Charlie seemed to drift far away but finally said, "My mom died when I was little, so I was raised by a nanny."

"I'm so sorry."

"I don't have very many memories left of my mother, but what I do have are good ones. I remember her smile . . . and her fragrance. When she tucked me in at night, I remember always looking into her eyes. They were so clear and pretty. I used to call them 'the wide blue yonder.' There was such love in those eyes. And she smelled like . . . well, I'm not sure of the scent, but it was as sweet and soft as *she* was."

"That's lovely, the way you remember her."

Charlie smiled but said no more on the subject.

Franny gave her pole a slight tug, trying to entice the fish. "So it's just you and your dad, then?"

"And my brother, who's three years younger than me."

"A brother. How wonderful. I always wanted a brother or sister to get into mischief with."

"It's a great thing, but my father kept some pretty tight restraints on us. I should say, he had Nanny make sure there was little room for mischief . . . *or* fun."

"That doesn't sound good. So, you and your brother didn't go fishing with your father?"

Charlie's shoulders sagged. "We did once. Never went back."

"What happened?"

"My father . . . he isn't really a fisherman, but my brother and I begged him for so long that he finally relented. My father couldn't just take us fishing like this. He had to rent a big boat and a guide with all the best equipment. What should have been fun turned out to be . . . well, my father's discontent."

Charlie winced. "Anyway, after all the trouble he went to, we caught nothing. He was furious, since he liked to win at everything, even if the victory was over something as unassuming as a fish. The boat came to the dock and, well, as he stormed off I heard him say, 'We don't need to go fishing. I can afford to have fish flown in and served to us like kings.' And that was the first and last time the Landaus ever went fishing."

"Oh my." Franny's heart ached for the little boys who never knew the joy of fishing with their dad. "It must have hurt your heart . . . then and now."

"The pain does ease with time, but my father isn't the easiest man to love even now. He'd rather be revered. The honorable Landau—he craves it like some people do the bottle. I honestly don't know how my mother put up with him all those years she was alive, but she did. And I wondered how she could have fallen in love with him. I know they met in college and married after graduation. Maybe he had some joy back then. Maybe having kids made him angry somehow."

Franny reached over and touched Charlie's arm. "I wish I could make it up to you."

"You *are,* Franny."

The look he gave her could defrost a freezer. *Be careful, Franny.* She turned her attention back to the water.

"Look, I think I caught something!" Charlie lifted his pole . . . and there dangling on the end of his line was an old shoe.

CHAPTER TWELVE

Charlie set Franny's last suitcase in the back of the pickup and closed the tailgate.

"Thank you for helping me load my belongings," Franny said. "I appreciate it."

Charlie dusted off his hands. "You're welcome. Glad to be of service."

After three weeks of "heart-gathering," as her momma would have called it, and after sharing a warm and wonderful Thanksgiving, why were they both acting like they'd just met? Perhaps Charlie was trying to sever feelings to make the farewell easier. But letting go of Charlie now was going to be anything but easy. "Well, I guess I'd better go."

Charlie came around to the driver's side and opened her door. "So, are you sure this jalopy is going to make it all the way to Oklahoma City?"

Franny ran her hand along the window glass of her old International pickup. "My daddy said old Gertrude here should last fifty years."

Charlie didn't look convinced.

"The truck won't break down. I promise. I'm more worried about that old rattletrap you bought from Farley to chase back and forth into town with."

"He guaranteed it for at least a month and a half."

She grinned.

Charlie glanced at the sky. "Looks like a storm later. You'll be careful, won't you?"

"I will." She'd seen the clouds earlier and had wanted to postpone her trip, but staying would only prolong the pain. The three weeks were up, and they'd made no commitments to each other of any kind. They were both free to make it on their own now.

"Are you sure you have everything you need?" Charlie asked. "Really sure?"

Was there a deeper meaning to his question? Oh, how she wished there were. "I should be fine. I appreciate your letting me store my things here until I get a job and an apartment."

Charlie nodded. "Glad to do it."

"Well." Franny rubbed her hands together. "You've got my aunt's telephone number in the city in case something goes wrong here. So, that's good." She looked at him—really looked at him this time, since she wasn't sure when she'd see him again. "I have faith in you, Charlie. You'll make a fine farmer. And Farley Hansen is a hard worker. He'll give you some good part-time help until you get things under control."

Charlie clutched the back of his neck. "You know, you should have called your aunt so she knows you're coming. What if she traveled somewhere for Thanksgiving and she's not back home yet?"

"I don't think my aunt has taken a trip since the last World War." He was being such a mother hen and Franny loved it, but then, maybe he was just saying and doing what any close friend would say and do. "I didn't call Aunt Beatrice because I wanted to surprise her. She always said I could stay with her if I ever came to the city. If she's not at home, I have enough money to stay in a motel until I get settled. I'll be fine, especially now that I have extra money to live on. Thanks to you, Charlie."

"You taught me how to run a farm in three weeks. You were worth a lot more than what I gave you. I probably cheated you."

"I wouldn't have taken a dime more." What was with all the money talk? Even though they hadn't been out on any formal dates, they'd been growing closer by the day. All she could think of now was a good-bye kiss. "Charlie?" Why wouldn't he kiss her?

He took a step closer to her. "What is it?"

"Do you really think somebody at one of the radio stations will hire me?" *Why can't I at least kiss him on the cheek?* She could run a farm, survive all kinds of drought and hardship, and even stand up to the likes of Payton Dunlap, but in matters of romance she felt as sturdy as soap bubbles in a dishpan.

Charlie looked disappointed with her question. "You're smart. You learn fast. You have more charm than should be legal. Any radio station would be lucky to have you."

"Really?" Franny raised her shoulder in a shrug. "I hope they think so too. It's what I've dreamed of for a long time."

"I'll pray for God's very best for you."

Franny couldn't ask for anything finer, except it would be even more wonderful if the dream could include Charlie.

"*And* I need to say . . . that you look beautiful."

Franny opened her coat, did a little twirl in her navy polka-dot dress, and touched her gloved hand to the pillbox hat sitting on her head. "I found it in Lancaster. It's a whole lot better than those print dresses I sewed. I looked like a feed sack in those things. Don't you think?"

"No, you most certainly did not."

"So, you really do like the dress?"

"I do."

"And I have on eyeliner and pink lipstick. I hear that's what the women are wearing now."

"I believe they are, but I'm no expert." Charlie smiled.

Oh, that Charlie smile. She already missed him and she hadn't even left yet. "Please say good-bye to Henry again. He's asleep by the floor furnace, but I've already given him an extra breakfast and at least ten hugs. I hope he understands that I need to get settled before I can bring him with me."

Charlie kicked at a clod of dirt, breaking it into pieces. "He'll miss you, but I think he'll understand."

And was that how Charlie felt? He would miss her but he understood? It sounded so down-to-earth, so maddeningly sensible. "Thanks for taking care of him. Henry will keep you from getting too lonely out here. He's always helped me."

Charlie stuffed his hands into the pockets of his overalls. "Happy to do it. He's a good dog."

She stood there by the door of the pickup for a moment longer, not wanting to go, not wanting to say the actual good-bye.

"I will miss you, Franny girl." Charlie gave her chin an affectionate pat—a gesture she'd gotten quite fond of over the last three weeks.

"I will miss you too, Charlie boy." Her eyes

burned with mist. Her emotions were so close to the surface that she'd have to leave or risk making a blubbering fool of herself. She covered her mouth with the backs of her fingers so he wouldn't see her chin quiver.

Charlie stepped forward then and pulled her into his arms. Even though the embrace felt loving and oh-so-tender, it also felt final. Like the last hug. A real good-bye. Franny pulled away when she could stand the thought of it no longer.

CHAPTER THIRTEEN

Charlie watched as Franny drove off in her little turquoise pickup, as she sped down the long lane, and as she disappeared over the hill in a cloud of red dust.

The wind kicked up, blowing dirt into his mouth. He spit out the grit, not caring how ungentlemanly he looked. He had no one to impress now. The windmill groaned in agony. *My sentiments exactly.*

Charlie trudged toward the house simply because he felt like trudging. He was not in a good mood, and his disposition was bound to get fouler as the day progressed. Franny was no longer with him. He had a whole day's work ahead of him, but it didn't matter. He was going to have a mug of coffee and grumble for a while.

Once inside the glassed-in porch, he gave the

cistern a few rough cranks and filled the water bucket. When he set the bucket down in the kitchen, he stubbed his toe on a pickling crock, which made him stumble backward straight into the bucket, overturning it and making water go pretty much everywhere. *Guess I have a heavy touch today as well as a heavy heart.*

After mopping up the mess, he made some coffee and sat down in the chair with a *thud*. Henry looked up from his pillow by the furnace with big woeful eyes. Henry knew Franny was gone. Dogs were smart that way. He grieved too. Henry just wasn't as noisy about it.

"Everything's all right, boy. Well, no, it isn't. I'm not going to lie to you. Henry, it was all my fault. I should have given Franny flowers today and a note for her to read later, to tell her what she's come to mean to me. And to tell her that yesterday was the best Thanksgiving Day I've ever known, and that Christmas without her is going to be the loneliest. With other women, I've always given flowers and chocolates. But Franny is different. I don't know, she's kind of like this celestial being, and you don't give earthly gifts to angels. They have no use for them."

Charlie imagined her sweet face. "That day we were in the farrowing house, there was this light about her, just behind her head, giving her a halo. It's the way I will always see her in my mind: glowing." He loved that. In fact, he adored everything about her. "And then today, Henry, I stood there like a lump and did nothing when she left except give her a hug. Just a hug. I didn't even kiss her good-bye." He slammed his coffee mug down, making some of the liquid slosh into the air and splatter onto the table.

Henry whimpered.

"Sorry, boy." Charlie daubed up the mess with a tea towel.

The dog lowered his head again and stared at Charlie. He was glad Franny had trusted him with her dog, and yet having Henry here would only make him think of her all the more. Just like all the other little things she'd left behind, such as the red sled in the corner. Something she had no use for now, but it would be a reminder of her just the same. He could imagine her filled with laughter and delight, sailing down one of the snow-laden hills by the creek. But his mind-wanderings were only making him more miserable. Charlie shook his head. "I shouldn't have been so generous with her, paying her to teach me farming. The money only made it easier for her to go."

Henry seemed to give him a disapproving sigh. "Yeah, I know, not good, but at the moment I'm suffering from a serious bout of selfishness."

Charlie looked around the room, taking in other details he hadn't noticed before. By all rights, he should be excited. His father's attorney had taken care of the paperwork, and he was now the proud owner of a farm in Oklahoma. He should be ready to dig in and work, and he would. But right now, he felt lost.

Charlie took a swig of his coffee. The liquid burned his tongue a little, but he didn't care. "Henry, I should have begged her to stay, but what would I have said? Marry me? Isn't that too big of a leap after three weeks? She would have thought I was nuts."

Henry came over to him, wagged his tail, and curled up by his chair.

"You're a good dog, Henry." Charlie rewarded him with a scratch behind the ears. "In fact, you're a better dog than I am a man."

"But who am I kidding?" He wasn't going to stop Franny from fulfilling her dream. That was just what his father had done to him, and it still caused him anguish.

Charlie blew on the coffee and took a sip. His dream was to be a musician, but owning a music shop would be just as satisfying. Yet his father thought both careers were a waste of time and money. When would he ever break free of his father's domination? *Music is not a real business, son. You're supposed to put childish things away now. We indulged you with music lessons when you were a boy, but now you're a grown man.* No, when it came to dreams he wasn't going to hold Franny back. Not now, not ever. He would let her fly.

He just needed to run the farm, do a good job, and then perhaps when his father deemed him worthy enough to run Landau Enterprises, he could make some of his own choices. But Charlie also knew that Landau Enterprises would be his undoing; instead of freeing him, it would be the noose that would bind more tightly with each struggle. With each passing year.

Charlie looked down at Henry, his new friend, and smiled at his calm and faithful temperament. "I know. I need to be the best I can be without Franny. I'd like her to be proud of me in the way I take good care of her parents' farm . . . of *her* farm."

Henry raised his head suddenly, as if he'd heard something.

"What is it, boy?" Charlie sniffed the air. "What's that smell?" He jumped from the chair and ran from room to room, checking for the odor that seemed to be getting stronger by the second. "God help me. It's smoke!"

CHAPTER FOURTEEN

Franny sped along Route 66 toward Oklahoma City, and to keep from crying, she sang every Christmas carol, love song, and radio tune she'd ever memorized. She sang because she suddenly felt anxious about leaving—about driving away from all she'd ever known. She sang because it was one of the ways she communicated with her Creator, and she sang because she already missed Charlie Landau something fierce. Too bad people didn't have telephones with them at all times. Sounded fantastic and bizarre—like something from the television show *One Step Beyond*—but if portable telephones were possible, she'd call him this instant.

After about an hour and a half of driving, the dark clouds had finished their debate on whether to become a storm, and the outcome wasn't good. Fortunately, she'd stopped long enough to put all her suitcases in the cab, but it made for a tight squeeze while driving. At least they'd be dry if it started to rain. Or snow.

She glanced over at her suitcases bulging with her belongings. It was obvious that she wasn't going away for the night. It was for always. She'd called everyone before she left—her neighbors, her old high school friends, her pastor and his wife. Some of the church folk had wanted to have a going-away party, but she'd left too quickly for any real good-byes. As far as her few semi-close friends, they seemed sad to see her go and wished her well, but they were far from devastated. Perhaps the endless farmwork had kept her from cultivating close friends. Maybe that was a problem she could rectify in the city.

Lightning flashed, and the crash of thunder

rumbled all the way to her bones. She hoped Henry wouldn't be too frightened, back at the farm. Henry hated storms as much as she did. But Charlie was there; surely he would watch out for him.

Franny's stomach growled. She'd planned to stop in El Reno for some of their famous six-for-a-dollar hamburgers—the ones smothered in fried onions and love—but she didn't dare stop now for fear of being engulfed by the storm. She drove on as fast as her old International would take her, hoping she could outrun the weather.

Within minutes the wind picked up, battering the pickup so hard that she had to make adjustments in her steering. Drops of rain fell on the windshield . . . the big spattering angry kind, the same kind she'd always seen before the hail. There was a pause, and then the clouds unleashed their fury, firing marble-sized stones of hail at her as if they were bullets. Crazy weather for November!

Franny took one of the bobby pins from her hair and chewed on it. Bad habit, she knew, but it wasn't a habit she could break in the next few minutes.

Even through the crashing noises, she could feel the next wave of trouble. Her pickup sputtered. The engine hesitated two more times. She hadn't gone through any deep water. Had she gotten some bad gas in Lancaster? *Lord, I can't break down now. This is not a good time, and you know how I am about Oklahoma storms.*

Franny slowed her vehicle, leaned toward the windshield, and gripped the steering wheel until her hands felt as if they were on fire. Her breathing sped up, and her mind seemed as though it might spiral out of control. What were these wretched sensations that took over her being, that always plagued her during a bad storm? She'd never been to a doctor with her malady, but she knew the episodes were attached to her parents and their accident. However, no matter how well she understood the emotional assaults, they still tormented her just the same.

Franny thought a scream might help her release some of the tension, but just when she felt like letting one fly, the hail ceased its attack, the winds died down, and the pickup seemed to cough up whatever was stuck in its throat. She relaxed her breathing, gave her old International a pat on the wheel, and thanked God for His tender mercies. Just to the north, the clouds broke their stronghold on the sky, and rays of sunshine forced their way through the gloom, creating a sunburst. Beautiful.

With renewed hope, Franny took the map and directions from her purse and unfolded the paper. Her aunt lived on the edge of Oklahoma City, so she would be there soon enough. Maybe in the meantime she could practice being a deejay. Then again, maybe not. She'd certainly rehearsed often enough on the farm. Of course, the hogs never had any feedback. Maybe the radio stations would have a script. Even if they didn't tell her what to say, wouldn't it be easy to spin records and talk about music? A tiny crack formed in her confi-dence, but she wasn't about to let it slow her down.

Once Franny had made all the right turns and found the correct street where her aunt had always lived, she cruised slowly as she counted the numbers to make sure she had the right home. Within moments she sat in front of what had to be her aunt's house. But the home looked dilapidated, the sidewalk was cracked, and several of the pine trees had died. Nothing looked right. What could have happened? Franny opened the door to the pickup, and with an anxious spirit in tow, she made her way up the stone path to the porch and then to the front door.

Franny sent up a little prayer as she rang the bell. But she already suspected that her aunt no longer lived there. A woman from next door came out onto her front porch. "Hey, you lookin' for old Beatrice?" The neighbor talked as if she had a mouthful of pebbles.

"Yes, ma'am, I am. She's my aunt."

"She ain't lived here for over a year." The woman pulled some silver tinsel from her hair and stuffed it into her pocket.

Franny moved closer to the edge of the porch

to hear the woman better. "Do you know where she moved to?"

"No sirree. She never told me where she went off to, and I never asked."

"She wasn't ill, was she?"

"Old Bee was so tough, you couldn't kill her if you ran her over with a bus." The woman wiped her mouth with her housedress.

Franny stepped back a little. Not the best neighbor for Aunt Bee. "That's a relief, to hear she's doing—"

"Looky here, I'm decoratin' my tree and got banana-nut bread burning in the oven." The woman went back inside her house and slammed the door loud enough to sound like a shotgun blast. Then that was it. She never came back out to finish the conversation.

Well, that wasn't very neighborly. Franny sighed. Guess she should have kept up with her aunt better, but Beatrice was a loner and Franny had been so busy on the farm that keeping in touch wasn't easy. Franny shook her head at herself and got back into her pickup.

There was nothing to do but keep rolling with her plan—to apply for a job at every radio station in town and then find a motel for the night. Franny removed another piece of paper from her purse and studied it. Using an Oklahoma City map, she'd written out directions to all six stations in the area. If she hurried, and if she skipped lunch, she'd be able to apply at every one of them before closing time.

One by one, Franny drove to each station. Each time before going inside she put on more pink lipstick, tidied her dress, and prayed every kind of prayer she knew how to pray. But each time she went in to apply, the manager of the station said they weren't hiring. Not even for a receptionist, let alone for a disc jockey. She'd checked out the big ones and little start-up ones as well as the fancy new FM station in town. Nothing. Not a hint of hope. No one even wanted to hire her as a janitor.

There was only one radio station she hadn't been to—one that was so tiny, it hadn't even made it onto her dream-job list. The station, K-BOM, probably didn't broadcast any farther than a block, but she would give it a try since there was nothing left for her to do.

When she pulled up in front of K-BOM Radio, she laughed. The structure was built with gray cinder blocks and had a tower the size of a child's toy, but she still felt determined. She straightened her little hat, looked up to the heavens beseechingly, and strode inside.

There was no receptionist to greet her, so she followed the dark hallway to a glowing red light. When Franny got to the door, she watched the deejay through the glass window. The young man—who had a modified beatnik look, a short, cropped beard, and hair long enough to look just like a woman—sat as still as stone behind a console and two turntables.

The man smiled when he saw her. Well, at least that was something. After the queued-up record began to play, he took off his headphones and popped his head around the door. He slid his dark glasses down his nose, which revealed blue eyes that looked a bit glazed. "What's going down, little momma?" The smell of smoke nearly gagged her, and it had a strange odor she'd never smelled before.

Franny tried her best not to cough in his face and instead put on her best smile. "Hi, I'm Franny Martin."

"Lester Ivy. Gimme some skin."

"Skin?"

Lester reached out his hand, and she shook it. "Sorry, I didn't know what you meant."

"Don't sweat it."

Franny twiddled with her pillbox hat and then admonished herself for fidgeting.

In the meantime Lester looked her over. "Nice rags."

She smiled but was puzzled, since his insult didn't seem to fit his friendly tone.

Lester leaned against the door frame, looking a little discombobulated. "So, where you from?"

"A farm near Hesterville."

"Far out."

Franny nodded. "Yeah, it really is. It's sort of like living on the moon."

"I'm getting some good vibes here." Lester wiggled his eyebrows. "Hey, I'm a jazz musician from Haight-Ashbury. Man, we got this new thing going down . . . spicy tunes, good energy."

"Cool," was all Franny could think to say in his vernacular, but she had no idea where Haight-Ashbury was. She blurted, "I would like to apply for a job."

"I dig. Everybody needs a gig. But I don't have anything." He pulled out the lining of his pockets and then stared at them as if they were infinitely fascinating.

"That's fine. Thanks . . . anyway."

"I know, bummer, right?"

"Yes, bummer." Franny nodded. Lester didn't rush back inside, so she stayed put, just to take one last look through the window before saying good-bye to the silliest dream she'd ever cooked up. Actually, it was the only dream she'd ever cooked up. She looked at him. "I just love music, you know? Ever since I can remember. Crazy, right?"

"Yeah . . . craazzy."

Franny twisted the straps on her purse. "Well, ever since I heard Daddy playing his harmonica and Momma singing along, I felt smitten with music."

"Right on." Lester did some kind of Egyptian

gesture with his arms and hands. "I got my love of music from my old man and old lady too."

Franny shrugged. "I just wanted to be near the music." She dropped her gaze to the floor as she felt a full day of "no-thank-yous" weighing on her spirit.

"Just hang loose there, little momma. Something'll come along."

"Thanks."

"Got a request?" Lester pointed to the shelves of records.

Franny licked her dry lips. "Maybe something Christmasy."

"What's your pleasure?"

"Sinatra's 'Have Yourself a Merry Little Christmas.' "

"Mmm. That's bad."

"Bad?"

"You know, groovy choice. Love Sinatra's music. I met him once. Cool cat."

"Groovy. Thank you."

Lester looked inside the studio. "Hey, gotta jam." He slipped his shades back on. "Later."

"Later, man." Franny grinned, having only a vague notion of what she'd just said.

The deejay gave the door frame a few fast thumps as if it were a bongo drum and then headed back inside his world—near the music.

Franny stood there for a moment as she tried to recover from her encounter with Lester. Was that the way folks talked in other parts of America? She hadn't even heard people on TV talking that way. Apparently she was unaware, concerning the ways of the world. But then, her sweet mother would have told her that naïveté wasn't a sin.

Lester pulled a forty-five out of his wall of music, rested it gingerly on the turntable, and queued it up to play. After a brief advertisement for the Sunnyside Up Diner, Lester cozied up to the silver mic as if he were about to kiss it and said, "This song is for a gal I just met, a real hip chick named Franny, who loves to be near the music. Yes, nothing can swing the mood like a Christmas tune. This is for you, sweet momma."

Within seconds, "Have Yourself a Merry Little Christmas" was playing, and right away it took her back to Charlie—when she'd first met him. The song reminded her of everything she'd left behind. What had she done? Was it all gone forever? Now she could no longer imagine herself as a deejay. The fantasy fizzled right before her eyes. She had little hope for a merry Christmas this year. She'd be alone in the city—without a friend.

Franny wondered if the sound of it could be heard—the sound of her heart breaking. She didn't look back as she fled to her pickup and soundly shut the door behind her. She moved her little Brownie camera to the floor. She had hoped to pose for a photograph on her first day of work, but there was no job, and not even a hint of one.

There was a telephone booth on the corner. How she wished she could call Charlie. He'd give her the understanding and kindness she craved, the comfort she longed for. But it was too soon, and the pain of the day's rejection was too palpable. Too sharp. She'd hoped to call him someday soon with good news. But obviously, it was not meant to be after all.

God, help me. Any nerve or willpower or uprightness I ever gathered in my years has all been spent in a day. Or perhaps this day proves that I never had any of those qualities at all. I am running on the fumes of a fool now. I am emptied out, and in great need of Your mercy.

Franny stayed in the general neighborhood, driving around aimlessly, feeling like a marble rolling around on the floor. Never had she imagined such utter failure. She'd always believed that once people saw her enthusiasm and energy and determination, they would hire her. At least as a receptionist. They hadn't even allowed her to fill out an application. What could have gone wrong?

Franny's stomach grumbled in rebellion, so she stopped at a local diner, one that couldn't be missed since it had a gargantuan hamburger on its roof. She sat at the counter, hearing and smelling the grease splattering on the grill, and finally ordered a foot-long chili dog. When it arrived, hot and overflowing with chili and all nestled in its little red basket, she suddenly didn't have much of an appetite. She took a sip of her root beer instead.

Flashbacks of being with Charlie those three weeks began frolicking through her head. Even though there was a bittersweetness that went with them, one by one she let the scenes play. Like the time they'd helped the sow birth her piglets, and when they were fishing side by side. When they took their TV trays into the living room and watched *The Ed Sullivan Show*. The times Charlie played Christmas carols on his guitar, and when they listened to all their favorite records—folk, doo-wop, gospel, and rock and roll.

She was into some serious reminiscing when the young woman next to her asked, "Would you please pass the salt?"

"Sure." Franny handed her the shaker.

"Thanks." The woman wiggled in her seat.

"You're welcome." When Franny tried going back to her sweet memories it was useless. Now she was distracted by the woman's skirt, if a person could call it that. She wore black slick boots up to her knees, and a red cashmere top that showed her midriff! Her mother would have found some extra material to sew over that bare tummy right away. And wasn't she freezing in that thing?

Franny glanced around. No one else seemed

concerned about the woman's apparel. Guess she'd been living in the dark ages out at the farm.

While Franny went back to sipping her root beer, a man strutted out of the back room wearing a paisley shirt, a jade-colored sleeveless tunic, and a plaid fedora. The man was a walking carnival. Franny tried not to let her mouth fly open at the sight.

The man leered at the woman who was half-dressed and said, "How ya doing? I'm Arnold, the owner of this fine establishment."

Since the young woman didn't run the other way, the owner rewarded her with an exaggerated wink.

Surprisingly, the woman winked back.

My goodness gracious.

Arnold took one of the silver bells off the aluminum Christmas tree near the counter, jingled it, and then set it next to her.

The woman grinned.

Then he slid the stack of donuts over to her and leisurely removed the glass dome lid. "On the house for such a pretty lady. Your pick."

Hmm. Perhaps you ought to pick up some of that drool while you're at it, Arnold.

"No thanks," the woman said, wiggling in her seat. "I'm watching my figure."

At that point, anyone could read old Arnold's mind—he was watching her figure too. To his credit he didn't say it out loud, but Franny couldn't believe the owner would be so intimate with a woman who appeared to be a complete stranger to him. Didn't he have any sense of propriety? Guess not. And on another level, Arnold certainly hadn't offered *her* a free donut. In fact, he didn't even tip his silly hat at her or acknowledge her presence.

At thirty-three, maybe I'm getting old. Franny hadn't spent a lot of time thinking about her appearance or her age. She'd always been too busy with the garden and the animals to think about such things. But now with some time on her hands she wondered . . . and her wondering was as entertaining as a meat hammer on the toe. If Charlie was forever out of her life, would love pass her by altogether? Would she never have a husband or family? She hadn't been to the doctor in years. Maybe she was getting too old to conceive.

First things first, Franny. At the moment she didn't even have a job. A little surge of panic trickled through her. Even though Arnold seemed far from the ideal employer, she blurted out, "Are you hiring any waitresses?"

Arnold sighed and turned his attention to Franny. "Yeah, I am. Why? You need a job?"

"Yes, I really do."

Arnold went into the details of the position and what he expected, and since she was in agreement, she filled out a job application and handed it to him.

Arnold glanced over the paperwork. "All right.

See you at seven in the morning." He pointed at his eyes and then at hers. "Seven sharp."

"I'll be here. Thanks." Franny opened the door to the rest of the day, grateful to have some work. The rain had stopped, but it had left puddles of mud and patches of sloppy grass everywhere. Franny stepped off the sidewalk, trying to avoid getting wet, but as she made her way across the street a car drove by and splashed her dress and hat with dirty water. She let out a yelp, yanked off her hat, and slapped it against herself over and over. "Oof!" Now her clothes were filthy, and they were her best.

Someone honked at her from behind. "Hey, watch where you're going, lady. Coulda run over ya." The man cruised on by, but not before giving her an ugly look and letting his car back-fire right in front of her, nearly making her jump out of her skin.

Franny got back into the safety of her pickup, slammed the door shut, and rested her head against the steering wheel. She'd need to find a motel before it got dark. Time to go. She started the engine, and just as she was motoring along again, her pickup sputtered. And then it died. *No, not now.* She turned the wheel as best she could toward the curb. She'd landed in a residential area, but she had no idea where she was. Not a good time for the pickup to break down, but at least it wasn't raining.

Franny checked the gas gauge, but the fuel looked fine. She got out, lifted the hood, and looked over the basics. Could be the alternator or a bad fuel pump or a myriad of other problems, but she just wasn't sure enough of herself when it came to the mechanics of her pickup to try to fix anything. She would need to find a garage.

Something wet splashed on her forehead. Rain? She looked upward. There was one cloud left in the sky—and it dangled right above her.

The full force of the day hit her. No dream. No home. No Charlie. The pickup was busted, and it was starting to rain. Again. It could not get any worse. How could she have sold the only home she'd ever known? She didn't love farming, but she didn't hate it either. She'd taken it all for granted—the inheritance that her parents entrusted to her. She'd swept it away with her own hand. Not from bankruptcy or idleness, but for a childish pipe dream that could go nowhere.

Oh, dear God, what have I done? I sold my livelihood. My heritage. All for some mad fantasy. I acted so silly when I was a teenager, and now I see remnants of that in me still. Guess You'll need to send a miracle to get me out of this one.

A train roared by the neighborhood, blowing its whistle. The blaring horn startled Franny, making her lose her balance. She tried to grab onto the front of the truck, but to no avail. She swung her arms to regain her equilibrium and then screamed for good measure. But all her efforts to slow her descent to the ground were in vain. With visions of white polka dots dancing in her head, Franny fell facedown into the mud. *Oh, Lord, that's not what I meant by a miracle!*

CHAPTER FIFTEEN

Franny had reached the summit of emotional readiness for a good old-fashioned cry. Or as her mother used to call it—a fit of bawling. The city had officially lost all its luster. Living near Hesterville, out in the middle of nowhere, was looking better by the minute.

"Lord, have mercy," Franny heard a woman say just above her. The stranger took hold of Franny's arm and helped her out of the muck.

Franny took her momma's handkerchief from her pocket, wiped the mud from her eyes, and blinked back into awareness. The stranger, an older woman, wore a plain print dress, and her face was as smooth and richly hued as coffee.

"Oh, child, how did this happen to you?" the woman asked.

"I've just had the most pitiful day of my life. And to make matters worse, I am completely out of good sense."

"Well, I don't have much to spare, but I'll loan you some of mine. How about coming inside, and I'll help clean you up. I'm Noma Jefferson."

"I'm Franny Martin. Thank you. I'm so grateful to you." She reached out to shake her hand but then thought better of it. She certainly didn't want to cover her benefactress in more mud.

The woman escorted Franny up to her front door and then into her small entry. It looked to be an old house, as far as Franny could tell through all the filmy mud in her eyes, but it was kept up well and tidy with bits of homey furnishings.

"Why don't you leave your shoes at the front door and then come on back into the bathroom? You can clean up in there, and I'll give you one of my old housedresses to put on. How about that? And then later I'll have Thomas have a look at your truck. He's my neighbor, and he's the best mechanic on this side of town."

"Thank you, Noma. I don't know how to repay you." Grateful tears filled her eyes and coursed down her cheeks, mingling with the mud. "Actually, I can pay you. I do have some money, and I'd really like to—"

"Shh, now, there's no need for talk like that." Noma touched her shoulder. "It's all right."

Noma guided her to the bathroom, where Franny cleaned up and slipped on the housedress before finding Noma in the kitchen with two bowls of beef stew. Her kitchen was small and simple but friendly, and it smelled of fresh homemade bread. The best kitchens always did.

There were warm touches like the gingham napkins and tablecloth and a crocheted wall piece just like her momma used to make. And right in the middle of the kitchen table was a tiny manger scene. Franny already felt at home.

"Here, now, sit and eat. You're going to be bones and blow away if you don't." Noma set a loaf of bread on the table and sat down.

Franny took a seat opposite Noma. "You are my good Samaritan."

"Now, now. I feel blessed for doing it. Let's pray." Noma folded her hands, pressing her knuckles together in a fervent gesture of supplication. "God bless this day, this food, and this fellowship. Take care of Your servant Franny. Hold her steadfast in Your precious hands, which were pierced for our sakes . . . for our deliverance from this life and into Your glorious presence. Amen."

"Amen." Franny picked up her spoon. As she studied her rescuer, she saw that she was younger than she first imagined, maybe early fifties. Her long hair was dappled with gray and done up in braids around her head as if a crown of laurels. And it was easy to tell that Noma Jefferson had peace like a river running through her veins. Wouldn't need more than five minutes in her presence for anybody to sense that about her.

Noma dipped a hunk of bread into the stew. "While you were cleaning up, I washed your dress in the sink and hung it out to dry. It should be all right in the morning."

Franny bit her lips to keep from getting emotional again. The act of washing out her dress reminded her of something her momma would have done, and she realized then how much she'd missed the affectionate attention of an older woman in her life.

"You look hungry. Eat up now."

Franny dipped her bread in the thick stew and took a bite. "Homemade. Ohhh."

"Glad you're enjoying it. It was my momma's recipe. She could have cooked circles 'round any of those fancy chefs, enough to make 'em dizzy. That is, if she'd been given half a chance."

Franny sensed there was much more behind her comment, but since Noma didn't volunteer any more information, she let it go. "Well, it's the best I've ever had."

"Thanks." Noma dug in with gusto as if she were truly hungry.

"Earlier, you asked me how I came to be here like this." Franny looked at Noma. "I'll tell you, if you'd like to know."

Noma had such a sympathetic smile that Franny told her the whole long story. It took all the stew, all the bread, and a pot of tea to tell it, since it was quite a tale of woe.

"Lord, have mercy," Noma said. "That is something. But it could have been a whole lot worse."

She picked up the tiny wooden baby Jesus out of the manger and clasped it in her palm. "You could have gone through all this without knowing God."

Franny had to admit that what Noma said was true, although she still wondered how God was going to finish cleaning up the mess she'd made. She certainly deserved to wallow in it for a while longer. "That's a lovely manger scene."

"My father carved it himself. Gave it to me on my thirteenth birthday."

"Looks like a treasure."

"More than you know." Noma placed the baby back in the manger then looked up at Franny. "My father faced a lynch mob once. He'd done nothing wrong but fish in the river, and for that he found himself staring at a rope and a tree. But my father was good with words, and even though he was scared that night, he stood up to those angry men. He talked them right out of the evil they was about to commit. And this manger scene was carved from the very tree those men was going to hang him on." Noma ran her finger along the wooden star. "I will always remember my father saying, 'Sometimes you gotta show people what you're made of.' "

Franny stared at the manger scene, her eyes blurring with mist. "That's a great story."

"That it is." Noma put her hand to her throat and took in a deep breath. "So, what will you do now?"

"Well, I did manage to get a job today . . . as a waitress. I'm supposed to start tomorrow morning at seven at the Sunnyside Up Diner."

Noma picked up the dishes. "Being a waitress is good honest work."

As Franny helped to clear the table, an idea occurred to her. "Noma, I would love for you to be my guest at the diner tomorrow. I want to thank you for—"

Noma waved her off with a chuckle. "Hon, there's no need for that."

"You'd be doing me a favor, since I'd feel a lot less lonely on my first day if I knew you'd be dropping in for lunch."

Noma filled the sink with water and added a dash of dish soap. "I do have a little time between jobs, and the Sunnyside Up Diner is an easy walk from where I clean houses."

"So you'll be my guest, then?" Franny hoped she'd say yes. It would make her first day not nearly so friendless.

Noma paused and then nodded. "Yes, that might be nice." She handed Franny a towel and then scrubbed away with her dishrag. "My little sofa makes into a bed, so you're welcome to stay the night. There's nobody here but me, so I'd enjoy having the company."

"Thank you." Franny began drying the dishes. "You just keep rescuing me, but I just keep needing it." She touched Noma's shoulder.

"Well, God comes to my rescue daily, so I'm just following in His ways." She rested her hands on the counter.

Both of Noma's hands were scarred with what looked like old burn wounds. Franny wondered about the disfigurements, but she didn't bring up the subject.

While Noma washed the dishes, she began singing the spiritual "Go Tell It on the Mountain." The sound of it was lush and soulful, and it connected Franny's spirit to another world—the heavenlies. Uncle George used to hum that tune, and hearing Noma sing it made her wish she could have said good-bye to him. Franny savored the sound of the spiritual and tucked it away in her memories.

It was easy to tell that her new friend's singing was tied to anguish as well as victory, but while Franny knew of suffering, she'd never known the kind that kept a person in an ever-present bondage. Even though her day had been a bad one, it wasn't the kind of day Noma might experience when people turned against her. Franny had never lived with the color of skin that could bring malevolence, the kind that banned people from businesses and churches and even whole towns. She'd been outraged on their behalf and yet she'd never really felt their plight. *God, help me to know—to see through Noma's eyes.*

Later that night Franny tossed and turned; she

seemed to have a whole host of reasons why she couldn't get drowsy. She fretted about the piglets, and she wondered if Henry had calmed down after the storm. And Charlie, dear Charlie, did he miss her as much as she missed him? She hoped so.

In the midst of her farm worries Franny thought about Noma again. God would surely answer her prayer as quickly as a hummingbird lighting on a flower. She could feel it coming. The Almighty was going to allow her to get a glimpse of what life was like for Noma.

CHAPTER SIXTEEN

Charlie limped his way through the weekday lunch crowd at the Sunnyside Up Diner and found a seat at the back. He was in no mood for chitchat with any of the other customers. He was in no mood for lunch, since he'd lost his appetite. He was just in the mood to find Franny, even though the news he had to tell her wasn't good.

And then just like that—in an answer to the most fervent prayer he'd ever petitioned heaven with—the woman he'd been searching for stepped out of the kitchen and into the light as if she were the very sunrise. Charlie attempted to rise to get Franny's attention, but a searing pain in his leg sent him back to his seat. For a moment he just watched her, relieved to finally have located her and content to once again take in the object of his affection.

Franny was dressed in a waitressing uniform with an apron and a lace headband, which gave him another pang of sadness along with his own personal grief. After only one day, had Franny already been turned down by all the radio stations? That kind of a blow would have devastated most people, and yet there she was, smiling and greeting one of the new customers as if she were an old friend. That was Franny—to have made friends even after one day. He continued to watch the scene, mesmerized by her. Charlie leaned forward to hear the rest of the conversation.

"So, it wasn't too far for you to walk, then?" Franny asked the customer, who was an older Negro lady wearing a maid's outfit. Charlie noticed that the woman carried a heavy-looking basket full of brushes and cleaning products, and she shuffled a little as if her feet were hurting her.

"No, it was just fine," the woman said, smiling. "I'm used to walking."

Franny motioned for the woman to sit at the front counter.

A few of the other patrons stared at her but didn't say anything.

The woman settled in at the counter next to

the display case and glanced around as if in awe of the diner. "I surely am hungry, though. Thank you for the invite."

Franny handed the woman a menu. "That's good, because we've got a blue-plate special with turkey and dressing and green beans . . . with pumpkin pie for dessert."

"That sounds mighty fine, hon."

One of the older male customers at the counter ground out his cigarette in the ashtray as if he were killing an insect, got off his stool, and strode out the door.

"Sir, you forgot your change." Franny started to run after the man who left suddenly, but it was too late. She shrugged, put the change in a jar, and poured her friend a cup of coffee.

Then Charlie saw a guy—apparently the owner—barrel out of the kitchen, combing his hair and glancing around. He was a real greaser type who was dressed like a buffoon and had enough goo on his gangster hairstyle to fry a carton of eggs. "Franny, what's going on? How come that customer was angry?" the man asked. He slid the comb into his back pocket and put his hands on his hips, waiting for Franny to answer.

The owner was so gruff that Charlie almost rose again, hoping to come to Franny's aid, but then thought better of it, since the last thing he wanted to do was make things worse for her.

Before Franny could answer, another customer

at the counter, who had an annoyingly pointy chin, turned to the owner and said, "Arnold, you used to run a respectable business here. Looky what's come in the front door. No one else is brave enough to speak up, but I am. You'd better clean up your diner, Arnold, or you're going to lose *all* your customers." Then the man slapped down his menu and raised his chin, which was made pointier by his spiky facial hair. Charlie thought the man's ducktail beard looked befitting, since he had to be a real birdbrain.

Arnold turned his attention to the Negro woman Franny had befriended. "Sorry, ma'am, I'm gonna have to ask you to leave. There's a café for *you* folks over on the next block."

The Negro customer he addressed slowly took a sip of coffee, placed her cup back on the counter, and said, "I will go, but the good Lord is watching all this, and He may ask for an accounting of it someday."

Arnold lowered his gaze and rubbed his chest as if trying to figure out how to counter her remark.

"This lady is my guest today," Franny said to Arnold.

"I'm sorry." Arnold put his hands on his hips. "If I let that woman stay, the rest of my customers will walk right out of here. Folks will tell their friends and they'll stop coming to my diner. I didn't sweat for ten years to build up a business just to see it demolished in one day. Not by you or anyone else. Savvy?"

Franny yanked off her headband and apron and placed them on the counter. "Then I quit." She turned her focus to the male customer at the counter who'd just demanded that Arnold clean up his diner. "Excuse me, sir?"

Charlie held his breath, knowing that Franny was about to set the record straight, and he didn't want to miss a second of it.

"You say you're not afraid to speak up, as if you're brave in some way," Franny said. "But your comments weren't courageous . . . they exposed you as a coward."

The man at the counter huffed. "People have a name for white women like you," he said loud enough for everyone to hear. "You're nothing but a—"

"Don't you dare foul up this café with your filthy words." Franny slammed her hand on the counter.

"Ha. You're the one guilty of bringing in the filth with that woman." The man stroked his devilish beard and looked around as if expecting a round of laughs from the other customers.

A few people rewarded him with a few chuckles.

Then every last soul in the diner went as silent as the grave, and every gaze, except for a squirming child or two, was locked on Franny.

"Sir, that woman is Noma Jefferson, and she is

my guest here, because yesterday she came to my rescue when I needed help. Her kindness toward me will always be remembered. Will *your* little speech be remembered?" Franny asked. "What you said was as valuable as a soldier fighting on the wrong side of the war."

Shaking with emotion, Franny addressed the crowd, "We are better than this . . . aren't we? Better than herding our brothers and sisters around as if they were cattle." She looked around the room as if to affect every willing soul. "The Declaration of Independence reads, 'We hold these truths to be self-evident, that *all* men are created equal.' And you know deep down in your gut that 'separate but equal' is a lie and that the Jim Crow laws are inhumane."

Franny picked up a ceramic Christmas tree off the counter and raised it in the air. "Hasn't this season of grace and love and goodwill toward men done anything to soften our hard hearts? What are we so afraid of? The evil we dread isn't in our black brothers and sisters, but it's in the hate-inspired laws *we've* created against them. God Almighty *is* watching us . . . and it's time we wake up and see how far we've strayed from what is right and good. Deep down we all desire to be decent Americans, but that right must never be presumed—it must be earned!" Franny set down the ceramic Christmas tree on the counter and dropped her shoulders as if exhausted.

If air could tremble in awe, it would have.

A kid at the counter gave his candy cigarette a pretend puff and said, "Neat-o."

A teenage girl snapped a photograph of Franny with her Polaroid camera.

Charlie released a half sigh, half chuckle—feeling an ocean wave of emotion, of pure joy. Unable to hold back for another second, Charlie put his hands together in loud applause.

Gradually others joined in, until the diner thundered with cheers. He eased himself out of the booth to give Franny a standing ovation.

The door flew open from the cold wind and the paper menus took to the air. Franny picked up a few and handed them to Arnold, who stood behind the counter with a dumbfounded expression.

Franny finally looked in Charlie's direction, and for the first time since he'd entered the diner, their eyes met. She gasped.

CHAPTER SEVENTEEN

Oh, Charlie boy! Franny had never been happier to see anyone in her life. What was he doing here? She wanted to run over and throw her arms around him, but first she stopped to make sure Noma was all right. "I'm sorry," Franny whispered to her friend. "I didn't mean to bring so much attention to you."

Noma touched Franny's cheek. "You've got a good heart beating inside you, and God bless your parents for raising such a fine child. But I wish you hadn't quit your job."

"Well, sometimes you gotta show people what you're made of." Franny and Noma exchanged smiles, and then Franny looked at Charlie. "I see a friend I want you to meet."

"Be happy to." Noma followed Franny to Charlie's booth at the back.

He looked so handsome in his tailored suit with his fancy gold tie-pin. Too bad she hadn't had time to freshen up in the little girl's room. As she approached Charlie, she was suddenly in a quandary about her greeting. Since they weren't dating, perhaps she shouldn't throw her arms around him. But in the midst of her indecision, Charlie pulled her into an embrace. "It's only been a day, but it feels so good to see you."

"I missed you too." *More than I ever imagined.* Franny hugged him back and breathed him in, expensive cologne and all. He was real. *How in the world did you find me? I must know everything.* But first she wanted him to meet Noma. "Charlie, I have a new friend I want you to meet."

When they eased apart Charlie gave Noma his full attention but said nothing about the scene he'd just witnessed. "I'm honored to meet you, Miss Jefferson."

"Call me Noma."

After Franny finished the introductions, Charlie invited them both to sit down in his booth.

"Thank you for the invitation, but I think I'll go back to my seat. I'd love to sit at the counter in this fine diner for a meal . . . to know how it feels." Noma dabbed at the perspiration on her forehead with a handkerchief, which she slipped back into the pocket of her maid's uniform. "And besides, I can always tell when a couple needs some time alone."

Charlie chuckled.

Franny raised a hand. "But we're not—"

"Maybe not yet you're not, but just you wait. . . ." Noma walked back to her spot at the front counter as Arnold arrived with her blue-plate special.

Franny sat down in the booth.

Charlie lowered himself halfway into the seat across from her but then sort of fell the rest of the way.

"You're hurt. What's happened to you?"

"It's a long story. But first I want to tell you how proud I am of you. You know, what you said here today. I didn't want to say anything in front of your friend in case it would cause her more embarrassment, but your parents . . . well, they would have been proud too."

"That means a lot, Charlie, but how did you—"

"Franny?" Arnold arrived at their table with her headband and apron. "I guess you can still have your job." He scratched his head. "You're kind of spunky. You remind me of my granny. But, hey, that little speech you gave, it's not going to be this way every day at the diner, is it?"

Franny wasn't sure what to say, but she at least owed her employer an honest answer. "I don't know. No guarantees."

"Hmm. Well, we'll see how it goes. I need the extra help around Christmas." Arnold set Franny's headband and apron in front of her. "And you can have your thirty-minute lunch break now. Looks like you and your boyfriend need a minute to yourselves."

"But he's not my . . ." Franny didn't bother finishing the explanation, since Arnold was already headed back to the kitchen.

Charlie laughed.

Franny wasn't sure if he was laughing because the idea of being in a relationship with her was a silly notion or because he wanted it to be true. She wished she knew the whole story. It might make a difference in her day—her life. "Now tell me what's going on with your leg. You're hurt."

"It's only minor." Charlie leaned toward her. "But what I need to talk to you about is *how* I got injured."

"Yes?"

"I fell while I was trying to put out the fire."

"Fire?" Franny crossed her arms on the table. "What fire?"

Charlie flinched. "The one that burned down the barn."

"The barn? It's gone?" The shock of his announcement ran through her like a cherry Kool-Aid spill on a white tablecloth—swiftly and deeply.

"Oh, Franny. How can I tell you how very sorry I am? And it happened on my watch." He reached out and touched her sleeve. "None of the animals got hurt. In fact, it scared the cows so much they broke through the fence."

"Oh my."

"But the cows are fine. I rounded them up. The fire department said the fire started from a short in the wiring. It started not long after you left."

"Oh, my, my, my." Franny imagined what the farm landscape must have looked like as the flames took the old building down. Not caring about her lipstick any longer, she pressed her fingers to her mouth and squashed her lips together.

"It was so odd, don't you think? That it happened the moment you were gone . . . as if the whole farm was in an upheaval, not wanting you to go." Charlie gave her a weak smile. "Please say something. You're welcome to holler at me."

"How could I be upset with you? I mean, it's *your* farm now. And they said it wasn't your fault anyway. Mice probably chewed through the wiring. You'll need to buy a cat."

Charlie's pained expression didn't soften.

"I promise you, I'm not upset. I'm just stunned. And I'm awfully glad you weren't seriously injured." *Thank You, God, that he didn't perish in the fire, trying to save the barn.* "You have some good insurance, better than what I had, so you'll get a brand-new barn. That old barn was beyond its prime . . . so rickety it could barely hold itself up anymore. It'll be all right."

"So you're not furious with me?"

"No, of course not."

Charlie steepled his fingers together and leaned toward her. "Good, because there's more to my story."

"Oh?"

CHAPTER EIGHTEEN

"Well, my hired hand, Farley he hurt himself."

"Badly?" Perhaps these mishaps were her fault, for leaving Charlie too soon.

"No."

"So he hurt himself in the fire?" Franny tried to remove the alarm from her face, since she didn't want to add to Charlie's grief.

"No. Actually, Farley hurt himself at home. He fractured his arm by falling off his daughter's rocking horse. Unfortunately, he won't be able to help me now. I went into town and asked around at the diner, but everybody's busy with their own work."

Franny tried not to grin. "So, Farley injured himself falling off his daughter's rocking horse? Farley never did have very much horse sense. Folks will pray for him as hard as they'll howl with laughter." She put up her hand. "Sorry, it's not funny." She leaned toward him. "So, Charlie, who's looking after the piglets? Did you remember to give them their iron shots? And who's watching out for Frutti? Is she starting to nest yet? If you don't watch her carefully, she'll end up having her babies in the field, and you know—"

"Everything is all right. Farley's brother is there watching over everything . . . for now. But he only promised to take over for today and tomorrow. I have to go back tomorrow evening." Charlie touched Franny's apron. "So, what happened at the radio stations?"

Franny hated to pile her unhappy news on top of his, but he would have to know sooner or later. "The truth is, no one wanted me. Not even as a receptionist. After I thought about it, I realized they were pretty wise in their decision. I have no college education. No background in radio. I have an Oklahoma accent and a voice that goes squeaky as a rusty windmill when I get excited. I was so sure of myself, and yet this was the most foolish thing I've ever done in my life." She picked up the apron and tied it around her waist.

She reached for her headband, but Charlie held onto the other end of it. "I admire the fact that you *did* try."

"You do?"

"Yes." Charlie let go of the headband. "In fact—"

"Wait a minute. Hey, how did you find me? Aunt Beatrice doesn't live at that residence anymore, so the telephone number I gave you was bad."

"I know." A smile warmed Charlie's features. "Well, I had a little help from my Friend." He pointed upward. "Hey, that'd make a good song. Anyway, miraculously, I heard your name on the radio. I could hardly believe it. The announcer mentioned this diner and, well, I didn't know where else to go. I took a chance since it was close to the station and I thought you might be hungry."

"It was a miracle you found me, since I could have stopped at any diner in the city." Franny picked at the lace on the headband. "Any diner at all."

"But you didn't. You stopped here. And I couldn't be happier about it."

"Me too."

"The thing is"—Charlie loosened his tie—"if you don't love your waitressing job, I wish you'd come back. You're good at farming, and I'd pay you very well to help me. Of course you'd stay in the house."

"Oh." Franny scrubbed her knuckles against her chin. "So that's the real reason you came to find me—to save the farm?" She had a sudden need to play with the salt and pepper shakers, so she woodpecker-tapped them together, impatient to know Charlie's real reason for his fanatic search to find her.

"No, it isn't at all." He caught her gaze, which wasn't easy to catch, since she was avoiding his scrutiny. "I missed you, Franny. The farm has no life or color without you. I doubt the potatoes would grow in the spring without you. And the pigs were getting a serious case of melancholia. It just won't do, Franny."

She sighed a little inside, thinking he'd redeemed himself. A little. "I have to confess that I missed the farm after I left. And I missed you."

"I'm glad." Charlie picked up the ketchup and mustard containers and bumped them together just like Franny had with the salt and pepper shakers.

She grinned.

"So, tell me, do you regret selling me the farm?"

"I would hate to put it that way." But how would she put it?

He set the containers down but continued to grip them. "Here's the way it is . . . I want you to come back, but I'm equally sorry about your dream. I want you to know that I wasn't rooting for your failure. Except now, I admit to a little selfish joy

118

on my part. But I assure you that I'm very repentant for it. Well, I'm trying to be."

Franny loved the way Charlie talked—loved his ways in general. "I believe you."

"And I promise I didn't burn down the barn just to get you to come back."

She chuckled. "I'm glad about that too."

"Good. Now will you come back? Just say those words. Please."

"Yes, I just might."

"Sorry, it suddenly got so noisy in here that I couldn't hear what you said."

"Yeah, I know. There's a bunch of ladies laughing up at the front. Women can be such cackling hens."

"What?"

"I said, women can be such cackling hens," Franny almost screamed the words just as the diner got quiet. A few people looked their way.

Charlie and Franny laughed.

"My answer is yes."

"Very good. Well, then, I think you're going to disappoint old Arnold. He was looking forward to working with his grandmother."

Franny chuckled. "Cute." She gave his hand a little pat. "Arnold will recover."

Charlie took her hands in his. "I want to ask you for another favor."

What could it be now? "Yes?"

"As you know, my brother and father live here

in the city and, well, I'd like for them to meet you. We could go after lunch. That is, if you want to."

"I would love to meet your family." Franny looked at her uniform and remembered the dress hanging in the back room. "I'll have to turn in this uniform, and that new dress I bought got a little mangled yesterday."

"You're perfect."

Now that sounded pretty fine. The man in the booth behind them blew smoke their way, and just as Franny waved it right back to him, Noma arrived at their table with purse in hand. "You're leaving already?" Franny asked her friend.

Noma clutched her purse and bin of cleaning supplies. "That was a mighty good meal, and I thank you for it."

"You're welcome, but it's me who's grateful."

"I usually don't take but a few minutes to eat my lunch, but today was special." Noma squeezed her eyes shut for a second as if trying to control her emotions. "You're always welcome in my home."

"Thank you, Noma." Franny stood. "I made a decision just now. I'm going back to the farm."

Noma looked at them, concerned.

"We won't be living in the same house." Franny grinned but felt her face go as hot as firecrackers.

"I wasn't worried about you two." Noma's face knotted into a forlorn, resigned kind of expression. "I was thinking how much I'd miss my new friend."

Franny gave Noma a bear hug. "I will miss you, but any time I'm in the city, I promise I'll drop by. And you're always welcome at the farm. It's five miles straight east of Hesterville."

"Someday I may hold you to that promise." Noma hugged her back and then released her. "But you're right in returning to the country. It's a good place to raise children."

The temperature on Franny's face heated up again, but Noma distracted her by turning to Charlie. "I've got a soft spot for this girl, Mr. Landau, so you take good care of her."

"Yes, ma'am." Charlie grinned. "I have a soft spot for her too."

CHAPTER NINETEEN

After a quick bite of lunch, a change of clothes, and letting Arnold know about her new plans, Franny found herself riding along toward Nichols Hills in Charlie's Rolls-Royce motorcar. She also found herself jiggling her purse, fidgeting with her dress, and twiddling with her hair. *Should I have put on more lipstick?* She was accustomed to being in the company of hogs and cattle and chickens, not the aristocracy. She felt so keyed up she could barely enjoy the ride, which was a shame, since she would probably never ride in such luxury again.

"It'll be all right, Franny. We'll only be there for a few minutes."

What was the matter with her, anyway? She could face pigheaded and tough-talking bigots, but she couldn't even say hello to Charlie's father without fear. Was it the wealth that intimidated her? Surely she wasn't so shallow. However, even though she tried to be earnest and steadfast at times, she also acknowledged having equal amounts of silliness.

He turned the corner and looked over at her. "Sometimes you go quiet, and I can't imagine what you're thinking. But I'd love to know."

Franny gripped the seat. "You wouldn't always want to know what's going on in my brain. It's a real mess in there."

"Mine's pretty shambolic too." Charlie tapped the steering wheel with his thumb. "Is that a real word?"

"If not, it should be. My brain sort of shambles, like a lost child . . . always in the wrong direction, though."

"You're not convincing me." Charlie turned another corner, and the houses went from homes to stately mansions with immaculately kept grounds and fountains. He drove through a large brick portico toward the back of the house.

"This is your home? It's so beautiful, Charlie. I can't imagine growing up this way."

Charlie came to a stop in front of a large statue

and looked at her. "My home is now a farm, but this is where I lived before that."

Franny blew the bangs off her forehead. "Why do I feel like I'm going to my execution?"

Charlie laughed. "I guess I've told you too many stories about my father. He's not *all* bad. He just can't remember how to live. Maybe you could teach him." He tugged on her sleeve. "Does that make you feel any better?"

"Do you want an honest answer?"

"With that look in your eyes, probably not." He grinned. "Stay put. I'll come around and get you." Charlie went to the passenger side and opened the door.

She grasped his outstretched hand and slipped from the car, trying to remember all the ladylike advice she'd gathered through the years. She straightened her shoulders and lifted her chin.

Charlie put his hand at her back as they walked along the stone path, and she welcomed his touch by leaning into it. But his limp made her cringe. "How's your leg?"

"It still hurts, but being with you works like a painkiller."

She chuckled. Their time together felt more and more like a date, which made her more and more nervous. But like a morning glory unfolding in the light, Franny was opening her heart to the possibility of falling in love with Charlie. Perhaps she'd already fallen a little in love, but along with caring for another person came the potential for worry and concern that something unfortunate would disrupt those first stirrings of tender affection.

As Charlie opened the back door, Franny felt the first twinge of concern—that something was about to go wrong.

CHAPTER TWENTY

Once inside, they were engulfed by hallways full of shadows and echoes that came from their footsteps on the marble floor. The whole effect was disconcerting and lonely and not a bit like what a person would want home to feel like. Maybe the velvet mattress of wealth really was full of spurs.

"My father will be in his office." As Charlie led Franny through the house, they passed a majestic entry with a spiral staircase as well as a type of medieval statue, which appeared to be guarding the house against intruders. The statue was falling down on his job, since she was surely an intruder. Franny glanced around at the expensive paintings and tapestries lining the walls and alcoves. Everything was elegantly decorated for Christmas, but the cheery look of the garlands and wreaths was swallowed up by the gloom. "So, you grew up in this house."

Charlie leaned down to her and whispered, "Well, I think I grew up in *spite* of the house."

"Oh, I see." Franny wondered why prosperity so rarely joined hands with joy. "To see it for the first time, though, it is breathtaking." She touched a dial telephone. "I noticed you have a lot of these. And so, do you have a color television set?"

"Not yet. My father thinks black-and-white has more character. I think he's just being cheap."

But not one thing in the house appeared to be cheap. Not a thing Franny could see.

They arrived at a set of imposing double doors, which were embellished with polished wood and stained glass. "Well, this is it." Charlie gave her a brisk nod. "Let me go in first, and then I'll come back for you and introduce you."

"All right." Franny blinked back her surprise at the formality.

He shut the doors behind him and Franny remained in the dark hallway, glancing around, feeling a little wobbly. It seemed unnatural for her to stand there, looking around, waiting like a peasant trying to enter the royal court. Memories from her youth came to her, ones where she would burst into her father's tiny study in the attic and run into his arms. The oak chair would squeak as he leaned down to kiss the top of her head, and the scent of Old Spice would tickle her nose.

Even when Franny got older and brought her schoolmates home, she still did the same thing, rushing into his room to share her friends, her excitement, her life. She had hundreds of those moments, a treasure chest of memories—all of them beloved, but at the time, all taken for granted. Now, standing outside Mr. Landau's office door, she realized how truly blessed she'd been and how sad she was to have lost it all.

Charlie opened the door, his eyes bright with what looked like excitement mingled with something else. Could it be fear? "Father is eager to meet you."

Franny waved her perspiring hands in the air. "Good. That's good."

"By the way, Father doesn't do hugs. Not the hugger type, if you know what I mean. So it would be best to just shake his hand."

Franny had rarely met anyone who wasn't a hugger, but she didn't want to upset the apple cart. So, no hugging Charlie's father. What other rules and protocols were there to have a proper audience with the great and powerful Mr. Landau? *Now, Franny.* She got her attitude back in check and followed Charlie inside the office. Mr. Landau sat behind a sprawling mahogany desk—the kind she imagined in the office of the president or some sort of dignitary—and tried to disengage herself from all that Charlie had told her about him.

After Charlie made the appropriate introductions, Franny shook hands with Mr. Landau, who, on first impression, looked like the photographs she'd seen of Sigmund Freud with his balding head, sculpted white beard, and little round eyeglasses. Perhaps they'd entered the fifth dimension . . . *dunn-duhh* . . . *The Twilight Zone.* She hid her amusement. Her uneasiness was making her a little goofy. To her pleasant surprise, in spite of Mr. Landau's intimidating appearance, the encounter felt reasonably welcoming. "It's nice to meet you, sir."

"Please sit down." Charlie's father made no mention of his son's limp. Odd. He motioned to the chair where he wanted her to sit. "So, you are Francine Alexia Martin, the woman who sold her farm to Charlie."

"Yes. That's me." Franny shrugged. She wasn't used to people using her full name. "The meaning of the name is—"

"Yes, I know, it means 'from France.' " Mr. Landau tapped his fingers together, looking pleased with himself.

"It's a place I've always wanted to visit, and—"

"Mmm, yes. Let's talk business for a bit, shall we?"

Franny could tell it wasn't a question, so she remained silent.

Charlie's body stiffened like the hardbacked chair he sat on.

Clocks ticked from every corner and crevice of the room. How Mr. Landau could think straight in his office with so many distractions was a mystery, and who would want such an incessant reminder of time?

Mr. Landau shuffled some papers on his desk. "From the information I've gathered, you had a well-run farm . . . considering. One doesn't usually think of a farmer as being female, though." His eyes tapered with sharp awareness, reminding Franny of a hawk. "So, I've been deliberating, trying to figure out how you did it . . . how you ran the operation by yourself."

"Well, after my parents died, I had some—"

"Upp!" Mr. Landau raised his forefinger. "I gave it some serious thought, and I came up with the answer."

"You did? I'd love to know how I did it." Franny bit her tongue, admonishing herself for her flippancy. "I mean, I feel honored that you spent the time to try to figure it out."

"Please indulge me," Mr. Landau said.

"Sure." Franny could tell she had no choice in the matter, but she was curious about his discoveries. She had no idea why anyone would bother studying her comings and goings so closely.

"For most women it would have been impossible, especially starting out so young." Mr. Landau marked something on a notepad with a fountain pen, as if keeping score. "But I think I found the secret. It's in your character. You're not afraid of years upon years of relentless, bone-tiring, mind-numbing work. That routine behavior either comes from someone who is witless and void of ingenuity, or it means you're shrewd. You know what you like, and you're not afraid to work hard to keep it. I'm impressed. And I'm not a man who is easily impressed."

"Thank you." *I think.* Franny gave herself the luxury of relaxing her shoulders. "But I do want to—"

"Upp!" Mr. Landau's finger took to the air again. "But then you surprise me still, because after all your hard work, you sold the farm. Just like that. Now why is that, Miss Martin?"

"Father." Charlie leaned toward the desk. "I didn't bring Franny here to—"

"It's a simple question, Charles. Miss Martin doesn't have to answer it if it makes her uncomfortable."

Franny looked at Charlie, who gave his head the tiniest of shakes, giving her permission to let it go. But it was, after all, a reasonable question, and even though it caused her pain, it was a query she couldn't hide from.

She looked at Mr. Landau, whose bushy eyebrows were raised. "I had this dream surrounding music." The blood rushed in her ears. "I see it as foolish now. I wanted to sing and play the guitar professionally, but my parents couldn't afford the lessons. It wasn't their fault, of course. Someone loaned me a guitar and a lesson book some years ago. I tried to teach myself, but it was hopeless. I don't think I have any natural ability. Since I could never *play* the music, I still hoped to be a part of it somehow. So I decided to move to the city to find a job at a radio station."

Mr. Landau rose from his chair as if he were alarmed about something she'd said. "You were right to think this dream in the city was beneath you."

Is that what I said? Franny shrugged. "Well, no one would hire me anyway."

Mr. Landau seemed absorbed, staring at a photograph of an elderly gentleman. Perhaps it was a picture of his own father. With care, Mr. Landau sat back in his chair. "Music is like a rose. It's beautiful, but we don't need it to survive." Then he suddenly gazed at her with a sharp expression, as if awakening from a trance. "So, are you regretting the sale of your farm now?"

"Father, we have a deal worked out. Franny will move back to the farm, and I'll pay her to be my farmhand. I'll be living in the apartment, of course."

His father rose from the chair again, looking agitated. "And you, Miss Martin—you would agree to this arrangement? To work as a hired servant on the very land you owned as your birthright?"

Choose your words carefully. Franny offered her most genuine smile. "I don't think I have to own a farm to enjoy its merits."

Mr. Landau eased back into his chair but didn't look satisfied. "This, I can't understand." He patted the handkerchief in his suit pocket, which was a perfect white rectangle.

"I can see why Franny would feel that way." Charlie picked up a brass spyglass from the desk and fingered it. "We think we can control things in this life, but in the end we possess nothing. Maybe the pursuit of joy comes more easily when we hold the reins less tightly."

"Hmph." Mr. Landau glared at the spyglass as he fingered one of his cuff links. "When did my son become a philosopher?"

"I think it was the day I met Franny." Charlie set the spyglass back down.

Franny warmed at Charlie's declaration, but the lovely sensation faded as she watched Charlie and his father share a barbed look that appeared to convey meanings far deeper than Franny could fathom. She wondered what baggage had been stacked between them—the history they were battering each other with.

Charlie rested his fingers on his eyelids as if he were getting a headache. "And another thing." He looked at his father. "I don't think the word *shrewd* fits Franny's personality."

Mr. Landau reached over and readjusted the

spyglass that Charlie had just set back on his desk—but he only moved it by a fraction of an inch. "And why not, Charles? It's a perfectly good word."

"Because *shrewd* has the connotation of someone who's scheming. And Franny is anything but that. She is guileless and brave and . . . well, unforgettable."

"Unforgettable. Hmm." Mr. Landau leaned forward in his chair and gave his son a good long look. "Well, I see you've spent some time together. Miss Martin, I would enjoy getting to know you better. I insist that you attend a dinner party I'm having with a few of my friends this evening."

"I would like to, but I'm Charlie's guest, so I should leave it up to him." Franny had no idea if she were breaking some kind of protocol and yet it didn't seem right to accept an invitation without getting Charlie's input.

Charlie looked over at her, smiled, and then looked back to his father. "Yes, that would be fine."

"Excellent. It'll be formal, by the way, so you'll both want to change. It won't be a problem, though. Charles, your bedroom is still full of your clothes. Nothing's been changed. And the housekeeper always keeps a selection of cocktail dresses in one of the bedrooms in the east wing. Miss Martin, you're welcome to use any of those."

"Thank you. That's very kind."

Mr. Landau looked as though he might disagree but said no more. Wasn't he used to people calling him kind? She had no idea, since everything she'd experienced in the Landau house seemed as foreign as though she'd traveled overseas.

"Father, I hope Willie will be here tonight. I'm eager for Franny to meet him."

Mr. Landau went back to shuffling papers. "No, he has other plans this evening."

"Oh?" Charlie said. "His plans . . . or yours?"

Mr. Landau glared at his son. "Now, Charles. Let's make the most of our evening with Miss Martin. Why don't you give Franny a tour of the house before you both dress for dinner? I've got some urgent business to attend to right now."

For the first time, Franny noticed a mark on Mr. Landau's left cheek—similar to the angular shape of a broken twig. It was an enflamed crimson color at the moment, so perhaps the redness was fueled by his sudden agitation . . . and perhaps there was more of it to be had just under the surface, an anger that his eyes were trained to hide.

"Of course." Charlie didn't look away from his father. "But if I give her a tour, I'll be turning on all the lights as we go along. This house has been dark for too long."

CHAPTER TWENTY-ONE

Charlie chose to give Franny a grand tour, deliberately missing, of course, all the family portraits covering the walls. To him they weren't so much family as dark memories longing to be forgotten. So he just breezed her right by them toward the conservatory.

"I have a surprise for you. I've saved the best for last."

"It's hard to envision anything more wonderful than what you've already shown me."

Charlie stood facing her in front of two French doors, and then with his hands behind him he opened the doors, not wanting to miss a second of Franny's reaction. He flipped some switches and the room came to life with all its usual dazzling beauty and elegance. Ever since he was a kid he'd thought the room looked magical with its black-and-white marble floor and glass atrium ceiling. But even as an adult he still thought the room special. Not just because it held his music but because it was a safe haven, a sanctuary away from his father's world.

"Oh, my, my, my." Franny gasped at the sight. "Look at it all. It couldn't be more perfect." She strolled to the middle of the room, looking at the tropical plants and flowers and at the large

Christmas tree in the center of it all. "This is by far the most beautiful room in the house."

"I'm glad you think so. I do too." Charlie took one of the pink roses from one of the many flower arrangements in the room, handed it to her, and bowed like a butler.

"Why, thank you, Charles." Franny accepted the rose with a curtsy.

"Oh, please." He grimaced. "That's what Father calls me."

"It does sound a little less endearing than *Charlie*. You know, I see some of the things in your father's personality that you mentioned, but are you sure he's truly an ogre?"

"Uh-oh. This could be a dangerous turn of events." Charlie grinned.

"How so?"

"He's getting to you." His grin paled.

"What do you mean?"

"Let's just say that my father and the word *Machiavellian* have a lot in common."

"I believe everything you've told me." Franny twirled the rose under her nose. "But I would like to think better of him."

"So would I." Charlie scrubbed his finger along his chin. "We can talk about happier topics, if you'd like."

Franny sat down at the grand piano and ran her hands along the keys. "How long did you take lessons?"

"Until I was twelve." Charlie sat down next to her on the piano bench. "But as an adult I've taken it up again. I just never bothered mentioning it to my father."

"I'm sorry you can't tell him about it . . . share it with him."

Franny had such a wistfully sad look, he wanted to kiss it away, but instead he turned to the ivories and began to play "The Holly and the Ivy."

Franny swayed to the music, and each time she came near him she brushed his arm. "People don't play that tune much at Christmas. It has such a forlorn sound to it, but it's comforting too. Kind of like a warm coat on a cold day."

After a moment he stopped playing, but he left his hands on the keys.

Franny touched his hands. "Why did you stop playing?"

"Well, there is this distraction."

"I'm sorry."

"Don't be." Charlie smiled. "It's such a lovely distraction."

"You play with such emotion. I can tell that you love music like I do. But why did you stop taking lessons when you were twelve? Because of your father?"

"Yes." Charlie heard the earnestness in her question, so he answered, "You heard what he said. Music is a pretty thing, but not a necessary thing. And so when he saw that my lessons were becoming too important to me, that there might be a chance I'd want to make it my life's work, he stopped them. He discouraged me from playing and instead took me to work with him as often as he could. His enterprises were paramount in our family. Business fed us all, not music, he would remind me. Art was the dessert you enjoyed if you cleared your plate first. But my father always made sure I never cleared my plate."

Franny rested her hands in her lap. "I'm so sorry. That's not good. Not at all."

"My father has just become an easy excuse, I think."

"But why do you continue to work within your father's parameters, then? I mean, if you succeed at farming, then your reward isn't music, it's more business . . . *his* business. Isn't that what you told me once upon a time?"

Charlie looked at his hands. They had a slight tremor. "That craving for our parents' approval is like a steel cable, even if what the cable holds is something that was never intended for us." Charlie started playing again, only this time "What Child Is This?" was the tune. "Sometimes I wonder if my father hasn't extinguished all the passion in me. Out at the farm I felt like such a pile of, well, wet ash might be an apt description."

"I don't see you that way at all." Franny placed her hand on his arm.

Charlie's pulse beat faster at her touch.

"I mean, if you didn't feel obligated to prove yourself to your father and eventually help run his enterprises, what would you do? If you could choose anything at all. Music?"

Charlie didn't even have to think about the question. "I'd run a small music store. Sell instruments and hire a couple of teachers to give lessons. Teach some myself. It would be pretty simple, but it would be wonderful. Wouldn't it?"

"Yes. It would be wonderful."

He covered her hand with his. "In fact, I need to ask you something. If I hadn't begged you to come back, would you have stayed in the city and continued pursuing your dream? Have I interfered with your life like my father has meddled with mine?"

"No." Franny paused for a moment. "But if you hadn't asked me to come back, I would have stayed here in the city. I would have continued to be a waitress. And I would have kept trying to break into radio. But . . . well, let's just say that I've been confused."

Charlie removed her hand from his arm but held onto it. "It's my fault, this bewilderment you feel."

"Yes, it's all your fault, Charlie." Franny had the cutest glimmer in her eyes.

He grinned. "But something's happened between us."

"Yes. It's like in a movie when the music builds, and . . ."

Charlie lifted her hand to his lips and kissed her palm. "Go on."

"And you get swept away in this Never Never Land of the heart."

"Yes, I've gotten quite swept away too." She was so close to him then. So very close. Perfect timing. Charlie leaned down and kissed her. He'd never known that lips could fit so perfectly together—like moist petals clinging to each other. He'd kissed dozens of women over the years, too many women, and none of them were as inspiring as Franny.

When he finally released her from the kiss, instead of looking dreamy-eyed like most women, Franny tugged on his skinny tie and asked, "Why, Charlie Landau, didn't you do that the day I left the farm?"

"Because I was a fool?"

"Correct answer. I suffered without that kiss." Franny looked a bit exasperated but grinned anyway.

"Hey, I suffered too." He tried to gain her sympathy with his most doleful expression.

"Well, maybe we could do with a little less suffering around here."

Charlie leaned down to her lips again, so they could both be put out of their misery.

Then, like the annoying tinkling of a bell, Charlie heard his name yoo-hooed in the form of a familiar and nagging voice. "Charlieee?"

Franny broke off the kiss, and they both looked toward the door.

Charlie disengaged from his embrace and groaned inwardly when he saw his old girlfriend. "Sylvie? What a surprise. What are you doing here?"

CHAPTER TWENTY-TWO

"Just watching," Sylvie said with a wink.

Charlie tried not to frown, but his brows might have puckered a bit.

"Sorry." Sylvie held up her hands in mock surrender. "I came in for the view and got lost in another one." She meandered into the room in spite of Charlie's lack of enthusiasm. "You two make a darling couple, by the way." She took off her cat-eye glasses and gave him a good stare. The kind of gaze you give someone when you think no one is looking. Yes, Sylvie was an odd egg all right—and a bit scrambled.

"Thank you." Charlie rose and introduced the two women.

Franny was cordial.

Sylvie came off as cryptic as always.

After the two women shook hands, Sylvie turned to Charlie and mimicked a kiss in midair. He'd never liked that gesture. Too social-elitist for his taste. It had always been a token that promised warmth but left one cold.

Charlie tried to absorb the lingering pain in his leg and not limp in front of Sylvie. He was in no mood for her lectures. Or her coddling.

"It's no secret that Charlie and I used to go out," Sylvie said to Franny as she whirled about the room lighting the tips of her fingers on all the fineries, "but please don't worry. I assure you I'm not a threat, Francine. I was never meant for the institution of marriage. I never was, nor shall I ever be."

Charlie was beginning to think he must have been a pretty one-dimensional person to have ever been charmed by Sylvie. When had he seen the light? He already knew the answer before he'd even finished the thought.

Franny rose from the piano, smiling at Sylvie. "I wasn't worried."

"Glad that's all clear." Sylvie struck a few random piano keys, making a discordant sound. "Love is like this piano. It's grand until it goes out of tune, which happens even to the finest instruments." She gave Charlie a sad look as she smoothed the thing sitting on top of her head. He guessed it was called a wiglet, but to him the thing was as attractive as a dead squirrel.

"So, Sylvie, are you here for the dinner party?" Charlie's greatest hope was that his old girlfriend would go find a different part of the house to haunt. He felt eager to get right back to what he was doing on the piano bench. Which had nothing to do with music.

"Yes. Your father invited me." She let her mink stole drop off one shoulder as she pursed her lips. Sylvie was forever posing even though there were no cameras. "And as usual, I brought along Barkley Irons. You remember him, I'm sure."

"Vaguely." Wasn't he the one with the big ears and small IQ? Or was he the one with the satin jackets and bow ties who thought he was Frank Sinatra? Charlie felt bad for his sudden nasty mood, but nothing ever went right when he was at home. He rubbed the back of his neck, hoping he wasn't getting a headache. Yes, he was hoping for so many things, the least of which was a conver-sation with Sylvie—especially when he could see that the wolf had on sheep's clothing tonight while Franny was looking too much like a lamb. "Where is old Barkley anyway?" *And shouldn't you be with him about now?*

"Barkley? I think he found your father in his office and they're arguing about a doomsday market crash or some such twaddle." Sylvie pulled out a pack of cigarettes from her purse, lifted one from the container, and didn't bother lighting it. "Barkley, dear old Barkley. Yes, he's like my pet poodle . . . follows me everywhere. Imagine that." She chortled. "Most of the Landau dinner parties are full of people who are as tiresome as a drippy faucet."

"Sounds about right." Charlie offered her a mollifying chuckle.

"Except for Charles here. He's our exception." Sylvie pointed at him with her cigarette.

Hmm. He was kind of curious how Sylvie had shown up out of the blue. What his dear Franny didn't know was that Sylvie lived two houses down the street and there would have been just enough time for his father to add her to the dinner list. Perhaps his father welcomed Franny on the outside but was plotting against her on the inside. It would be typical of the way the Landau household worked.

"However, I just heard from your father that Francine is anything but tedious, so I'm looking forward to some lively conversation."

"I hope I can live up to it," Franny said. "So, what do you do, Sylvie?"

"Do? I don't *do* anything. I guess I'm as boring as the rest of them. My father has a trust fund for me, and I live off that. Oh, and I dabble in writing. I have two publishers asking me to write something for them. They love my voice. In fact, I've been told . . . and I hesitate boasting about myself . . . but *they* say I'm a female Hemingway. Imagine that. It's just . . . well, I can't think of a subject worthy enough for my attention."

Franny laid her rose on the table. "You must enjoy reading too."

"Oh, I do. Fitzgerald takes my breath away."

Sylvie gave Franny her full attention. "Who's your favorite?"

"Harper Lee," Franny said.

Charlie smiled. He hadn't discovered that fact about Franny, but he could have guessed it.

"Good choice. Lee's a brilliant writer, and her Atticus Finch is one of the most memorable and heroic characters of all time." Sylvie offered Franny one of the black cigarettes from her pack. "They're Russian."

"Sorry, I don't smoke."

"Oh, no need to apologize. I've been trying to quit ever since I developed a cough." Sylvie slipped the cigarette pack back into her purse. "Why is it we always love what isn't good for us?"

Charlie studied her, hoping she wasn't about to open old boxes from the attic—ones they'd both put away long ago.

Sylvie caressed the shiny gold tip of her cigarette. "I don't smoke them very often . . . I just like to keep them around to play with. One of my older physicians still assures me they're good for my lungs. Imagine that. But then they used to promote bloodletting too. So what we think is good for us turns out to be bad and vice versa." She gave her wrist a flip in the air. "C'est la vie."

Franny started to speak, paused for a moment as if changing her mind, and then said, "You said you were looking for something to write about. Have you considered the civil rights movement?"

"No, I haven't. Tell me more, Francine."

"I believe . . . well, I hope there's a tidal wave of change coming to this country." Franny crossed her arms. "And I also believe that words can change the world. Think of it—you'd have a chance to be a part of the change."

Sylvie stood silent for a moment, which Charlie was always happy to see, and then nodded. "What a fine idea, Francine." She linked arms with Franny and began to lead her from the room. "I want to hear more, much more. Say, Cook has a pot of chocolate fondue bubbling in the kitchen, so why don't we spoil our dinners while you tell me how I could change the world. Let's . . ."

Charlie didn't hear another word, since Sylvie had strolled out the door with Franny. The evening was deteriorating fast. He let out some steam and headed after them.

CHAPTER TWENTY-THREE

Later that evening, Franny stood in front of a full-length mirror, gazing at herself, turning this way and that, which was an activity she'd had little time for over the years. She'd never seen herself in a cocktail dress before. *Hmm, not bad*—black taffeta with a flared skirt, puffed sleeves, and a square neckline. The best part was, she didn't look overly ridiculous in it. Was this what women were wearing to fancy dinner parties? She had no idea.

Franny did a little whirl in front of the mirror and then curtsied with her forefinger touching her chin. She let out a giggle. Funny sound, coming out of her mouth. She'd never been one for giggling, but the day was turning out like the show tune "Some Enchanted Evening." It was a good thing she was alone, though, since her primping and gazing felt a little silly.

Franny slipped on black lace gloves as she glanced back at the bed, where she'd found the evening dress and accessories laid out for her. It had been an unexpected sight, especially since Mr. Landau had told her that she could choose any of the dresses in the closet. It mattered little to her, and yet it had been a curious thing to see. Charlie wouldn't have chosen the outfit for her, she felt certain of that. But didn't Mr. Landau have more important things to do than select a woman's clothing for a dinner party?

Then she remembered Charlie's warning about his father and his controlling ways. Perhaps there was much more to Mr. Landau, many more layers of his personality yet to see. Maybe a maid had set out the clothes and her imagination was getting the better of her.

Franny sat down at the vanity table and smoothed her simple hairstyle, wishing it were in a bouffant, which looked more sophisticated and less matter-of-fact. She picked up a can of hairspray and used it liberally until she sputtered and coughed.

She picked up a bottle of perfume on the mirrored tray and took a whiff. The smell reminded her of the fragrance Sylvie was wearing. She gave the pump a squeeze, letting the spray mist her neck. Nice scent even on a farmer. *Imagine that.* Franny batted her eyelashes like she'd seen Sylvie do.

She fingered the bottle and then set it back down, wondering if Sylvie's dressing table looked similar to this one. Charlie's old girlfriend seemed accustomed to a luxurious lifestyle. Certainly her evening dress had been modish, a navy chiffon with an off-the-shoulder V-neckline. Striking, just like her personality.

Franny had to admit, Sylvie was attractive—the kind of woman men would want to take to the movies, but also the kind of woman who could be *in* the movies. And Sylvie was a mystery too. Her facial expressions and playful banter showed that she still cared for Charlie, but no matter how fascinating or trendy Sylvie came off, one thing was certain—she was not a good match for him. *Let it go, Franny.*

A tube of lipstick sat front and center on the vanity table as if it were for her particular use. Someone had thought of everything. She pulled off the gold cover and rolled up the stick of color, which turned out to be a rich ruby red. But wasn't pink the latest? Hard to know, since she couldn't afford fashion magazines.

Franny leaned toward the mirror and smeared the tint on her lips. Totally different effect with the black dress. She touched her mouth, recalling Charlie's lips against her own. Perhaps before the evening was over, there would be time for making more of those good memories. Which were even better than chocolate fondue.

Franny glanced around the huge room that was probably bigger than her living room and kitchen combined. In spite of all the furnishings and elegantly decorated alcoves to explore, she headed to the closet, curious about what was inside. She expected to see a row of spectacular evening dresses. To her surprise the closet was empty except for one item. A porcelain clock sat on the wooden floor like an abandoned toy. A tiny painted violin adorned the top. It was so pretty and delicate. She wound it up, placed it next to her ear, and listened for the ticking sound. It still worked. She set the time and looked at it again, fingering the gilded instrument on top. In the midst of her wonderment, the tiny glass violin broke off into her hand.

It took a second for the misfortune to register. *Oh my. What have I done?* Broken a family heirloom? A rare antique. A priceless relic! The horror of what she'd done struck her, and she nearly doubled over with pain. How would she ever tell

Charlie? Since she couldn't replace the treasure, Mr. Landau would surely order her out of the house. The incident made her feel as though she didn't belong in such an elegant world—Charlie's world.

On the other hand, how could the clock have broken so easily? Well, no matter the consequences, sometime during the evening she would have to find the right time to tell Charlie what she'd done.

Franny gently placed the broken clock on a shelf and closed the closet door, reprimanding herself for her inquisitiveness and wishing she had a bobby pin for a good chew. What had Momma always told her about her habit of nosing around in other people's things? That it would get her into trouble one day. *Guess that day arrived.*

She looked at a clock on one of the end tables, not even daring to touch it, and read the time. In five more minutes she would meet Charlie in the dining room.

The remaining minutes gave her time to study the room from a safe distance with her hands folded safely in her lap. The bedroom was no less than a masterpiece of beauty and elegance. The furnishings would make even the most level-headed woman drool over all the loveliness.

Was she falling for the opulence and the romantic living that would come from great wealth, where anything seemed possible? The thought struck her as superficial but honest. It reminded her of a passage from a Jane Austen novel she'd once read—*Pride and Prejudice*. When the heroine, Elizabeth Bennet, first admitted to falling in love with Mr. Darcy, it seemed to be connected to the moment she saw the beautiful grounds at Pemberley. Was that admission a flaw in Lizzy's character, and if so, was Franny succumbing to the same weakness?

CHAPTER TWENTY-FOUR

The various courses of dinner went well and were only fraught with minor hiccups. Mr. Landau had insisted that Charlie be seated across from Franny throughout the dinner instead of next to her. Even though Charlie didn't seem too happy about the request, he recovered and was jovial in general, especially when he looked her way.

Charlie looked like a prince, adorned in his double-breasted jacket, but she hoped the formal-wear wasn't too appealing on him since Sylvie was seated right next to Charlie.

The supper itself came off spectacularly, like a fantastical dream, one Franny knew she would never forget. She'd done her best not to embarrass Charlie in front of his father, and hopefully, she'd accomplished her goal. All that remained of the evening was to consume the dessert—individual red-velvet cakes, each adorned with a chocolate swan.

The way the guests escorted her into the conversation with such cordiality astonished Franny, and the fact that Charlie's father didn't seem to mind his son having affection for a woman with such humble beginnings was also a welcome surprise.

On a more realistic level, it felt too good to be true, like fleecy clouds concealing a cyclone. Franny took the last sip of her coffee and let her shoulders relax. Of course, she still had to figure out a way to tell Charlie about the broken clock. That thought took some of the sweetness out of the cake.

"I have one last question for you, Francine. About the farm." Mr. Landau dabbed at his mouth with his linen napkin. "Charlie mentioned a large orchard and garden on the farm. Do you take advantage of this commercially?"

"No." Franny set down her fork. "I've never sold the produce."

"And why is that? You can't eat it all by yourself." Mr. Landau chuckled but seemed to focus all of his attention on her reply.

Perhaps he wanted to top off the evening with his toughest questions. "I've continued my father's tradition of giving away the surplus fruits and vegetables to the needy in town."

Sylvie raised her cup in Franny's direction, making her dangling snowflake earrings shimmer. "Well, I think it's commendable, Francine. Here, here. I would do the exact same thing . . . that is, if I had a charitable heart."

Chuckles trickled through the room.

Mr. Landau stroked his beard, ignoring Sylvie's lighthearted comment. "It's generous of you, Miss Martin, but if you do this service for the locals year after year after year, won't you hurt them more by keeping them in ignorance? How will they ever learn to take care of themselves? It will no longer be charitable but an impediment to their education."

Franny took a sip of coffee to swallow the cake that had lodged a complaint in her throat. "I see your point. And it is a good one."

"Thank you. Now don't disappoint me. I know you have a rebuttal." Mr. Landau's voice seemed buoyant enough, but something in his eyes appeared foreboding. Was it her imagination?

Charlie offered her an encouraging smile.

"It's just that the people I've helped over the years, well, many of them work hard. I'm not giving the nod to slovenly behavior or taking away their desire to work; I'm just trying to have some compassion for people who aren't given a reasonable wage. It's the employers who are in need of an education on ways not to be so scrooge-like." Franny set the cup down, since her hand was about ready to shake the coffee right out of the dainty cup.

"Bravo." Mr. Landau patted his hands together in silent applause. "Your reasoning is faulty, of course, since even Jesus said the poor will always be with us, but you have such sagacity and conviction it's hard not to applaud."

Franny's jaw twitched in indignation, but she kept a civil tone. "It's rude to argue with one's host, but I think you're taking the Lord's words out of context." In her flustered state, she dropped her napkin on the floor.

Barkley reached down and picked it up with some formality and handed it to her with a wink. She had no idea what that was all about.

Charlie made a wad of his napkin and set it next to his untouched dessert. "Father, we've all grilled Franny enough for one evening, don't you think?"

Perhaps Franny had missed Charlie's rising emotions. Apparently she had, since he looked like he was about to blow.

"Now, Charles, the banter was all done in the spirit of fun."

"Well, perhaps Franny could do with a little less of the Landau brand of entertainment."

Mr. Landau ignored his son's comment and said, "As the guests in this room know, I don't enjoy the company of a great number of people, so you are an anomaly, Miss Martin."

Barkley raised his glass. "Well, here's to this evening's lovely anomaly."

Everyone chuckled, including the other two guests, Horace and Harriet—the pensive ones. They raised their glasses like dutiful guests. Franny suddenly felt more naive than brave. An anomaly meant *irregular,* after all. She looked at the tiny swan on her plate. Franny had been saving the best for last, but seeing the hapless expression on the bird's chocolate face, she couldn't devour it after all.

Mr. Landau scooted his chair back. "Charles, it's getting too late to travel back, so you'll both need to spend the night. Separate wings, of course. I think you said you have someone watching over the farm until tomorrow. If that's the case, then you both may have breakfast here and get an early start in the morning."

"Fine." Charlie scooted his chair back.

"Glad you all could come this evening." Mr. Landau rose from the table and everyone did the same, as if the final curtain had now come down and the theater was closing.

Mr. Landau's audience of six said their pleasantries and good-nights, and then Charlie took Franny by the arm and whisked her down a long corridor.

"Charlie, what is it?" Franny held on for dear life as he propelled her down the hallway without saying a word.

Charlie opened the doors to what looked like a large family library.

Franny strolled inside and glanced around at the sumptuous room, which was complete with its own flocked Christmas tree. How lovely. She walked over to it and touched one of the snowy boughs. Hundreds of multicolored bubble lights illuminated the tree. It was enthralling to watch the bubbles dance as they moved up the little tubes. She'd seen such newfangled decorations in the stores but had never been able to afford any of it. Seeing the tree, though, brought back sweet memories of holidays on the farm—the laughter around the kitchen table as they made handmade ornaments, the snow melting on her cheeks as she and her father chose that one special tree, the candlelight service on Christmas Eve, and her mother's never-ending flow of wassail. She sighed, missing it all.

Franny sat on the sofa, which was situated cozily in front of a great stone fireplace. A low fire popped and crackled pleasantly, creating a festive mood . . . not to mention a romantic air.

"I thought the dinner would never end." Charlie unbuttoned the top button of his shirt and loosened his tie. "I don't think I could have endured my father badgering you for another minute."

"It was all right." Franny rested back on the cushy divan. "I was beginning to get used to it."

"That is the last thing I want, for you to have to

get used to my father's bullying." Charlie paced the floor a few times.

Franny patted the seat next to her, and he melted into a smile.

Charlie sat down. "I'm just so glad to have you by myself for a moment to talk. Barkley and Horace were so busy falling in love with you, *I* didn't get a chance."

"To talk or fall in love?" Franny grinned.

"Neither."

Oh, how Charlie could make a girl smile.

Charlie went over to the hearth, threw a few more logs on the sputtering flames, and poked at them until the logs blazed.

"Where did the fire come from?" Franny got up from the sofa and sat down on the floor near the fireplace.

"I told one of the housekeepers we'd need one after dinner."

Just like that. "This is such a different way of life than the farm."

"I know, but I don't mind the work out there. It's freeing." Charlie sat down next to her on the rug and touched her gloved hand. "And I don't mind building my own fires."

Franny chuckled. It was obvious he was trying to be amorous, but her mirth from the apparent joke could not be squelched. "Well, you do have a way with fires."

Charlie appeared puzzled, and then he chuckled.

"I dug a hole for myself on that one, didn't I? The barn. The fire. Right. I am *very* good at building my own fires."

Franny wilted inside. How could she be so cruel? She needed a harness on her tongue. "That was an unmerciful thing to say. I'm sorry I brought it up, especially—"

Charlie tugged on the sleeve of her taffeta dress. "It's all right. It really is." He removed his jacket and laid it on a chair. "By the way, right before dinner I told my father what happened . . . about the fire."

"What did he say?"

"Not a word, but I could see his look of disapproval."

"I'm sorry about your father. And I'm sorry I laughed just now." Franny reached out and gave his arm a solid squeeze. "I'm way too outspoken. Will you forgive me?"

Charlie looked at her. "There is nothing to forgive, my dear."

My dear? Oh my. That sweet talk went down like cream on freshly picked mulberries. No one except her parents had ever called her by such an endearing name. A quiet settled between them—the good kind. Franny could almost imagine a lifetime of Charlie's nearness. It was getting easier to envision all the time. But she needed to ask him a question—one that had been fermenting like pickle juice all evening, and one that had the potential to be more uncomfortable than the loss of a dilapidated old barn. And much more uncomfortable than the porcelain clock she'd broken. "Charlie, there is another kind of fire we should talk about."

"Yes?" Charlie scooted closer to her. "I'd love to hear more about this topic."

Franny covered his hand with hers. "I think Sylvie is still in love with you."

CHAPTER TWENTY-FIVE

"Oh, that." The last thing Charlie wanted to talk about was an old flame. He'd been working steadily to get Franny alone all evening, so chit-chat about Sylvie was more than superfluous; it was irksome.

However, the idea that Franny seemed concerned about his earlier dating life was a favorable sign. "Sylvie only thinks she's in love with me. Her daddy's trust fund gave her too much freedom, so she's had more money than purpose. For the last few years she's been like a mighty ship at sea—a great force of power with very little rudder. But you gave her an idea tonight. Something she could think about, something she could write about. A real purpose."

"I didn't do it to distract her from you. It was just an idea."

Charlie pulled back at the thought of it. "Of course not. You're not a manipulating kind of woman. And I would know. I've seen plenty of them in action over the years, believe me." He gazed into her smiling eyes. "Besides, I don't love Sylvie. I never did."

Franny made little circles on the rug with her finger. "But I hope her heart isn't still hurting."

"No, I don't think so. I think she loves whatever man is in the room at the time. Did you notice how she also doted on Barkley at dinner? As well as Harriet's date?"

"Perhaps Sylvie was trying to make you jealous. I'm not completely ignorant of the wiles of women, you know." Franny raised her chin, but the gesture only made her look all the more innocent.

Charlie wrapped his arms around his knees. "What you don't know is that, months ago, Sylvie was the one who dropped me. Not the other way around. Of course it came at the right time, and so I was grateful to her."

"You don't think she's changed her mind?"

"No. She just loves drama in every form. And for her to cling to the notion that there's still something lingering between us is perfect theater for the heart. She's a writer, after all. She lives for witty dialogue and intriguing interludes, real or imagined."

Franny grinned. "I know it's silly for me to

bring it up. It's just, there we were, kissing and all, and then there she was, watching us in the doorway as if she wanted to be the woman on the bench kissing you instead of me."

"I promise, Sylvie will be fine. It's very thoughtful of you to worry about her, though."

"But it's more than that. I'm glad she'll be all right, but I was asking for selfish reasons too."

"Selfishness in Franny. I can't believe it." Charlie pretended mock horror.

Franny looked at her gloved hands, which were folded on her lap. "At supper I'm sure it was easy to make a comparison between Sylvie and me. She's so glamorous, and I'm so . . . well, not nearly as stylish or dazzling. At the table tonight, Sylvie must have looked like a peacock sitting across from a chicken."

Charlie tipped his head back, laughing.

"Hey, it wasn't *that* funny."

"I'm sorry, but . . ." Charlie had to catch his breath from the laughter. Franny had no idea how pretty she was, and that made her even more attractive. "May I say, you are no chicken, not in mind, body, or spirit. And even though you are beautiful, you are no peacock. I have no use for them anymore. They know how to strut around, but that's about it. All their flouncing gets tiresome. And besides, Sylvie has a mustache."

"She does not." Franny laughed and gave him a little shove.

"Can we talk about something besides Sylvie now? Please?"

"Well, what do you want to talk about?" Franny's eyes seemed to drift just behind him to an end table. He looked where she was staring and noticed the crystal bowl of truffles. "Would you like one?"

Franny nodded. "Yes, please."

"You have quite the sweet tooth, don't you?"

She grinned. "You noticed."

"Well, I've never seen anyone dig into a slice of red-velvet cake the way you did this evening."

"Sorry, that wasn't very ladylike."

"Times are changing. Who's to say what is lady-like? Some people would say that farming isn't ladylike, but then they'd have to argue with me." Charlie handed her the bowl and Franny took one of the wrapped truffles. She set the candy in her lap and fiddled with the buttons on her gloves. "I don't want to get chocolate on these lovely gloves. Although I hate to take them off."

"Why?"

"They hide my awful hands. In case you haven't noticed I have farm hands. My fingernails aren't manicured, and they don't have pretty red polish like I saw on the other women tonight. They're—"

"Here, allow me." Charlie turned Franny's hand over, unbuttoned the three tiny buttons at her wrist, and then with excruciating slowness eased the black lace glove off her hand. Charlie gave the same attention to her other hand, all the while leaning closer to her, so by the time the other glove slid off, Franny seemed to have forgotten all about her lack of polish and the chocolate truffle.

"You might find it interesting to know that some women never allow their hands to be seen uncovered. They even wear sleeping gloves made of silk," Charlie whispered into her ear. "And I want you to know, it's the silliest thing I've ever heard of."

Franny giggled. "But I wonder . . ."

"Yes?" He brushed her cheek with his lips.

Her mouth parted, but her usual resolve to verbalize her opinion faltered.

CHAPTER TWENTY-SIX

Just to make certain his prelude to a kiss had the desired effect, Charlie retrieved the truffle from her lap, slowly unwrapped it, and fed it to her in bites. "These truffles come from Belgium, by the way. They're dark chocolate filled with rose cream. What do you think?"

Franny swallowed the last bite. "Aromatic. Luscious." She licked her lips. "Extraordinary."

"Hmm." Charlie nodded. "Good evocative adjectives." Then he tilted her head with his finger and brushed his lips over hers. "I wonder if that's where the idea for a chocolate kiss came from."

She laced her fingers around his neck and pulled him down for a serious kiss. When they later disengaged—impossible to tell how much later—from their mystical enchantment, Franny found her voice. "Merry Christmas."

"Merry Christmas," he whispered back.

"I think I've waited my whole life for that kiss."

"Me too." Charlie eased away. "Your face has a rosy glow from being so close to the fire."

"The glow isn't from the fire. At least not *that* one." She gestured to the fireplace in front of them.

Charlie chuckled. "You know, sometimes you see a thing far away. You don't know what it is, but you feel drawn to it, because you know this thing will change your life. And the closer you get . . ."

"The closer you get?"

"I'm not saying this very well." Charlie gently took her face into his hands. "All I know is, well, those three weeks on the farm with you were the best three weeks of my life. And the day you were gone, well, it was the worst day of my life. And that's not even including the barn burning down."

Franny laughed.

"What's so funny?"

"For somebody who doesn't think he can say it right, you really said it right."

"I did?"

163

"You did. You could be a poet."

"A sad and sorry poet."

Franny kissed his hand before he released her. "But what are we going to do when we go back to the farm tomorrow? Things have changed between us. If the boss is dating the hired help, it could get messy."

Charlie kissed the tip of her nose. "I don't think the cows will be filing a complaint against us."

"No. They wouldn't dare. They love me too much."

"I guess we'll have to take it one day at a time. But know this: you're changing my life, Franny girl."

"And you've changed mine." She paused. "So tell me, is there any improvement in your leg?"

"Your kisses have cured me. Better than medicine. Look, no limp."

"That's because you're sitting down."

Charlie chuckled. "So I am."

They sat there by the fire, drinking each other in for a moment, when Charlie felt a pang of guilt, knowing that if Franny were to someday become a member of the Landau family, then he could no longer hide certain secrets from her. "You know, you were so fortunate to have had parents who were loving and generous and full of virtue. The way you talk about them moves me. It makes me wish . . ."

"Yes?"

"Well, when a person is ill, sometimes that person just needs a little help to get back to the place where he or she started. But if he's made to be confused, then it's hard for him to find his way."

"What do you mean?"

Charlie pointed to the picture of his brother, Willie, on the mantel. "It's about my brother."

"So that's your brother? I can tell. He looks a lot like you."

"Yes, people always say that about Willie."

"It's a shame your brother couldn't be here tonight. I would have enjoyed meeting him."

"I want you to meet him as well." He lowered his gaze. An odd little bug made its way across the floor. It would surely make their maid, Matilda, scream if she saw it, but he decided to leave him be. He couldn't stand to see another living thing hurt in this house.

"Is everything all right?"

Charlie thought of leaving the discussion for another evening. And yet he knew he couldn't hide their secrets forever. "No, things haven't been right in the Landau family for a long time. My brother, Willie, didn't make it here this evening because he's in a mental institution."

CHAPTER TWENTY-SEVEN

Franny paused for a moment, trying to figure out how to respond. "Has your brother always had these issues, or is it recent?" She touched his hand. "You don't have to talk about it if you don't want to."

Charlie rolled up his sleeves. "My father loaned you that dress this evening and everything to go with it. He just can't . . ." His voice drifted off as if he were out of words.

"Yes. I thought it was kind of him to help me out, since I had nothing appropriate to wear."

"You were fine the way you were. But my father had to make certain you were dressed the way *he* wanted you dressed for *his* evening."

Perhaps Mr. Landau had indeed been the one to set out her clothes. What an eccentric quality. "I guess your father has a need to orchestrate things for people."

"More than you can imagine. Only most people, like you, can handle his manipulations. They either follow through with his wishes or they ignore him. But what if there were someone who looked up to him, who wanted to please him more than anything in the world . . . but couldn't? What kind of mental trap would that be like?" Charlie rested back against the front of a chair.

"So your father's controlling nature has made your brother emotionally unsteady?"

"Exactly."

"That is so tragic. Have you talked to your father about it?"

"Oh yes. But he sees this as my brother's problem. Father has spent years trying to convince us that pursuing artistic endeavors will lead to poverty and mental instability. It's a lie, of course, just to force us into running his enterprises. Willie did fulfill his dream of becoming an artist, but his freedom is slowly killing him."

"I don't understand."

Charlie rose from the floor, leaned against the fireplace mantel, and watched the logs being consumed by the blaze. "From time to time Willie has suffered from bouts of depression, but nothing severe. Father tries to convince him that his depression is turning into madness. And the timing of our father's speeches are particularly cruel. When Willie is preparing for a new art show, Father usually insists that Willie check himself into the institution."

"Oh, Charlie. I had no idea." Franny couldn't imagine such a family nightmare. If only she could comfort Charlie or help Willie in some way. "Can't your brother at least refuse to admit himself to the institution?"

Charlie turned and looked at her. "My father has such a power over him. He's able to convince

Willie to admit himself. Well, that is, when my father feels it's necessary. He doesn't stay any longer than a few days at a time, but it's disruptive to his life. I hate to see him like this, but until I can break this merry-go-round my father has him on, I don't see much hope. Unless, of course, God sees fit to do a miracle."

Franny reached for the chair, trying to find a graceful way to rise off the floor in a dress, but before she could put in a struggle, Charlie lifted her up into his arms.

"I never would have guessed there was such turmoil in your family, Charlie. It's good you're going back to the farm. It's a place to be yourself."

"Especially with you by my side. Well, I'll be in the apartment, but you know what I mean."

"I do." Franny found herself caring more for Charlie and his family by the hour. She eased away to look at him. "Would it help your brother to come for a visit? To stay with us for a while? He might enjoy the peace of the farm . . . the fresh air and all the animals. It might do him a lot of good."

"I think it's a brilliant idea."

Franny rested against his shoulder, and the spot felt just right.

Charlie kissed the top of her head. "But let's give it a couple of days before we invite Willie out to the farm. I'm still not quite in the rhythm of things yet."

"You will be. It just takes time."

"It's not coming naturally to me, Franny. Not like it does to you. When you left, I felt as though I were wandering around in an empty room with the lights out and the doors locked. Let's see how much more grim I can make it sound."

"You'll fall into step with it. I promise."

"I did learn something out there. That I've lived a shallow life . . . and a soft life. Too easy. Not trouble-free emotionally when my father is around, but our money has diminished many of the hardships that most people face every day. Even though I don't think I'll be an exemplary farmer, the experience has been good for me." Charlie eased her away, kissed her forehead, and said, "You're welcome to stay in here and sit by the fire, but I need to go to bed."

Franny held onto him. "Do you have to go so soon? It was just getting cozy."

"I would love to visit the night away with you, but it's more important to impress you with a good day's work tomorrow." He winked, but he looked like he meant it.

"All right." Franny nodded. "As a fellow farmer, I can respect that. I should hit the hay too."

Charlie picked up his jacket off the chair. "Shall we, then?" He placed his hand at the small of her back. "I'll escort you to your wing."

"Before we go . . ." Franny fingered his rolled-up sleeve. "I have something I have to tell you." She'd tried to keep her fretting at bay all evening concerning her encounter with the porcelain clock, and she'd mostly succeeded, but now was the time to confess her transgression. To come clean with her deed. "I've been putting it off all evening. It might be nothing, and it might be something terrible. Only you can tell me which one it will be." Franny mashed her lips between her two fingers.

Charlie grinned. "You always do that duck thing when you're upset."

"What duck thing?"

"What you're doing right now with your lips."

Franny removed her fingers from her lips, mortified that she'd been looking as feminine as waterfowl. "Oh."

"Whatever it is, I absolve you from your guilt right now. It can't be that terrible."

"But I haven't told you what it is yet," Franny said.

"I don't care. There's nothing you can say that will make me feel any differently about you than I do right now. Nothing unless you tell me you are married."

She laughed. "No, we're safe with that one."

"Then please tell me, so we can go to bed."

Franny blushed.

"In separate wings."

"I broke a clock. There, I said it. I didn't mean to. I promise."

Charlie looked relieved instead of upset. "Well, it'll be one less clock for the maid to dust. I'm sure she'll want to thank you in the morning."

"But you should at least know *which* clock." Franny picked up her gloves and fiddled with them. "When I was in the bedroom getting ready for this evening, I got curious about what was in the closet. You know, all the other dresses that your father mentioned. I guess closed doors always intrigue me. Not such a good trait, I'm sure."

"That's debatable, but go on." He grinned.

"So I opened the door, and to my amazement the closet was empty except for a small porcelain clock on the floor. When I picked it up and fingered it, the little violin on the top broke off in my hands. I'm so very sorry, Charlie. I shouldn't have—"

He quieted her by placing his finger over her lips. "I don't care. That's the nature of the Landau house. Things get broken. But I care nothing about porcelain clocks."

"But what about your father?"

"I doubt he cares. We have way too many knick-knacks around here. I'm glad to be rid of some of our old junk."

"Are you sure?" Franny sighed. "I felt terrible about it."

"You should be worrying about what's important."

"Like what?"

Charlie waved his hand. "I don't know . . . like worrying that we'll have too much rye grass in the wheat this year or that the next litter of piglets will get milk fever."

Franny pulled back in amazement. "You sound like a real farmer."

"I can read." He cocked his head. "Your father left some farming books around."

Charlie offered her his arm. "Now, my lady, if you're ready, I'm going to escort you to your room. And then I'm going to give you a good-night kiss that will make the wallpaper blush."

Ohh, such a great line. Franny was going weak at the knees just thinking about that very kiss when a shadow moved at the end of the hallway. But it was no shadow. It was Mr. Landau, and he'd been caught staring at them with the most malignant sneer. He quickly backed away into an open room. Fortunately Charlie hadn't seen anything, but Franny would surely stay awake half the night wondering why Mr. Landau seemed friendly on the outside, but in an unguarded moment, his expression had darkened into malevolence.

CHAPTER TWENTY-EIGHT

Sugarplum-fairy dreams danced in Franny's head all night, intermingled with mysterious beasts that lurked in every corner, poised and ready to lunge at her with the faintest provocation. Sleep could be such a brain stew of leftovers nobody wanted.

In the morning, breakfast at the Landau house turned out to be more pageantry than plentiful, and Charlie's father felt it his duty to give them enough farming tips to choke a cow—maybe a whole herd. Mr. Landau was indeed a man who enjoyed being governor of all his affairs as well as his family's.

After several weary farewells to the household, Charlie and Franny finally set out on their trip, disappointed that they had to make the drive in separate vehicles but grateful to be traveling back to the farm.

After Franny pulled up in the yard at home, she jumped out of her pickup truck and ran to the house to give Henry a hug. He welcomed her home with so many slobbery kisses that she toppled over laughing. "It's so good to be home, Henry." Nothing smelled or felt as good as home. "Merry Christmas a little early, boy."

Charlie and Franny dismissed their temporary

farmhand, thanking him profusely, and then changed into their work clothes.

A bit later Charlie and Franny stood in front of what was left of the barn. "Well, here it is," he said. "Not much left but ashes, a piece of a wall, and a few blackened farm implements."

The wind blew over the mound of rubble, making a sad, sighing sound as if it were mourning over the passing of an old friend. It certainly wasn't a happy sight to see.

"I managed to save the tractor." Charlie removed his hat and looked at her. "Someone from the insurance company has promised to come out." He tugged on the pocket of her overalls. "Are you terribly disappointed to see it? Is this what you imagined? Or worse?"

"To be honest, it's worse than I thought it would be, but it doesn't matter, since we'll enjoy watching a brand-new barn go up." She ruffled his hair.

"Good. Well, I guess we'd better do our chores, since the cattle are lowing." Charlie grinned. "I don't even know what that means."

"It means they missed us," Franny said, "and they're hungry."

Side by side and all bundled up for the cold, they completed a multitude of farm chores, laughing and chatting through each task. Feeding the cattle. Slopping the hogs. Checking on Tutti and Frutti and their piglets. Gathering the eggs.

Cleaning out the chicken house, which meant scooping manure out the window. Charlie's leg had improved so much that he didn't seem to even notice the chores. If he had any lingering pain, he never mentioned it. Perhaps the farm air had revived him.

Later, they drove into town for chicken feed as well as five bales of hay, since all the straw had been consumed by the fire. Charlie did the bulk of the loading while Franny wondered how she'd ever done all the work by herself. And more importantly, how she'd done it without the camaraderie of such a wonderful friend.

Just friend? Not at all. She thought of their growing relationship—the sweet tendrils of affection that connected their hearts and pulled them closer each day. She hadn't even realized how lonely she'd been before Charlie. He made her see all that she'd missed, all that she longed for in a companion.

By afternoon they were exhausted but happy. Charlie wiped his hands on his overalls and said, "I've been wondering about your childhood. You know, what you did for fun. I'd love for you to take me to your secret places."

What an endearing request. "All right." Franny set her feed bucket down and dusted off her gloves. "We have some time before it gets dark." She looked up and paused to consider a stormy patch of sky, but since the blue-black clouds appeared to be rolling in the opposite direction, she ignored them.

With delight, Franny showed Charlie all her childhood hangouts. She took him to her shabby but beloved tire swing, where as a girl she'd tried to fly high enough to snatch pieces of cotton candy from the sky . . . although back then, she'd done little more than bruise her behind as well as her pride. Franny showed Charlie where the wild plums grew and then the gypsum cave, which wasn't very big but held infinite possibilities for pretend adventures when she was growing up.

Charlie still wasn't bored—amazingly—so she took him to the shallow pool where she'd made wedding cakes out of mud pies. And where she always found a gazillion tadpoles each spring. She'd called them her precious brood and nurtured them into frogs with bits of dried oatmeal and tender supplications. It had been a blissful life. Still was.

Charlie seemed fascinated with their explorations, so Franny kept going, taking him to an ancient metal barrel where her family had always burned their trash and where she'd hurled strings of firecrackers just to hear the chain of *ka-bangs*. And then—saving the best for last— Franny took him to her most secret place—the tree house nestled in the old elm where she'd spent most of her time dreaming. It became her summit, her castle, where all things were possible. Franny looked up at what was left of her tiny chateau—perhaps just the right size for little girls and an occasional elf or two. She grinned.

"So this is it, huh? Not bad. Even the roof is still there."

"Did you and your brother ever build a tree house?"

"No, my father didn't want anything to mar his trees." Charlie shrugged and chuckled.

Franny sighed. "I wonder if your dad ever had a tree house when he was a boy."

"I have no idea. He doesn't talk about his childhood very much." Charlie placed his foot on one of the lower limbs of the tree. "Come on. Let's have a look at your house."

"But I haven't been up there in years. The wood is probably rotten."

"I'll be careful, Mommy." Charlie dangled from a limb and grinned.

She watched him as he hoisted himself up to the tree house. Franny shivered, but she wasn't sure if it was from the chilly temperatures or the concern that he might fall.

Charlie opened the latch on the makeshift door, stooped down in the little entranceway, and then disappeared inside. The floor groaned with his weight, but no boards gave way. He opened the crudely constructed windows, stuck his head through one of the openings, and looked down at her with a smile. "It appears to be sound. You built a sturdy little house. Come on up."

Franny grabbed the first big limb, and then, remembering her old routine, she pulled herself up on the tree's nooks and crannies, which had always been her footholds to the loft. When she got to the tiny portico, Charlie drew her inside.

She glanced around the wooden structure and remembered how grand it had all been in her youthful imagination. The kitchen and dining hall to the right. The living quarters to the left. Even a skylight, which was little more than a hole left behind from an overly zealous hailstorm. Franny laughed at the memories as she wiped away the cobwebs and an old wasp's nest.

She flung open the back doors, which led to the veranda—that term being used in the loosest sense. "It's so strange being up here after all these years." She looked out the tiny doorway. "Charlie, would you like to sit a spell on my porch?" She motioned toward the precarious boards and railing just beyond the tiny doors.

"I'd be happy to." He eased himself down on the wooden extension and held onto the railing as he let his legs dangle over the edge. "Nice view."

Franny sat next to him and rested her arms on the railing. Just as the moment took on a sweet glow of rightness, the memory of Mr. Landau glaring at her from the shadows morphed her glow into a sickly garish hue. Her mother always said that fretting was the pastimes of pagans, so perhaps she should put Mr. Landau out of her mind. For now. "In the summertime, the fireflies would come out. Daddy would play his harmonica on the open porch, and Momma would sing along." She took in a deep breath. Memories of her youth wafted around her like a sweet breeze. "As a kid, I thought this view was paradise."

"And now?"

"Still paradise." Without thinking, she started to hum "White Christmas." She chuckled. "Sorry . . . habit of mine. Do you hum too?"

"No, but I've been caught whistling from time to time. Some women don't like it. They think its juvenile or old-fashioned or something. So I don't do it much anymore."

Well, I don't think it's juvenile or old-fashioned. "The farm is a great place to whistle." The breeze hurried through the elm tree, making the last of the brown leaves rattle. Franny looked above her. "The leaves are very chatty today."

"What do you think they're saying?"

"I guess all the things people are too afraid to say." Franny reached up and touched one of the leaves, but it crumbled into pieces and blew away in a puff of wind.

"I'm curious about something. When you were little, did you always color inside the lines? Wait a minute, let me guess. You didn't.

You told the teacher that lines were for people who had no imagination. So, am I right?"

"You're pretty close. When the teacher asked me why I didn't color inside the lines, I said that the people who made the coloring book put the lines in the wrong places."

Charlie chuckled.

"And did you?"

"Color outside the lines? No. But my brother never even used coloring books. He liked to color on everything, including painting swirling stars on the bedroom wall."

"I bet your nanny was thrilled."

"Not as thrilled as Willie. At five he thought he was van Gogh. Then when he got a little older, he wasn't content with a small paint set. He always said that God had made so many more colors than what he saw in his little tray. And he wanted to paint with them all. So, he went outside and started mashing up leaves and dirt and whatever he could find in nature to mix with his paints. Didn't work very well, but he was so passionate about it. I've always loved that about him."

"I'm sure I'll love him too."

"But not *too* much I hope."

"No." Franny smiled. "Not too much."

Charlie went quiet and seemed to study her. "So, did you ever invite anyone up here to your tree house?"

"No one but God."

He grinned. "Then I feel honored, although I invited myself."

"I'm glad you're here."

"I still can't figure out how you did all this by yourself. I don't mean the tree house—I mean everything. Weren't you ever lonely? It seems like a forlorn way to live . . . that is, without a companion all these years."

I didn't know how forlorn I was until you came along, Charlie. She wanted to say the words, but the timing didn't feel right. "Some days were easier than others. I would open my window at night, and I could hear all kinds of things . . . the coyotes howling or a distant train or the bugs humming their little hearts out. And on Sundays I might sit out on the porch and listen to the rain pattering on our tin roof. Sometimes these sounds were music to me, and then at other times they made life almost unbearable. It might have made me stronger, but I *feel* more breakable. But that doesn't make a lick of sense. Kind of like that silly idea I had to go to the city and—"

"Now, Franny, I wish you wouldn't keep tormenting yourself for having a dream."

"Honestly, my head was so stuck in the clouds, I couldn't see my own nose. It embarrasses me."

"I have plenty of humiliating stories to tell that make me look ridiculous. Would it make you feel better if I told you some of them?"

"It might." Franny grinned, wondering how

many men would allow themselves to look foolish just to put someone else at ease. If Charlie only knew what he'd done to her heart. She was in danger of losing it altogether. "Do you ever play the 'What if' game?"

"What do you mean?"

"Well, like, what if my daddy and momma hadn't gone up to latch that cellar door? What if your father had encouraged you as a musician?" *And what if you hadn't come to dance with me?* "You know, that sort of thing."

"The 'What if' game can get pretty scary. And what good can it do anyway? It only keeps us bound in the past." Charlie sputtered out some air in a chuckle. "Listen to me talk. I'm the worst—"

Thunder rolled over them and turned into a deep, throaty growl. Franny looked toward the north; the sheet of sky behind them had darkened as if it had been dipped into a bottle of bluing. "We'd better get inside."

Charlie helped her up.

"I have to warn you—when it comes to storms, I have as much backbone as a filleted catfish." She maneuvered through the tree house and then down the staircase of limbs and branches even faster than she had as a child.

When Charlie made the final step down with a jump, she looked at the churning storm and said, "This doesn't look good." She pointed toward the north. "The clouds over there . . . they seem to be spinning. We'd be safe in the cellar, but I haven't been down there since my parents died. It's not fair to ask you to use the hall closet when there's a cellar, though." Fear engulfed her.

"It's all right, Franny. I'll be with you." The wind suddenly lashed at their clothes. A spray of red dust whirled at them, and a tumbleweed bounced though the yard as if it were a rubber ball. "Those clouds mean business." He grabbed her hand. "Let's go." Lightning—red as blood and as sharp as a devil's claw—made its presence known with an assault so fearsome that it shook Franny to her bones.

CHAPTER TWENTY-NINE

Drafts of frigid air curled around them like wraithlike fingers. The gusts hit them with a blistering force, imploding with fury.

Hand in hand they ran toward the house, the wind battering against them all the way. Once they were inside, within the safety of the enclosed porch, an object slammed into the side of the house. Franny gasped but couldn't move.

Charlie took hold of her shoulders. "We need to be belowground." He looked toward the far end of the long, narrow porch, toward the cellar door.

Franny's face went numb, and her whole world swirled along with the storm. "I can't go down there. You should go, you and Henry, and yet I'm scared for you. I don't know what we should do, Charlie."

"Look, if the wind is bad enough to knock a piece of wood against the house, then it's too dangerous to stay up here. There might be a funnel cloud right above us."

Henry whimpered by the kitchen door.

Charlie slapped his leg. "Henry, come, boy."

The dog scurried toward them. Henry stopped at Franny's side, nudging at her.

Leaving her for a moment, Charlie opened the cellar door and flipped a switch. "Go on, boy."

Henry trotted down the stairs into the cellar.

Franny mumbled something, but she could barely decipher her own words.

Charlie turned her head to meet his gaze. "Stay with me, Franny."

Dizziness seized her, and her foot faltered.

He grabbed her hand. "Do you *hear* me?"

Her air felt cut off. Where was all the oxygen?

"Franny?"

She tried to concentrate on Charlie's voice. "Yes. I'm here."

"One step. Just one. All right?"

"I can't. I just can't. I'm sorry."

Charlie descended a couple of steps on the concrete stairs and turned back to face her. "I need you to do something. I want my guitar."

"What?"

He pointed toward the open closet next to the mouth of the cellar. "My guitar is right there in the closet. I want you to reach over and grab it."

Franny moaned in exasperation, but she moved slowly toward it and clasped the instrument by the neck. "Now what?"

He took hold of her free hand. "I'm going to teach you to play."

"Right now?" Franny twisted her hand in his, trying to squirm free.

"That's right." Charlie took a step down into the cellar and gave Franny a tug.

"But there's not enough light. We can't." Instead of going down the step she just leaned over.

"We'll use candlelight. And Henry and I are going to tell you stories."

Unable to break free from Charlie's grasp, Franny took one step downward and then another. "Stories? This isn't a good time for stories."

After a few seconds Franny's head cleared enough for her to understand what Charlie was doing. While she clutched the neck of the guitar and fumed over his goofy comments, he was ever so slowly leading her down the cellar stairs.

"Look at this," Charlie said. "You're getting there."

Franny stopped on the stairs, unable to move. "This is where they died. Right here." *Oh, God in heaven, is their blood still on the stairs after all these years?* Had the neighbors cleaned everything as they had promised? Or was it still visible? She glanced downward but saw nothing. The stairs were covered with dust but no more. The neighbors had respected her wishes. They had honored her parents.

"You've got to come the rest of the way down. I'm going to carry you down if I have to. Franny?"

"Yes?"

Something crashed at the other end of the porch—what sounded like shattering glass.

She jumped. "Oh, God, no, please. It's happening again."

"Now, Franny." He gave her a firm tug. "Move!"

She hurried down the rest of the way while Charlie lowered the door and then joined her in the bowels of the cellar.

"You did it, Franny." Charlie took the guitar from her and rested it against the cement wall.

Franny clutched at her heart. "I think I'm going to be sick."

"I'm not going anywhere." Charlie wrapped his arms around her, pulling her into the warmth of his embrace. "I'm not going anywhere even if you throw up all over me."

Franny released a nervous chuckle. "I just might."

Charlie held her even more tightly. "I'm right here."

After a moment or two Franny's heartbeat

slowed into a natural rhythm. When she felt she might be able to sit on her own, she moved to a wooden bench in the corner.

"You all right now?"

"Better." She nodded.

"Sorry I yelled at you."

"You're forgiven." Henry came over to her and curled up by her side. "Good boy." She gave him a scratch behind the ear and a gentle pat.

"It's kind of dark on this side of the cellar." Charlie took some matches out of a canning jar and lit the candles on the wooden table.

Franny dabbed at the perspiration on her forehead with her sleeve. "We used to sleep down here when things got bad." She pointed to one of the bunks. "Until that night."

Charlie sat across from her on one of the mattresses. "Do you want to talk about it?"

"I think I told you most of the story. It really was the worst storm I'd ever seen. Some of the porch windows right above the cellar were shattered by flying debris, so the cellar door got the full force of the winds. That's what made it bang up and down. Anyway, Momma and Daddy both went up to try to secure it. But the door was too much for them. And I guess before they could head back down the stairs, an elm tree fell. And that was it. The force of the blow was enough to kill them. I witnessed all of it. Those last moments are impossible to forget. The only blessing was that their suffering didn't last long, otherwise . . ."

Charlie took her hands in his. "I cannot even imagine such a thing. How hard that must have been."

"I will never forget the looks on their faces. The very people I'd loved most in the world . . . watching the life drain out of them."

Charlie squeezed her hands but didn't say anymore, waiting for her to go on.

"I knew this was the safest place for you and Henry to be. I knew it was the safest place for me, and yet . . ." Franny crossed her arms over her middle. "It's strange about irrational thoughts. There's no accounting for them. They cause us to toss all common sense out the window. You convince yourself that the tragedy could happen all over again. I thought of this cellar as a place of doom, not a refuge."

"It's all right, Franny. I've never met anyone yet who didn't have some secret place in his or her heart that wasn't hurting. And *everyone* is afraid of something."

The glow of the candlelight flickered against Charlie's face. Such a fine face. With Charlie there she didn't mind the dank, musty smells of the cellar or the way the small space closed in around them.

Franny glanced down at Henry, who appeared to be sleeping in spite of the storm.

They both reached down at the same time to

give him a stroke, and their hands touched in midair.

"Your friend has become my friend," Charlie said.

She smiled and hummed a few bars of any song that came to mind, trying to blot out the sounds of the storm that raged above them, raged against the elms, the house, and her spirit like some dark entity. Then, other anxieties took their turns gnawing at her.

Franny got up from the bench and settled in next to Charlie. He draped his arm around her, and she snuggled close to him. What if Charlie were taken from her—either by storm or by some other means? Even with the best scenario, Charlie was only meant to be a farmer for a time, just to prove to his father that he could succeed as a businessman. And then he would be gone to run his father's enterprises. Would he offer to sell the farm back to her? What did she dread losing the most? What was it she desperately needed—more than the farm, more than the music? With every passing hour it was becoming easier and easier to answer.

Charlie.

She was falling in love with Charlie. But did she really believe he would propose? He needed her, but why? Was it only to run the farm, or did he feel that same rush of love?

A silence drifted between them, and she

wondered about his thoughts. "I hope we won't have too much damage from the storm."

"Well, at least I'm covered. I might have more than one claim to file with the insurance people now."

She looked up at him. "You promised me a story, something embarrassing."

"I did indeed, Franny girl."

"But I want the worst one."

"You are so cruel." Charlie grinned. "I will do my best. This is one of the most pinheaded, ungentlemanly things I've ever done." He cleared his throat. And then coughed.

"You're stalling."

"Of course I am. Are you sure you want to hear this?"

"Yes! More than ever now."

He paused as if he might change his mind. "All right. When I turned eighteen, I had a bet going with my brother."

"Hmm. What kind of bet?"

"I had a bet going . . . that I could kiss one hundred girls before I turned twenty-one."

You did what? Franny had to admit that just for a moment, she wasn't paying much attention to the turbulent weather above her head.

CHAPTER THIRTY

Charlie regretted telling Franny his revelation the second it came out of his mouth.

She pulled away and looked at him. "And who won the bet?"

"I did." He groaned. "Man, I wish I hadn't told you. It turned out to be more embarrassing than I thought it would be. Shows how self-serving and phony young guys can get about affection."

"I did lots of things in my youth that I regret now. Too many to count." Franny moved back over to the bench and gave Henry a pat.

"Nothing that harebrained, I'm sure." Charlie took off his tight boots and leaned against the cement block wall.

"So what did you win?"

"Win?"

"In the bet you had with your brother."

"Five dollars."

"That's pretty funny."

"Father had us on a strict allowance."

Franny lit a few more candles. "I'm curious about your motivation. Besides being competitive with your brother."

It wasn't Charlie's favorite subject, but he supposed he deserved the question. "I guess I got confused, thinking that if a kiss equaled love then I wanted to have as many kisses as I could get."

"And did you discover anything else from your ordeal?"

"Well, I wouldn't *exactly* call it an ordeal."

She grinned.

"But I did learn something valuable besides needing to keep ChapStick on me at all times." Charlie bent his knees and draped his arms over his legs. "I learned that a kiss is meant to be more than just an act or an exploit. So much more than entertainment. A woman should not be approached nonchalantly with a kiss. One should feel truly drawn to her first. Then, it's not an exhibition but an exalted act—a divine gift." *Just as you are a divine gift to me.*

"That was beautiful, Charlie."

He smiled his thank-you to her. The candlelight glimmered, illuminating her face just enough to make her look like the angel she'd become in his mind. Perhaps it was a good time for a little music by candlelight. Charlie went to get his guitar and then offered it to her.

"You meant it? You're going to teach me how to play?" Franny put her hands behind her back. "I must warn you first, I'm hopeless."

"Nobody is hopeless."

"I'll give it a try under one condition." Franny held up her finger.

"What is it?"

"That you give up on me if you become too frustrated."

Charlie frowned. "Now what happened to my invincible Franny? I know she's around here somewhere."

"Will you teach me about shape notes?"

"Yes."

Franny grinned. "All right." She accepted the guitar and placed it in her lap as if she were hugging it. "What's first?"

Charlie sat down across from her. "Place the curl of the body of the guitar on your right leg, and avoid the urge to lean over."

Franny sat up straight.

"That's it. Good posture. Now use the tips of your fingers to press down on the frets."

Franny did just as he said.

"Try not to clench your fingers. Relax your hands. All right."

"Now what do I do with my right hand? Wow, these steel strings are painful."

"They will be until you build up some calluses. Now have the back of the guitar pressed up against you."

"Oof!" She gave her bangs a puff of air. "What a lot to remember all at once."

"I promise I'll help you. You'll get to know the guitar so well that it'll become your best friend, and it'll happen faster than you imagine."

"Sounds nice." Franny got into position and

then looked up at him. "Thank you, Charlie."

There was such trust in her eyes, such sweetness. Had he ever known such a look, such a face? And then he knew it—he wanted to wake up to that face for the rest of his life. *I love her. I love Franny.* How had it happened so quickly, so completely? But then, maybe it was just a matter of recognizing what he'd been searching for all along.

Franny lost her smile and went very still as if listening.

"What's wrong?"

"It's so quiet. There's no more pressure against the house. No wind or rain. Why did it stop so suddenly?"

CHAPTER THIRTY-ONE

Charlie did think the sudden quiet felt peculiar, the way the wind got swallowed up. "Maybe I'd better go up and check."

"Please don't." Franny set the guitar down. "It may not be safe yet."

"I think the squall has blown over. I could just raise the door and take a quick peek."

"All right, but be careful. Please?"

"I will." Charlie smiled. "Maybe this is a good time to ask you something. That is, something I've been wanting to ask you all evening."

"Yes?"

"Do you have a soda shop in town?"

"You're kidding." Franny chuckled. "What a question. You want to know that right now?"

"Yes, right now."

"There is one in Lancaster."

Charlie rose. "Tomorrow is Saturday." He placed his hand over his heart. "Would you give me the honor of allowing me to drive you into town to buy you a milk shake?"

"You're asking me out on a date?"

"It would appear so."

Franny twirled her hair. It was a gesture he hadn't seen her use before but one that looked adorable on her. "And could we share the milk shake with two straws?"

"I don't know." He scrubbed his finger along his chin. "Just as long as the locals don't think it's indecent."

"I think it'll be all right." Franny grinned. "They have a jukebox, and they will have loaded it with all my favorite Christmas tunes by now."

"We'll have to make use of the dance floor if they have one."

"They have one."

Tomorrow will not come soon enough.

The stillness above them remained steady, so he asked, "Now what do you think? Ready for me to go up and have a quick look?"

Franny nodded.

Charlie headed up the stairs. He couldn't figure out why the storm and rain had passed so quickly. Could they be in the eye of a tornado? Seemed unlikely, but he took his time going up the stairs. Once he made it to the top, he lifted the cellar door. The pulley system gave the door some extra oomph, which made it rise faster than he'd intended.

"Charlie?" Franny ran up the stairs just behind him.

He looked through the porch windows and saw something he'd never expected to see—snow. "It's all right, Franny. Everything has gone as white as heaven."

"Do you mean the ground is covered with hail?"

"No. It's what William Strode called the 'feather'd rain.' We've had our first snowstorm of the season." He smiled down at her. "Come on up."

The look of worry on Franny's face turned into delight as she joined him on the porch. She placed her palms on the window. "Glorious snow. It's Christmas already. I don't ever remember seeing snow after a thunderstorm. Will Rogers said, 'If you don't like the weather in Oklahoma, wait a minute; it will change.' It's so true."

The reflective glow from the snow mixed with Franny's awe and lit her face. He never wanted to take her smiles, her passion, or her wonder for granted. He wanted to cherish them always. In fact, *cherish* was the perfect word to describe the way he felt about Franny. That concept would make such a great song. He needed to write that down.

Charlie followed her gaze to the other side of the porch. Looked like the storm had left its calling card in the form of a few broken windows. "We do have some damage."

They walked over to the other end of the porch and assessed the pile of wood and glass. "It's not as bad as I thought it would be," Franny said.

Together they swept up the mess and nailed boards over the two openings.

When they were finished, Franny dusted off her hands. "That should take care of it, for now, anyway."

Charlie's attention drifted back outside. "You know, I'm kind of like a kid when it comes to the white stuff. I never get tired of seeing it."

"There's a farm tradition around here when it comes to the first snow. We always watch it from the ridge." Franny took her coat off the nail hook and slipped it on. "Besides, we need to check the farm for damage."

"Good idea." Charlie grabbed his coat. "So where's the ridge?"

"It's on the north side of the creek. You haven't seen it yet. But we'll follow the path past the mulberry tree, beyond the meadow, and then there it is . . . at the top of the hill." Franny touched his shirtsleeve. "I'm sorry I never showed it to you. I was so busy getting you acquainted with the farm that I didn't spend enough time encouraging you to fall in love with the land. *Your* land."

Oh, I was busy falling in love, all right, just not with the land. He grinned to himself. "We can't break tradition, now, can we?" He couldn't think of anything finer than taking a walk with Franny in the middle of a snowfall. They got Henry settled into his usual cozy spot near the kitchen furnace, and then they bundled up with all things warm and headed outside into the pristine wonder of the early evening.

They checked on the animals and went over the farm buildings, looking for damage. When none could be found, they followed the path toward the ridge. Apparently, the footpath was really a trail the cows had made on their journeys back and forth from the feedlot to the pasture.

"The cows are pretty smart. *They* know when to come home," Franny said, but it seemed as if she were talking more to herself than to him.

The snow came down more heavily now, in eddies of white, and started to collect in patches here and there in the winter wheat and in the crevices of the trees. "So, tell me more about this ridge."

"It's pretty up there, and kind of special. Every time something momentous was about to happen on the farm, something sort of historic in our family, we always took it to the ridge. When Momma found out she was pregnant with me, she told Daddy up on the ridge. When my father made the last payment on the farm, they celebrated up there, toasting with sarsaparillas."

Charlie enjoyed hearing Franny talk about the farm and her family. There was such a history here, a string of stories chronicling people's lives, and so far beyond what anyone could imagine just by looking at the property. It was still very much Franny's home.

After a brisk walk, enough to warm them up, they came across the lone mulberry tree Franny had mentioned. "So, did your father plant this?"

"We never knew how it came to be here. But I do know it gives the sweetest mulberries. Mom used to call them purple candy." Franny reached out and fingered a dormant branch. "I hope this tree is loaded in the springtime. You shouldn't miss a chance to have mulberry pie."

"What do mulberries taste like?"

"Like what blackberries dream of being."

"Oh." Charlie smiled. "Too bad spring is so far away, then."

A flash of disappointment crossed Franny's face. Did she think they wouldn't be together by springtime? He wanted to talk to her about it, but the wind picked up enough that talking became more difficult. "Would you like to go back? The temperatures seem to be dropping pretty fast."

"We should be fine." Franny shrugged and pointed eastward. "It's not too far now."

Charlie hoped the snow wouldn't get so heavy that they wouldn't be able to see their way back home, but he let go of his fears and continued following Franny down the path and then through a wide pasture. Even though it was still autumn, the approaching twilight season made its presence known by draping the fields and pasture and trees in the most elegant ermine coat. Hmm. Franny would be stunning in an ermine coat. Maybe he could buy her one as a gift. He would love to dress her in furs and jewels—the very best. But he could almost hear her saying, "I'm as simple as Jane Eyre, so I have no use for all that regalia. I'm just Franny." Charlie chuckled at the thought.

Franny didn't hear his laughter though, since she'd broken into a run across the pasture. "There it is, up there . . . the ridge. You'll love it," she hollered back at him.

Charlie ran to catch up with her. When they'd gotten to the highest point, they stopped just a few feet from the edge of a cliff.

"You're right. This is beautiful, especially in the evening light." Charlie sat down on a boulder and gazed out across the landscape, taking in the scene —the red-rock canyon, the cedars and willows, and the winding creek below. The wind calmed and a quiet settled over their world. It was a profound stillness that could only come from being covered by a snowfall in the countryside.

If all the important events happened on the ridge, then someday he would find the perfect time to bring Franny up here with the sole purpose of asking her to marry him. Charlie took the cold air into his lungs, but he felt far from cold.

Franny sat down next to him on the boulder. "I wasn't kidding about the land. It gets under your fingernails, but it gets into your heart too."

"This land . . . it's still in your heart. I can tell."

"I guess it's all right to love this farm and love music too. God made our hearts big enough to love all sorts of things. In fact . . ." Franny pointed to the other side of the canyon. "If you'll look over there by that cluster of sumac, you'll see the perfect Christmas tree. I spotted it some years ago, and now it's ready to cut."

"We should get it sometime soon." Charlie leaned toward her and pointed in the same direction. "Look. Coming out from behind that tree. Deer. Two of them."

"A mother and its fawn. You know, it's really hard not to love this place."

"So, there are no regrets about coming home?"

Franny turned to face him. "I like visiting the city, but to live there, well, maybe it's too bustling after all. Too much exhaust. Too many ashtrays. Too much noise."

"I'm glad you came home. You belong here." Charlie reached up and caressed her cheek with the palm of his hand. "Your face is glowing pink. Are you too cold?"

"No, not now."

He wanted to kiss her, but he also hoped Franny had forgotten about the bet he'd made with his brother. *Please let her forget my foolishness.* The snow continued to fall, but now it came down with less ferocity and swirled in fanciful circles around them, wrapping them in a cocoon of white confection. The snow almost whispered to them, urging them closer. He took off his gloves, wanting to feel her skin next to his. "Franny girl?"

"Yes, Charlie boy?"

"If I'm not mistaken, right above us in that big tree is some mistletoe. Hey, that's got to be some kind of sign."

"Maybe, except that we have mistletoe growing all over the farm."

"Even better." Charlie leaned down to kiss her, and the moment sealed them off from the rest of the world. It became just the two of them and the whirling magic. Had it been the same for Adam when he kissed Eve? Was there ever snow just to romance them? He couldn't be sure about earth's first kisses, but he knew their own moment felt blessed. God created. God inspired. And God sanctioned. And it was going to take every ounce of his willpower not to propose to her right now.

But he would wait and plan and make it a day so beguiling that the only word she could think to utter was *yes*.

When their kiss came to a close, Franny said, "It's hard not to wonder how my kisses compare to all those other women—"

"Oh, Franny. How I wish I'd never told you my stupid story. Why did I tell you?"

"Because you were trying to make me feel better."

"I don't think I did." He took hold of her hands. "But always remember that the finest kiss, the most passionate kiss, the most memorable kiss comes from here." He took her hand and placed it over his heart.

When Franny opened her mouth to speak again, he kissed her. Then he eased back and whispered, "Your kisses are real to me. All the others were years ago and are barely even remembered. They were as genuine as a plastic ring out of a Cracker Jack box."

"I always loved those rings. Always thought they were real." Franny grinned. "I was wrong to bring up the bet." She touched his cheek. "I won't mention it again. I promise."

"That's a relief."

"But I also want you to feel that you can always be honest with me . . . about everything. All right?"

"It's the best way to build a relationship."

Charlie raised his chin. "But you know, now that we're on the subject, what about all those farm boys around here? I'm sure they were very interested in you. Still are, I'll bet. And I wonder how many kisses they've enjoyed on these fine lips."

"I've had a few, but they were all like smooching hog lips."

"And just how many hog lips have you kissed? Wait a minute, hogs don't have lips."

Franny took his hand in hers and kissed his palm. "Seriously, I have kissed very few men, and not one was good enough for a second helping."

"All right. I guess we can put it to rest, then."

Franny stood up, raised her hands toward the sky, and did a dancing twirl. "It's like we're inside a snow globe and someone has given us a shake."

Charlie laughed.

"And it will be so pretty tonight when the moon comes out. The snow will look as if it's been sprinkled with blue glitter." She patted her hands together. "I know what we should do. When we get home, I'm going to make you some vanilla ice cream out of snow. Did you ever do that, growing up?"

"No, but I'd like to try it." *When we get home.* He found himself loving those four words.

Franny looked out over the ridge and gave one big sigh, and together they headed back toward the house just before nightfall. The moment was close to perfect, but instead of rejoicing in his spirit, the moment gave Charlie pause. Throughout his life, his very sunniest hours were usually followed by something somber. And it usually included his father. All at once he felt deeply troubled that his father, once he discovered Charlie's intentions to marry Franny, would find a way to poison his dreams. His father had done it over and over through the years, and he wouldn't hesitate to do it again.

Lord, please don't let my father come between Franny and me. You've placed us together. Please don't let my father tear us apart.

CHAPTER THIRTY-TWO

On Saturday, Charlie kept his promise by driving Franny into Lancaster for a treat at the Doo Wop Malt Shop. When he parked in front of the shop in his Rolls-Royce and then helped her out of his car, there were more gawks from the customers than there were tunes inside the jukebox. *I must be dreaming.* Franny tried not to swoon too much over the attention, and for the most part, she thought she kept her grins to a minimum.

Charlie had become less guarded about his family's name, and so it wouldn't be long before people were chin-wagging about "that Landau boy" trying to be a farmer. Oh well. There was no putting the brakes on the gossip once the locomotive had gotten revved up.

The weather had warmed a bit, and the last of the melted snow had turned into glistening diamonds in the sunlight. Franny adjusted her wool dress and the matching bow in her hair. So nice *not* to wear overalls.

Charlie pulled a nickel out of the pocket of his trousers, fed the parking meter, and then placed his hand at her back. Just as he was about to open the door for Franny, he pointed next door. "There's a music store. Do you mind if we go in there first?"

"Don't mind at all."

Once inside Finnegan's Music Store, an elderly man, who was Mr. Finnegan himself, came out from a back room. She remembered him from her youth. He'd aged over the years and wrinkled, but he wasn't craggy, just seasoned.

Organ music played over the speaker system. Too bad Mr. Finnegan didn't modernize his store's music a bit—he might get more customers.

The older gentleman looked up from his work at an adding machine. "May I help you two?"

"Oh, I'm just looking around, sir. But I like everything I'm looking at." Charlie touched the strings on a guitar and murmured, "Mmm. Fender Stratocaster."

The older man's face creased into a smile. "I

think I know a kindred spirit when I see one. So, you play?"

"Yes, the guitar and the piano. But not as well as I would like."

"Ahh, yes." Mr. Finnegan took down the guitar that Charlie had been fingering and handed it to him. "That's what I've said about my playing for the past fifty years. One thing I've learned is that true art can never achieve perfection. It's impossible. Man is flawed, and therefore art is not without flaws . . . but that is also the beauty of it. The reason?" He raised his finger with a little shake of fervor. "Our defects help to draw attention to the One who is perfect, without failings or limitations."

Franny smiled at the older gentleman, absorbing his wisdom. She'd always remembered that about him—his wise sayings and kind face. Mr. Finnegan didn't seem to recognize her, though, from all the times she'd frequented his shop as a kid. Perhaps his eyesight wasn't as sharp as it used to be.

"I couldn't agree with you more." Charlie handed the guitar back to the man. "And this is a beautiful instrument."

"That it is."

Charlie sat down on the piano bench but merely touched the keys. Franny walked past a display of trumpets and French horns and then fingered one of the acoustic guitars with wistful imaginings. *Hmm. Someday . . . maybe . . . with Charlie's help.*

The older man spoke up again. "I've been trying to retire for a few years, but nobody wants to take the business off my hands."

Charlie turned back toward the man. "Really?"

"I have just enough students to keep the place running, and I haven't had the heart to close it down. Not yet, anyway. Too many kids would suffer, since we're the only place like it in the whole area. But I can't hang on forever. I'm getting a little brittle around the edges. You know, as old as Methuselah. So I ask everyone who comes into the shop if they know of anyone who might be interested in it."

The skin prickled on Franny's arm. She could feel it in the air—God was up to something wonderful. She waited and listened.

"I see. Thanks for letting me know." Charlie went quiet for a moment as he stared at the keys.

"I'm offering a very reasonable price," the older man singsonged. He went back to polishing the old wooden counter, but he seemed to have a twinkle in his eyes.

Charlie looked across the store to Franny.

She nodded at him. *This is it.* This was the music store Charlie had been dreaming of.

He joined her on the other side of the store, away from Mr. Finnegan. "So, what do you think?"

"I think God has been working on this for

some time, putting this together for you. Charlie, you were meant to be here today to hear this." Franny tugged on his sleeve, hoping and praying he wouldn't walk away from such divine orchestration.

"But how will we do both . . . run the farm *and* a music shop?"

"I'm sure God has that worked out too. You just don't know how yet. But if you continue to lease out the wheat acreage and cut back on the number of hogs and cattle you raise, you should be able to do both."

"Franny, you're not using the word *we,* and it's getting me a little worried. I have to know what *you* think about this."

"But it's *your* farm, Charlie. And it will be *your* music shop. You shouldn't allow me to have too much say in what you do. This is a big decision." *And I don't know if your heart is as lost in love as mine.*

At the moment, technically speaking, Franny was still the hired help. Of course, the hired help was dating the boss, but with no real commitments. Charlie had made no declarations of love. Nor would she force any promises or announcements. It wouldn't be right. Love would need to flow naturally from his lips or not at all. Perhaps if things didn't work out between them, she could buy her farm back and Charlie could have his music shop. But that thought wasn't easily managed. The idea of not sharing her life with Charlie seemed unbearable now.

"Franny, look at me." With his forefinger he raised her chin to meet his gaze. "That's no longer the way I see things. Trust me."

He had a look in his eyes she couldn't quite make out, but it made Franny's heart beat a little faster.

"So, please tell me, how do *you* feel about this shop? I want to know."

"Well, I've always loved it in here. I even love the way it smells. I used to come here as a kid and pretend I could be like the well-to-do children who got lessons and learned to play. But my parents couldn't afford it, so I always went away dreaming." She glanced around. "There's a lot of potential here. If you advertised maybe you could build up the number of students. Hire more teachers. Maybe even offer a greater selection of instruments. It could be quite grand." Franny got lost in the moment, realizing how the shop could be her delight too. God really had made their hearts big enough to love all sorts of things. But the biggest stumbling block hadn't even been mentioned. Mr. Landau came to mind. "What about . . . ?"

"Yes?"

"Your father? With the way he feels about music, would he try to stop you?"

Charlie's smile faded.

CHAPTER THIRTY-THREE

Charlie always knew the day might come when he'd be forced to step out of the spotlight—the one his father had focused so intensely on his life. "Well, if I bought this music store, my father wouldn't be in the stands cheering for me. That is the one thing I'm certain of—but whether he'd try to stop me, I don't know. Franny, perhaps it's time to take my own course, make my own life. Even if it means going it alone, without my father's approval. Or his financial help. I do have some money saved. I have to do what I think is right, and this feels right to me."

"So will farming still feel like the right thing too?"

He wanted to brush her concerns away with a kiss, but words would have to do for the moment. "I don't regret buying the farm. I doubt I'll ever be a great farmer, but I am beginning to feel what you've been talking about, the way the land gets to you. And if I hadn't come to buy your farm, I never would have met you." He let his finger slide down her cheek and under her chin. "Both were a divine gift, and no man could be happier with them."

"I see." She smiled, touching his hand.

But the part he couldn't tell Franny was how

his father might react when he told him that he intended to marry her. Even though his father had been cordial to Franny at the dinner, there was no guarantee he would endorse their union. He sensed that the two new directions in his life might set off a clash that could escalate into an all-out war. *One battle at a time.* "I need to know . . . do I have your blessing to buy the shop?"

"Yes, you do."

"Then I think *we* have something to say to Mr. Finnegan." He offered her his arm, and she took it.

Charlie led her to the front of the store, where Mr. Finnegan still buffed away at the same spot as he tried to sneak glances at them. He seemed to already know what they were going to say.

"Sir?"

"Yes?" Mr. Finnegan chuckled. "I overheard you two talking. I hope you have some good news for me."

"We do." After Charlie introduced himself and Franny, he said, "I am interested in buying your business, but of course we'll have to negotiate the price and discuss the details."

"I assure you, you'll find me a most reasonable man to deal with." Mr. Finnegan shook Charlie's hand.

"I'm sure I will." Charlie handed him his business card. "Here's my information. My attorney will be in touch with you soon."

"Anytime at all would be fine. I'm always right

here." Mr. Finnegan patted his hands together like a small boy. "This is a very good day for me . . . for us all. You're an answer to my prayers. Thank you."

"You're an answer to mine as well, sir." Charlie shook the man's hand again, and the elderly gentleman put his soul into it, pumping his hand with gusto. *What a good man.* Too bad his father hadn't ended up a bit more like Mr. Finnegan.

"Merry Christmas." The older man gave them a little salute.

"Merry Christmas," they called back and headed out the door.

Charlie's spirit had never felt so light. "I think we should celebrate this momentous decision."

"What better way than the Doo-Wop Malt Shop?" The pink-and-green neon sign blinked its welcome to them as Franny opened the door.

This time Charlie walked through while Franny held the door for him. "Thank you, miss." He bowed slightly.

They got a few stares as they strolled through the door that way, which made them both laugh. Merriment was a new feeling for him, and he knew at once that it felt like a great way to live.

Charlie couldn't remember the last time he'd been in a malt shop. He glanced around at the chrome barstools, the jukebox, and the milk shake machine behind the counter. Quaint and cozy—a good place to be with Franny.

Once seated in the crescent booth at the front, Charlie ordered one white cow vanilla milk shake, and just as Franny suggested, he asked for two straws and chocolate sauce swirled on top.

When the waitress brought their malt, they slid their straws into the foam and leaned forward to sip their drink. Their noses touched, and Franny laughed. "This is good. I haven't taken the time to have one of these in about a year. Usually too busy with chores. And I'm happy about what we're celebrating. I really am."

Charlie wondered what she was leading up to. "Do I hear a 'but' in there somewhere?"

Franny went serious. "I promise I won't bring it up again, and I don't want you to think I'm not happy about the music shop. I'm thrilled. But please tell me one more time that I haven't interfered too much with your life. Your father might see what we're doing . . . you know, buying the music shop . . . as mutiny. I would hate to encourage you to do something that could drive a permanent wedge between you and your father. Family is such an important part of life, and I could never forgive myself if I caused a—"

"Franny." He took hold of her hands. "My father and I were struggling long before I met you, so please don't worry that you're causing a rift. But you have to understand that my father has made me jump through so many hoops over the years, I feel like an animal in Barnum & Bailey. I will continue to give my father respect. I feel God would want me to . . . but my father can no longer dictate my life."

"I understand." Franny relaxed her hands in his. "I'm with you."

"That's just where I'd hoped you'd be." Charlie gave her hands a squeeze and then released her. He took another swig from the straw, and she did the same. His talk had become bold, but somewhere inside he hoped he wasn't a prairie dog poised to run back into its burrow. It was hard to know how to be a man of integrity, and even harder to live it. When he'd had a few more minutes to think about the consequences of buying the shop, he realized there was a good chance his father would disinherit him. Where would his mettle be then—cowering in a hole? "So, you feel better then, about my father and our plans."

"Yes, I do."

"Good." Charlie took another sip of the malt and then slid out of the booth. "I think we need some music." He headed to the jukebox. He found the song he'd hoped for, slid a coin into the slot, and walked back to Franny. Elvis began to sing "Blue Christmas." It was a melancholy tune, but it brought back the memory of the day he'd first met her—when they'd slow-danced together. Now he would dance with her again as the woman he loved, and it would be unforgettable.

He stretched out his hand to her. "May I have this dance?"

"Yes, you may."

Charlie led her to the little checkered dance floor next to the jukebox. She placed her palm against his, and he placed his hand on her waist. Then they disappeared into the music, barely noticing the other customers grinning and nodding in their direction. Together they swayed back and forth, and with each intoxicating beat of Elvis's song, they were more deeply enveloped in a golden haze—just the two of them. Perhaps it was the sweet-sad lyrics or the unhurried and evocative style that worked its charm, but he doubted it. It was just being near Franny. That was all the magic he needed.

Her cheek, oh-so-soft against his, and the rose scent of her hair was a wonderful overload on his senses. Charlie moved her a little closer to him, feeling mighty glad that he wouldn't have to live the song's lament and be without Franny for Christmas. "A moment ago, you asked me if you'd interfered with my life. You have. You've interfered with my life in the most wonderful and profound way."

"Oh? I have?"

"Yes. You've made me fall in love with you."

CHAPTER THIRTY-FOUR

Even though Franny rode back to the farm in Charlie's Rolls, it felt more like hovering on a bank of clouds—the poufy, blissful kind that would never think of turning into a rainstorm. On the dance floor, when Charlie whispered his endearment, she had thought he'd said something else—maybe "dove" or "above." Surely not "love." But when she had him repeat the words to make certain there was no misunderstanding, she burst into tears. Charlie gave her his handkerchief, and in spite of her sobs she was certain it would be remembered as one of the most romantic moments of her life.

When Charlie helped Franny out of his car she got a little drifty, gazing into his dark brown eyes. How many sighs could a girl endure before she passed out from hyperventilation? But she'd have to come down from her dreamy state soon, since they had a load of not-so-dreamy chores to do before supper.

As they walked toward the house together, Franny glanced toward the lane. A car drove up the road at an alarming speed. "I wonder who that is." She shielded her eyes against the sun.

"Do you know the car?"

"I don't think so."

They waited for a moment until the car pulled

up into the yard and slowed to a stop in front of them.

The vehicle, on closer inspection, looked to be an ancient green Chevy station wagon, and it looked like it had been through a mud bath, which made the driver barely visible through the windshield. Franny walked toward the car as a woman got out. "Noma, is that really you? I can't believe it. What a wonderful surprise."

Noma chuckled as she pressed her palm to her forehead. "I'm mighty relieved that you're so glad to see me."

"Well, of course I am." Franny pulled the woman into a hug, and they stayed that way for a moment or two, rocking back and forth. Franny could feel the woman's bones through her thin coat, and it made her heart ache for the older woman. "I was afraid I would never see you again. I'm so glad God thought otherwise." When Franny released Noma she turned to Charlie. "You remember Noma from the diner."

"I'm glad you came," Charlie said. "By the way, how did you find us out here? There aren't any road signs."

"Well, I stopped and asked some people in town. They told me the way." Noma glanced away for a moment.

Franny touched her arm. "Did they treat you well in town?"

"Well, when they saw me, they got a little

absentminded about how to greet a woman, but other than that, they was just fine." Noma looked at Charlie and then back at Franny but said no more.

"What is it?" Franny asked.

"I guess I do need to tell you something." Noma licked her lips. "But I've just arrived, and I hate to burden you with my story. It's not pleasant to hear."

"You can tell us anything," Franny said. "I promise it's all right."

"Whatever you have to say, Noma, it's safe with us." Charlie walked toward her car. "Maybe we could get you settled and then you could tell us about it."

"Yes, that's a good idea." Franny looked at him with a grateful smile. "And we could sit in the kitchen with some apple cider."

Noma hesitated, looking worried, and then seemed to yield to the idea. "Thank you for your kindness."

"You're welcome, but we haven't done too much yet." She grinned, which made Noma smile.

Arm in arm, like old friends, they walked toward the house while Charlie brought in her one small bag. Perhaps he sensed that Noma needed the listening ear of a woman, because he disappeared outside.

When the two of them had gotten settled with

mugs of hot cider, Franny said, "Now, please, tell me, what's on your mind?"

Noma took a sip of the cider. "After I left the diner, well, I got fired from one of my cleaning jobs."

"Oh no. What happened?"

Noma gathered her hands into a knot. "Well, the lady who let me go, Miss Alice, she got it into her head . . . as awful as it sounds . . . that I was after her man. Her husband was almost old enough to be my daddy, so I don't know how she could get a thing like that stuck in her head. But facts don't matter much to Miss Alice once she gets going. Mm–mm–mm."

"How could she accuse you of such a terrible thing?"

"Well, those words came pretty easy to her. Rolled right off her tongue."

"But where was her proof?"

Noma sighed. "Miss Alice's husband don't stay at home much, and when he does come home, he's usually tipsy. And yesterday he came home drunker than a saloon skunk. I tell you, it was a sight to see him staggering and stumbling about, knocking things over. Expensive vases and knick-knacks and such. Anyway, I was upstairs dusting, not making any noise. Miss Alice doesn't approve of me singing or humming while I work, so I was quiet. But I was also keeping an eye on her husband, just to make sure no harm came to him.

Then I saw him teetering at the top of them stairs. He was about to fall down a long flight of steps. He woulda surely broken his neck. Just before he fell I grabbed his arm, just to steady him. That's all I did."

Noma shook her head. "That's all I did. But it's not what Miss Alice claims. She says I was encouraging him to . . . well, I will not fill the air with her words. They're lewd, and they're a lie before the Almighty."

"But what did her husband say? Did he take up for you at all?"

Noma cupped her fingers around the mug as if trying to take in its warmth. "Miss Alice's husband, he said nothing in my defense. He just went on to bed to sleep off the whiskey."

"That is so malicious." Franny's eyes stung with mist. "But you still have your other cleaning jobs, right?"

"I still had enough work, but all the other ladies are friends with Miss Alice, you see, and when she told them . . . well, they believed her. And so, that was the end of me."

CHAPTER THIRTY-FIVE

"They all fired you without even letting you defend yourself?" Franny moved her mug away, but she really wanted to throw it against the wall.

Noma nodded. "I begged them not to let me go.

I said I'd clean their houses for half the money. I thought they'd have mercy on me since Christmas was coming and all. But they said if I showed up for work again, they'd call the police."

"Surely there's something we can do about this." *God, why does life have to be riddled with so many injustices?*

Noma touched one of the little printed flowers on the sleeve of her dress. "It was enough that you were here to listen to my story. To be believed and understood . . . well, that means more to me than money."

"I know what you mean. To be believed is meaningful and necessary. But I'd still like to do something. They should be forced to do what is right." Franny tugged on her apron until the well-worn fabric tore. "It's so hateful, what they did."

"Justice is always gratifying. Yes. But it would be hard to stay in a place where you know you're not wanted. Folks like to feel welcome."

"Oh, I agree. I do." Piece by piece Franny put a workable plan together in her mind. "I know a place you would be very welcome: here on this farm." She knew it was no longer her farm, and yet she knew Charlie's mind well enough to know that he would want Noma to stay until she could get a job.

Noma looked at Franny, her eyes watering. "Your charity, your generosity, is appreciated, but I can't accept it. I could only consider staying under one condition, which is what I came to ask you both. I thought since you had a farm to run, maybe you needed someone to cook and clean for you. And maybe help with the chores. I don't need much money, only a little food and a place to rest my head. I could be happy just to be around folks who make me feel like I'm human."

"Actually," Charlie said as he opened the screen door, "that sounds doable." He held up his hand. "I promise I just heard the last part. I know you're in some kind of need, but whatever it is, I think we're in need of you more." He sat down at the table. "Franny and I would like to hire you with full pay. It's the only way we'd agree to your idea."

Franny gave him a rosy smile.

"I'm going to be buying a small business in town," Charlie said, "and we're going to need some extra help with the workload out here."

"Yes, that could work very well." Franny clapped her hands together.

They both looked at Noma, who seemed surprised at what Charlie had said. Then she smiled up at the heavens and nodded at them both. "Thank you." Her eyes shone with tears. "Such good news today."

"I'm glad." Charlie stuffed his hands into the pockets of his overalls, looking quite happy. "Glad it's all settled, then."

"And I have a nice place for you to sleep," Franny said. "I'm in the back bedroom, and

Charlie sleeps in a little apartment above the toolshed. So you may have my parents' old bedroom."

Noma drooped a bit. "I'm sorry to start out so contrary, but I don't feel it's right, taking your parents' room. Do you have another place for me? I don't need much."

"Well, there is a small bedroom in the attic, but it's not really fixed up very well, and—"

"That would do me just fine."

"All right." Franny reached out to Noma and squeezed her hand. "But the minute you change your mind, you're welcome to the other room."

"Thanks be to God. He's given me a place to work." Noma rose, picking up the mugs from the table.

"And a place to call home," Franny finished. "But what about your house? Who will watch over it?"

"That wasn't my home to keep," Noma said. "I just rented it from my sister, so now she's going back to live there. And it was her furniture too. All I own is in that bag. And in my pockets." Noma pulled out the tiny wooden manger scene from her coat pocket and set it on the table. "Over the years, I've found that what God sees fit to give me is always plenty."

Franny had never traveled through life as humbly as Noma had. She wondered what Noma's life had been like—finding blessing in simplicity and giving in the midst of shortage. And how must Charlie view Noma's life—was her poverty impossible to imagine from his affluent upbringing?

Henry whimpered from the porch and then barked, stealing Franny from her thoughts. "Henry carries on like that when he hears somebody pulling up in the yard."

Charlie got up from the table and went out through the screen door.

Franny and Noma followed him onto the porch.

"What in the world . . . ?" Charlie said.

"Who is it?" Franny asked. "Do you recognize the car?" Whoever it was, the person drove a very expensive vehicle.

"It's my father. He's come to check up on me."

Franny's mouth went dry as face powder.

CHAPTER THIRTY-SIX

Charlie didn't want to wait for his father to come to the door, so he grabbed his coat and headed out to meet him. Franny and Noma followed close behind.

Charlie went around the driver's side of his father's Bentley and opened the door for him. "Father?"

"Son?" He tapped his finger on the steering wheel and then got out of the vehicle.

"To what may we attribute your visit, sir?" What was his father doing here? Couldn't he trust his grown son to run a business even for a few weeks before the inquisition?

"I've come to visit my farm." His father picked up a leather folder off the seat and then smoothed his camel-hair coat. "I wanted to see what you were really up to out here."

Franny, her usual gracious self, made the introductions with Noma, and to his father's credit, he didn't create any embarrassing moments when Franny introduced Noma as a friend and not as a cook.

"Did you want us to give you a tour?" Charlie finally said to him, although there was little need to ask since his father already scrutinized the terrain with a skeptical eye.

"Yes, and I have a few questions about the operation." His father tapped his finger on the folder. "I have some ideas for improvements and expansion. It'll be a lot more work for you, of course, but you're up for it. Aren't you, son?"

Sooner or later his father would have to be told about their plans to buy the music shop. Maybe now was as good a time as any. "Well, it's good that you brought it up, since—"

"I would love to help show you the farm," Franny said to Mr. Landau, "but I'm sure Charlie would like to spend some time alone with you. I need to get Noma settled in the house. Please excuse us."

Charlie knew what Franny was up to. He'd have to thank her later. It might, indeed, be better to break the news about the music shop to his father in a more intimate way. The news would still work like gunpowder when he blew, but at least the firework exhibition would be in private.

Mr. Landau nodded to her. "Thank you, Francine."

Once they were alone, his father didn't say anything more. He merely marched toward the barn. At least what remained of the barn after the inferno—*inferno* being his father's word. Why did he always have to go for the jugular vein? "Wouldn't you like to change into something a little more appropriate? It's kind of dusty out here, and you never know when you're going to step into something . . . foul. I warn you, it's a mess that's hard to clean up."

He shot Charlie a frown. "I'm fine." He gave the bottom of his suit vest a jerk to straighten it. Something he did every hour on the hour. Charlie could set his watch by it.

"Are you angry about something?" Charlie asked.

"No." His father kept walking toward the blackened mess like a pointer to its covey.

The birthmark on his father's cheek appeared fiery, which was always a barometer of his mood, but Charlie had learned from childhood not to mention the birthmark. Ever.

They both stopped in front of the molten disaster.

His father stood there, stroking his beard. "Have you called the insurance agent?"

"Yes. It's all been taken care of, Father. It was an old barn, and we'll get a new one. No one is upset. Franny thinks it's a blessing."

"She no longer owns the farm, so I don't see how her opinion is necessary." His father seemed to study him. "How necessary has her opinion become to you?"

"Quite." He wanted to tell his father about his plans to marry her, but he hated to light too much dynamite all at once. They'd be blown to kingdom come.

"Oh? I see. Well, she's a woman with grit. I'll give her that."

Generous of you, Father.

"She is like a rag doll, though . . . too rough around the edges for decent society, especially in those dime-store dresses of hers, but maybe that can be fixed with some serious—"

"Fixed?" Charlie kicked at a rock he saw stuck in the ground. Instead of loosening it, he stubbed his toe. "There isn't a thing in the world I would change about Franny."

"That infatuated, are you? Hmm. I'm glad she doesn't mind hard work. She'll be a good helper in this expansion. I've been thinking about the fields in particular. Some of the ones that aren't suited for growing wheat could be used for a large hog farm. A piggery with hundreds of animals." He opened the leather folder. "Then when the operation is in full swing and making money, we can sell the farm and you can finally come to work for me. I've been putting this off for too long, so with these new plans we can speed things up a bit and move forward with our ultimate goal."

Charlie placed his fingers on his closed eyelids. He felt a headache coming on. A big one. He'd need some aspirin this time. "I have to tell you something. It's—"

"As far as Franny is concerned, when the time comes for you to sell, maybe she'll be tired of the farm . . . and, well, of you too. Then she won't be a problem. You'll both be able to make a fresh start all around." He snapped his folder shut as if that were the end of the discussion.

Charlie tried to remain calm, but it was getting harder by the second. Instead of inflaming the situation with wrath-filled words, his fingernails ground into his palms. He didn't know where to start with his father. There was too much wrong with everything that came out of his mouth. *God give me patience. I want to honor him, but I can no longer let him rule me.*

"Well, *say* something."

Charlie stuffed his fists into the pockets of his overalls. "I'm staying in the apartment over the toolshed . . . but not for long." He wasn't quite sure why he'd said the words, but it felt right to do so.

"I know you mentioned that when you were at home. I'm glad you've come to your senses. *You* should be in the main house and the hired help should be in the apartment. But what does this have to do with anything I've just told you?"

Charlie looked at his father, eye to eye. "My life out here started with a certain plan in mind." *Your plan.* "But Franny has changed everything. She's—"

"Upp." He raised his index finger. "I realize she's another one of your girlfriends, but—"

"No, I wouldn't put it that way." He straightened his shoulders, knowing he was about to put gasoline on the fire. "Someday I will be moving into the house, but it's not for the reason you mentioned. If she'll have me . . . Franny will be my wife."

CHAPTER THIRTY-SEVEN

His father's birthmark brightened. "You've come out here and you've been mesmerized by this woman. I can see it."

"I thought you *liked* Franny."

"She's an interesting woman. But we all know interesting women, and we like spending time with them. And eating dinner with them. But it doesn't mean we have to marry them."

"I've never met anyone like her. Sometimes she's just Franny, guileless and simple with a heart as big as the moon, and then sometimes she has these spirited moments when she seems almost bigger than life—as if she were, I don't know, an American icon."

His father slapped his hand on the folder. "That is the most irrational gibberish I've ever heard. She really has you spellbound, doesn't she?"

"You're listening, but you never hear me, Father." Charlie picked up a rock and threw it at a window on the barn. It was the sole remaining windowpane on the last standing wall. The sharp sound of it crashing through the glass felt unexpectedly painful, as if the stone had hit him instead of the barn.

"Perhaps I should remind you that you two are from very different upbringings, different educations, different families, and—"

"Is that why you invited Sylvie to dinner? To distract me from what is different?"

His father made no reply, so that left him with only one correct answer.

"And now that I'm thinking about it, you were probably the one who planted that clock in Franny's closet the night we all had dinner. You know, the clock that was ready to break when she touched it. You wanted to set her up. Make her look bad. I hope you hadn't planned on bringing it up while you're here, because—"

"Look, no matter what you think you see, Francine Martin is just a—"

"She's just what . . . a farmer? I was hoping you weren't going to say that. Farming is hard work and a very honorable profession. She's smarter than most men I know, and yes, we have different families, but after hearing about Franny's father and mother I feel a great loss in my life that I didn't get a chance to meet them. To know them. I'm sure my life would have been richer for knowing them, and I mean richer in the *nonmonetary* sense."

"I know what you meant. You don't have to belabor it."

Charlie glanced over the debris and noticed an old dartboard; it was charred almost beyond recognition. He could just imagine Franny playing the game with her father. They'd been so close. She'd been so fortunate.

"I'd like to see the rest of the farm now."

"All right." He knew his father well enough to know the real reason he'd changed the subject: he'd already dismissed the idea of Charlie marrying Franny. Charlie sighed, feeling old for the first time in his life. "Why don't you stay for dinner?" Maybe she could win him over. If anyone could, it would be Franny.

"All right. I will."

"Good." Charlie nodded.

His father walked off in the direction of the

farrowing house. "Then I can tell you *both* about my expansion plans for the farm."

Charlie thought he'd wait for dinner to tell his father about the music store. Of course, it meant the meal would be like an undigested bomb in his stomach. He would take no joy in Franny's cooking tonight.

"By the way, you'll need to get the barn up soon," his father said. "I'll crack the whip with the insurance company—"

"No need for any whips. It'll be fine." Charlie would need to change the subject yet again. "Let me give you the rest of the tour."

They walked around the farm, father and son, side by side, talking about farming issues . . . and from a distance they might have even looked like a good family team. But in spirit, the chasm between them was big enough to consume the entire farm. Charlie dug his fingernails into his palms. *God, I no longer know how to fix this great crack in our relationship.*

"I see you've hired yourself a cook."

Charlie kept up with his father's fast-paced stride. "What?"

"That colored woman."

"That woman you're referring to is Miss Noma Jefferson, and she's a friend of Franny's and soon to be a friend of mine. She was going to be our guest for a while, but she insisted on helping out. And she needed a job."

"Hmph. Well, I suppose you'll want to keep her in the main house along with Francine. Perhaps she'll want to stay in the master bedroom and she'll need her own personal maid too." He shook his head. "You young people have such outrageous notions. You're like the king who lets his peasants tell him how to sit and what to eat and where to sleep."

Give me strength, Lord . . . even if it's just for dinner. And then, hopefully, he won't want to spend the night.

After an abbreviated version of the farm tour, Charlie steered his father toward the house. He was surprised that he didn't put up an argument, but then perhaps the enticement of dinner sounded good, even if it wasn't five courses.

The minute they stepped into the enclosed porch, the aroma of home cooking greeted them.

"Something smells good," his father said, sounding a little less gruff.

"Franny is a wonderful cook." *Good start.* He'd find a special way to thank her later for all the peace offerings.

The second they were in the kitchen, Franny met Charlie's gaze and smiled. It was her attempt to encourage him, and it succeeded . . . at least a little. She and Noma were both working, running back and forth from the kitchen counters to the table with heaping plates of food—steak, mashed potatoes, and peas. "I'm glad you've come in. Supper's ready."

"Smells wonderful, Franny." Her face had a smudge of flour on it, and he wanted to brush it off with a kiss, but he also knew it wouldn't be the best timing for a display of affection. So, he just helped her by toting the basket of biscuits and the bowl of homemade butter to the table.

"This farmhouse never did have a dining room. I hope you don't mind eating in the kitchen," Franny said to Mr. Landau.

"This is fine."

"Please, go ahead and sit down, all of you," Franny said, taking off her apron. "I think it's all on the table now."

Mr. Landau pulled out the chair at the head of the table— the only chair that had arms—and sat down with enough regal pomp to impress royalty. "You don't dress for dinner?"

"No." Charlie sat next to his father. "It's easier to keep my overalls on, since I'll have to go back out later and do a few more chores."

"Oh," was all his father replied.

Franny pulled out the chair at the opposite end from Mr. Landau and stood behind it. "Noma, you are also a guest this evening, so this is your spot."

Noma glanced around the room and then backed away. "I don't think—"

The scowl his father wore appeared to be

keeping Noma from sitting down, so Charlie shot him a supplicatory expression. His father smiled, but something ran under the surface of his expression that told Charlie his tolerance for being maneuvered was close to the edge.

Mr. Landau looked over his glasses at Noma. "Miss Jefferson, the sooner you sit down, the sooner we can taste this fine cooking."

When Franny didn't appear to have any intention of sitting down until her friend was seated properly, Noma took off her apron, placed it on the counter, and slipped onto the seat.

Franny gave Noma's shoulders a squeeze and sat down across from Charlie.

Noma readjusted herself in the chair—and, as Franny might say, Noma looked as comfortable sitting across from Mr. Landau as a worm dangling in front of a catfish.

"Charlie, do you want to say grace?" Franny smiled at him.

That was what he needed—grace—a truckload of it. "Sure." Charlie bowed his head, wondering how the words should come out.

CHAPTER THIRTY-EIGHT

When the meal was almost over, Mr. Landau cleared his throat. "Charles, as you know, I have something I want to discuss about the farm."

Charlie cleared his throat even more loudly than his father. "Yes, I know, but there's something I need to say first. I know what you're proposing, and I think under normal circumstances it might be a good business move."

"Might be? Please explain." Mr. Landau ate the last bite of his second helping.

"Well, first of all, I've been listening to the farm-and-market report, and hog prices are so low that this might not be the best time to start a large operation with a commodity that's doing so poorly in the marketplace." He felt like a coward, skirting around the main issue, but at least the report wasn't a lie.

"Yes, yes, I heard the same report." His father waved him off. "Old news . . . but I've consulted with an expert in the business, and he says—"

"What?" Charlie put up his hands. "He says what, Father?"

Franny swallowed her food, and the sound of it could be heard across the table.

Noma dabbed at her neck with her napkin.

"Look, no matter what you do about the hogs, I

still think you should utilize that fallow land. It would be to our advantage." His father locked eyes with him.

Charlie gripped his utensils until his fingers went stiff. "True, but there is another factor to consider."

His father lifted his glass of sweet tea but didn't drink as he waited for Charlie to continue. Charlie glanced at Franny, who was busy buttering her biscuit—for the second time. He gave her a wink.

She smiled back at him but absently reached for a third dollop of butter.

"And what could it be?" his father asked. "This other factor?"

"Well, we'll keep running the farm, but I've also found a shop in town . . . one I'm interested in running. The owner is selling, and I've already told him I'll make him an offer." Charlie set his napkin down. Dinner was over. At least it was for him.

"Oh, really? And what kind of business is it, son?"

Charlie rubbed the back of his neck. "It's a music store."

Mr. Landau ran the tips of his fingers along the edge of the table. "Well, I thought we'd been through this before."

"We have, but my side of the story has yet to be heard." Charlie glanced at his father but then looked away.

Mr. Landau folded his napkin, and with ominous formality, he set it next to his plate.

They were at an impasse in the road with no sign of a detour.

Everyone stopped eating. Except for a hum from the refrigerator, all else went quiet.

"Pumpkin pie anyone?" Franny rose. "Noma was good enough to go into town for some ice milk to go on top."

"No, thank you," his father said. "Charles, we should discuss this in private."

"I think this is a good place to talk," Charlie said.

Noma rose. "I should go now, since—"

"You're welcome to stay, Noma." Charlie motioned to her chair. "Please."

Noma clasped her fingers around her throat and slowly sat back down.

"Well, now, Charles, you've got your allies around you, so I guess we may proceed." He made an exasperated gesture with his hands and turned to Franny. "Miss Martin, I can't imagine—"

"You're welcome to call me *Franny*." She took her seat.

"Miss Martin, surely you don't approve of this scheme that Charles has cooked up. The farm has always been your life. You did, of course, seek a wayward life of music recently, but you insisted that you'd made a blunder—that you'd learned a valuable lesson in the process. Wasn't this the impassioned little sermonette you gave at my house?"

"Not my exact words, but yes." Franny fingered her uneaten biscuit. "But the experience . . . my blunder . . . didn't lessen my love for music. It's difficult to reject a God-given dream outright. It keeps rising up until we follow through with it. And your son and I do have a plan." She gave Charlie a beseeching "please-give-me-a-hand" look.

"We do have a strategy, sir," Charlie said. "If we continue to lease out the wheat land and cut back on our herds, we would have time to manage the store. And too, Noma has agreed to work with us. With her help, there should be no problem with being able to get all the work done." No matter how rational the idea had sounded earlier—now when he placed it before his father like an innocent sacrifice—it looked weak and blemished.

"Time has nothing to do with it," his father said, impatience seeping into his tone. "It has to do with our ultimate objective, and that is for you to work at Landau Enterprises. This has been our understanding since you were thirteen."

Charlie stacked his dishes. "The owner, Mr. Finnegan, let the music store languish some, but with some advertisement and a little more merchandise I think it could succeed. It's the only music store in this whole area, so I think . . ."

"You didn't hear me at all." His father glanced

around the table with a look of incredulity. "Not a word."

That is how I've felt all my life.

His father stood up from the table, allowing his chair to scrub across the floor, which made a wrathful sound. "I am appalled at this turn of events." He turned to face Franny. "And you, young lady—I thought you'd come to your senses about this great offense done to your parents, trading in your heritage as if it were a used automobile. You sold off your inheritance, what your parents sacrificed to give you. You walked away from it, selling it all to my son with no debate or any thought. Just like Esau, who didn't bother to fight for his birthright. Where was your grateful spirit for this legacy? Where was your understanding of the lifeblood—"

"Father." Charlie ground his fingernails into his palms. "I don't think you—"

Franny put up her hand. "It's all right, Charlie. I don't mind answering your father's questions. They're valid." She closed her eyes for a second and then said, "I understand what you're saying, Mr. Landau, and you have a good point. I've had all these same thoughts, and I have grieved about it." She licked her lips. "But I have to live with my mistakes, and they were mine to make. I believe my parents would have respected that. They enjoyed having me by their side, working on the farm, but they also raised me to be independent in my reasoning and free to follow my heart."

"Hmph." His father smoothed his tie and took a step back from the table. "I hear a lot of 'feels right' and 'free' in your rebuttal and a copious amount of 'me.' It's the way of youth today, and such foolhardy behavior will not to be tolerated in *my* house."

Franny sat quietly, but Charlie knew his father's words must have struck her like an iron rod.

Charlie glared at his father. "Sir, you owe Franny an apology. I think—"

"You're mistaken. I owe nothing to anyone. It is you who owes *me*." He turned back to Franny. "Thank you for the meal. I will be driving back to the city now." And then, without even acknowldging Noma, he snatched up his leather folder on the kitchen counter and strode out the back door.

Charlie looked at Noma and then at Franny. "I'm sorry. I never meant for—"

"It's all right." Franny reached across the table and placed her hand over his.

Noma gathered up the dishes. "Your father seems to be a man with more purpose than peace. I'm sorry he's causing you so much pain."

"Thank you for that, Noma." Charlie rose from the table. "Excuse me. I'll walk him out to the car to say good-bye."

Franny nodded.

Once outside, Charlie ran to catch up with his

father, who was already sliding into his car. "Isn't there some way we can work this—"

"Now you listen to me." His father slapped the leather folder against his hand. "There will be no more talk of this music store. And there will be no more talk of marrying Miss Martin. You will do as I say, and that is all."

"Father, I'm a grown—"

"Upp! No more. This is your final warning. If you buy this music store and marry that woman, I have the power to—"

"Yes, I know. You have the power to disinherit me. I'm willing to accept it if you —"

"No. I knew cutting you out of my will wouldn't be enough to deter you from your nonsense, so I'm ready with another plan, one which will enable you to see more readily the error of your ways." He punched the back of his hand into his palm. "If you follow through with your plans I will be placing your brother in a mental institution, only it won't be for a weekend. It will be for years. The director and I are friends. He owes me a great deal. And once I say that your brother is a danger to himself and to others, they will lock him away. And *my* attorney, Jerald Winslow, will make certain it sticks. Do you understand me *now?*" His voice dissolved into a hiss.

"You can't mean that. I know you've never really loved us, and you've been harsh at times. But I never thought you were capable—"

"You are wrong on all accounts. All of this I do for love, not with any malicious motive. Someday when you're no longer full of reckless behavior and this weak-mindedness, you will thank me. Someday you'll know what I've done. What I've forfeited for you." He leaned toward Charlie. "Sometimes we have to do what is radical for the ultimate good of the beloved."

"But, Willie . . . he would die in there in that awful place." Charlie struggled to absorb what his father was proposing. His father's words seemed jumbled and his logic perverse.

"No, he would not. He would probably gain some much-needed clarity!" His father touched the birthmark on his cheek. It had gone blood-red.

"You can't mean this. It's Christmastime. Don't you have any mercy?"

"Of course your brother won't be going to the institution, because I know you'll do as I say. However, if you think for one minute that I don't mean what I've promised this evening, just try to become engaged to that woman or buy that music shop. It will all come to pass just as I have said, but if there is any guilt to be suffered, it will be yours and yours alone. Now please remove your hands from the car door."

Charlie hadn't realized he'd been grasping the door or that his hands had gone numb. He eased his fingers away and said no more. He'd learned from past experience that when his father got into one of his certainties, there was no talking him out of it, especially when he got his personal attorney involved. The attorney was, of course, the best in the city and a force to be reckoned with.

The engine purred to life and his father drove away into the night, leaving Charlie immersed in grief.

Had his father lost his mind? This went far beyond his usual manipulations. How could any lucid person say what had just come out of his mouth? How could anyone confuse evil with love?

God, why is this happening? In Your grand scheme of things, couldn't there have been a better way? If one parent had to die, why couldn't it have been his father? Charlie hated himself for the thought. It felt natural to think that way but also heartless—just like his father.

Charlie felt trapped with the ultimatum. How would he face Franny? He'd just declared his love to her. In his heart, he'd already proposed, and he knew she could sense his commitment simply by looking into his eyes. From every angle, the situation appeared to be hopeless.

He couldn't go back to the house. Not yet. Not until he'd figured things out. He needed a long walk in the fresh air. He stuffed his hands into the pockets of his coat and strolled around the farmyard aimlessly.

Charlie meandered here and there, doing the

chores and punting dirt clods across the yard as he shouted questions toward the heavens. When he finished those activities, he found an old golf club in the trunk of his car and whacked at cow pies in the full light of the moon until his arm ached. His roving and trouncing landed him in front of the windmill. He stared up at the tower, the blades, and the all-important wind vane, which kept the whole contraption facing the very thing that powered it. Franny said it was "for when the rains wouldn't come." Hmph. Good way to describe the Landau family legacy.

A gust of air made the windmill groan as it turned into the wind. The sudden wailing conjured up a scene from his youth—the time his brother was seventeen and had just come back from his first stay at the mental institution. Willie had been terrified. The peculiar reason Willie was admitted in the first place came from a bout of what his father called *waywardness*. Charlie released an anger-laced chuckle. His father had asked Willie once again to give up his art to accept a career at Landau Enterprises. Willie refused, so he was harassed and manipulated until he agreed with his father that he was depressed enough to check himself into the institution. No one could ever get away from their father's assaults. One became a fugitive with no place to hide.

On an impulse, Charlie grabbed hold of the windmill's ladder and climbed the metal rungs to the top. He got a little shaky on the last step, but the view was amazing, as from an eagle's nest. He could see more clearly up there, breathe more easily, even though his legs quivered. There on top, looking out over the farm world and beyond, Charlie made a pledge to his brother—that he would work harder to protect him from their father. And he knew no career dream or hope for love would ever make him break this familial vow.

But could God provide a way out of such a moral dilemma? Was there a way to sidestep such a tragic plan? What if he hired his own attorney to fight his father? What about giving the news to a hungry journalist who might want to make the most of it? The story was sensationalistic to say the least. Once everyone knew about the threats, his brother would surely be free.

But if it exploded into an epic family battle and was accompanied with scandalous publicity, what kind of toll would that take on Willie? Would it be even more painful in the long run than the alternative? He had no idea, and the not knowing was maddening.

There, under the bright stars and the heavens he'd just railed against, Charlie wept—not for his loss, but for the sadness Franny would feel when nothing changed. When he didn't follow through with the purchase of the music store, and when his promise of love never progressed into marriage.

She would wonder what had happened to change his mind. How could he tell her the truth?

Sickened with heartache and cold to the bone, Charlie slowly made his way back toward the house.

CHAPTER THIRTY-NINE

Franny looked at the kitchen clock and then at Noma. "I wonder why Charlie hasn't come back." Maybe the conversation between the two men had taken a darker turn. *Please, God, don't allow this conflict to close the door on their relationship. No matter how difficult things are, Charlie needs a father.*

"Maybe Charlie wanted some time alone to recover. His father leaves a mighty deep wake behind him." Noma handed her the last washed plate.

"So true. Never met anybody like him." Franny contemplated Mr. Landau's daunting nature. The man didn't seem to live in a world of reason but of might, like a bull in a lamb's pen. Not the best atmosphere for raising secure and happy kids. *Must have been really hard on Charlie and his brother, growing up that way.* Franny finished drying the plate and set it down on the stack. "Excuse me for a minute. I'm going to have a quick look." She went out onto the enclosed porch and gazed through the long row of windows. Nothing. She went into her bedroom and pulled back the curtains, hoping to see Charlie.

Instead of seeing her beloved, she saw a shadow move across the field and then disappear behind the brooder house. What was that? It appeared too far away to get a good look, especially since the yard light didn't illuminate that area very well. She thought of going outside to investigate, but moments later she heard the porch door open and close. It must have been Charlie. Holding her breath, she went back to the kitchen and waited for him, deciding to forget the shadowy figure.

Charlie looked at her when he came inside. His eyes were rimmed in red, and he looked as weary as a man who'd been on a long journey but had never made it home. She searched his face, trying to find the Charlie she'd fallen in love with. Where had he gone? He appeared so lost that her spirit ached for him. She wanted to throw her arms around him, pull him close, and tell him all would be well, but could she make such a guarantee? For a moment she too felt misplaced. Or maybe it was Charlie's sudden distant air that kept her at bay.

"I'm going upstairs for a bit," Noma said before disappearing up the back steps.

Charlie sat down at the kitchen table and placed his hands in his lap.

Franny draped the tea towel over her shoulder

and stood by his side. "Would you like to talk about it?"

He sighed. "I don't know."

Franny sat down next to him. "Your father said something else to you, didn't he? Something that changes everything."

"How could you know that?" Charlie's eyes held such sadness.

"I can see it written all over your face." Franny fidgeted with the frayed end of the tea towel, picking at it until the loose threads fell on the floor. After another round of quiet she said, "I remember one time, growing up, when there was this stray dog that wandered onto our farm. Daddy always tried to run him off, but he refused to go. We got very attached to each other, and after a lot of begging, Daddy said we could keep him. He was a good dog, but one time I made the mistake of cornering him. And to my surprise, he bit me."

Charlie shrugged. "So? What does that story mean? Are you trying to say that my father is a good man and I made the mistake of cornering him?" His expression held a glint of irritation.

"I don't think you're at fault, but I do think your father may feel trapped and scared." Franny wasn't sure if she should finish her story, but something compelled her to continue even though the sensation was like a ball of string unrolling willy-nilly down the stairs. "Years later that same dog, Ed, had pups. So I renamed her

Edwina." She offered him a shaky grin. "Anyway, we had the mother and her babies in the house during a thunderstorm, and she got so frightened that Edwina injured her babies while trying to shield them. They survived, but it was a struggle for them."

Charlie crossed his arms. "So, you're saying that some fear inside my father—perhaps something from his past—must be triggering these reactions?" He rose from the table. "I'm sorry, Franny. I know you're trying to help here, but I just can't see it. Even if my father is tormented in some way, he'll still need to make some serious adjustments in the way he fathers, or he'll have two sons stomped to death in the name of love."

"Charlie, I'm—"

"Maybe my father is just a terrible sinner with a hard heart. Has anyone ever thought of that?"

"Maybe you could show him what real love looks like, Charlie."

"That's a sweet sentiment, but it never works that way in the Landau house."

Henry came lumbering in from the bedroom, his nails tapping on the linoleum floor. He looked at both of them earnestly and then settled himself on the floor between them.

"Good boy, Henry." Charlie gave him a pat and then looked up at Franny. "For now, you'll just have to understand that you don't know the whole story. This kind of family landscape is unfamiliar territory to you. Be thankful for this, Franny."

"I am. But whatever it is, we can work it out." Franny didn't mean to let her voice get so loud and feisty. Was he slipping away from her? Did he regret his words of love? She reached out to him, but instead of touching him, she let her hand fall to her side.

Charlie must have sensed her distress and disappointment and felt moved toward compassion, since his expression softened into a half smile. She could even see a glimpse of the old Charlie. "You are a woman of words so earnest and warm they could thaw an icy lake. But this isn't anything that can be fixed with rhetoric. I'm sorry, Franny. I am." He backed away. "I think for now, I'd better say good-night."

Franny rose from the chair. "Please tell me . . ." She pressed the back of her hand against her mouth to keep her lips from trembling. "Please tell me that nothing has changed between us."

Charlie glanced upward, his shoulders slumping. "God, how can I do this?"

Franny, confused and bewildered, searched his face for answers. "I don't know what you mean." Charlie's troubled look made her want to cry. He had to be carrying a burden she knew nothing about, and one he seemed determined to carry alone.

Then, as if some stronghold broke loose in Charlie—as if he were now making up for what he'd been denied—he rushed over to her and scooped her into his arms. They held each other for a long time, close and safe and full of tender affection. Franny rested her head on his shoulder, wanting to dissolve into tears, but she held them back. She would save them for later in the quiet of her room.

After a few more moments, Charlie eased her away just enough to catch her gaze. "My darling, Franny, please know this . . . no matter what happens, nothing on earth could make me stop loving you. It is the way I'll feel until the day I die."

CHAPTER FORTY

Sunday arrived with the promise of a new and glorious morning, but Charlie felt little of it in his heart. He moved around the farmyard without his usual energy. All the goodness of the previous weeks, working side by side with Franny along with the hope of spending the rest of his life with her, vanished like smoke. Giving up the idea of owning the music store seemed trivial now, compared to losing Franny. His love for her had become both his treasure and his torment.

He looked upward and squinted into the sun. The glittering blue sky seemed like a painful backdrop against the night's travails. Joylessly, he'd finished most of the morning chores. Franny and Noma had gone on to Sunday morning services without him, which was best considering his mood. But being with Franny had become more and more complicated, since she knew something was wrong. She'd known from the first moment.

He remembered Franny talking about the ridge. She'd said that everything important happened on the ridge. On impulse, he set down the bucket and walked along the cow path, past the mulberry tree, and up the hill. At last, when he was just shy of the cliff, he stopped and looked out over the vista. The creek ran in quiet ripples in the canyon, lulling all of nature to sleep like a lullaby. The pale, promising colors of spring wouldn't come for months, yet he longed for them. Something, anything, to lighten his spirit.

His thoughts continued to spiral downward, becoming as dreary as the landscape. He could sense the unsettledness of time—the way life brought good gifts and great sorrows and everything in between. His previous life had known some of life's untamed rhythms, but not as keenly as he felt them now. But then, he'd never loved before. And he'd never had to walk away from it.

With every passing day he felt his life changing, taking this course and then that course as if he were being swept away on a swollen river without any way to steer or stop. But wasn't the whole world changing with him? It felt as though they were all moving along on that same river, being pitched around in an era of turmoil and vision, of marvel and miracle. It was a time when people went to bed with an image of the world and every morning it vanished like the morning mist, replaced by something they no longer recognized. His small boat floated among millions.

And yet . . . even in the loss of control and the unsure waters, he felt the sense of being watched over by something—Someone greater than himself.

Realizing why he'd really come, Charlie dropped to his knees. He'd come to the ridge to reaffirm where he stood with His master. God was not asleep. He was there in a world of turbulent waters, and He saw even the smallest boats thrashing about.

Charlie wasn't sure how long he'd been there, kneeling and then sitting on the boulder, looking out over the countryside, but he needed the time. To pray. To pause. And just to be. He hadn't known that state of being for most of his adult life—just to be. It was hard to know stillness amidst the bustle of the city. But here, in the quiet places, where the only clamor was the running of the deer or the rustling of cedars in the wind, here he'd found a sanctuary for his soul, and with God's help, he'd found his peace.

Charlie breathed deeply and took in the smell

of the rich earth. He picked up a clod of dirt and let it mold to his palm. Just like Franny had said, it was getting to him—the land—growing on him just as surely as the grass that took root in the pasture.

Amazingly, he'd even managed to reconcile with the squirrel living in his apartment attic. And *that* detail was a marvel in and of itself.

Maybe it was a good time to brush up on his whistling skills. Charlie cleared his throat, and without censoring himself he gave it a try. The action felt breathy at first, but when his lips finally found their shape, he whistled "Silent Night." Why had he ever stopped such a wonderful pastime simply because Sylvie and her friends had called it gauche? Guess he'd needed to figure out who he was and stick to it.

After whistling a few more favorite Christmas tunes, he rose from the boulder and turned to head home. At that moment, he witnessed what he considered a miracle, and it was one that he could not have imagined.

CHAPTER FORTY-ONE

His brother Willie was coming up the hill toward him.

"Willie?" His younger brother looked well and, with the grin on his face, happier than he'd seen him in years.

Charlie hurried down to his brother and pulled him into a hug. "It's good to see you. What in the world are you doing way out here?"

"I've come to see *you*, big brother."

When they released each other, Charlie asked, "How did you find the farm?"

"I took a few wrong turns. Story of my life. Right?" Willie chuckled. "But then I stopped at a farmhouse and got some better directions. So, here I am."

"Stay as long as you want."

"Well, I'm not sure if—"

"Come on. At least until Christmas. The accommodations aren't what we're used to, but it feels like home."

A pained look shadowed his brother's face. "Yeah, well, we know that feeling is hard to come by, so I'm glad you've found it out here." Willie brightened. "Look at you, with those overalls and that raggedy coat. You look like the real McCoy, man." He slapped him on the back.

"Fit and healthy. So, farming agrees with you."

"Well, it grows on you."

Willie grinned. "Guess so."

Charlie ruffled his brother's hair like he'd done when they were kids, and Willie jostled him right back with a punch.

Willie had changed too; he'd gone a little beatnik with his paisley shirt and Nehru jacket. Their father would hate it, but it looked good.

"Come see the view." Charlie headed to the top of the ridge.

His brother followed him, and they both sat down on boulders. The wind teased them with several bursts of air. "It blows like a dust devil up here sometimes."

Willie chuckled. "Yeah, well, it's always blowing somewhere in Oklahoma." He buttoned up his jacket. "This is invigorating. I like it up here." After a few moments of quiet between them, his brother looked him over with curiosity. "You've changed some. More than the healthy thing."

"How's that?"

"Just a few weeks ago, I doubt you would have thought that sitting on a rock was worth your time. But here you are."

"Do you think it's a good thing?" Charlie asked. "The changes?"

"Probably, yeah." Willie snapped his finger as he hit his palm. "So, what do you do for fun around here?"

"Oh, people do a lot of moseying."

"That bad, huh?"

"And a lot of backbreaking work too."

"Eww." Willie got up from the boulder, picked up several acorns, and studied them. "Well, you must be staying around for *her,* then. I met your Franny."

"You did? Never did take you long to meet my girlfriends."

His brother laughed. "You're right about that."

"How did you know she was *my* Franny? Did you weasel it out of her? You were always good at that too."

"Man, I was the best weaseler around. Still am. Used to drive our nanny crazy, though. Remember?" Willie slipped the acorns into his jacket.

"I remember." It was good to see Willie picking up things, taking an interest in life again. It meant he'd gone back to painting.

"In answer to your question, no, Franny never said a word about it. But she glows like a woman in love. There's no mistaking that."

"Franny's not like anyone else. She talks about crickets and candling eggs and shucking the corn and birthing piglets, but she also has a passion for music and, well, life. She forgives easily, finds joy in the smallest things, and loves with her whole being. I think if fire came from the sky and burned up the whole earth, she would be left standing, because Franny is a woman after God's own heart."

Willie whistled. "Man, oh, man, I hope *I* fall in love that hard."

"I've dated a lot of women over the years, so when I found some wheat among the chaff, well, it was easy to see."

"Truth?"

"Yeah, I want the truth."

"Well, I think she's a real darling, Chuck, and if you don't marry her, *I* will."

Charlie laughed. Willie hadn't called him *Chuck* since they were teenagers. It felt really good. "So how did Franny know where I was?"

"I don't know." Willie shrugged. "She just knew. You know how women are. They're intuitive."

Especially Franny. Charlie pondered that pleasant fact for a while and then said, "I've missed you."

"And I, you." He chuckled. "Did I say that right?"

"Sounds good to me."

Willie picked up a stone. "This is quite a cliff you've got here." He peered over the edge and looked back at Charlie. "So has our father been out here to harass you yet? To check up on your progress? If he hasn't, he *will* now, with me here. Pardon the lousy pun."

Charlie scrubbed his hand against his chin and wondered just how much he should tell his brother about their father's visit. He wasn't going to mention the threats. It would only cause his brother to go into a tailspin of depression. "Yes, he found me."

"I knew he would. He always does." Willie's hand twisted to the right as if it were deformed.

Charlie hated to see the straining contortion in his brother's hand, since it was one of the signs that he still struggled with past emotions connected to their father. "Should we change the subject?"

"No." Willie dropped the stone. "I need to talk about it."

"All right." Charlie wanted his brother to be healthy, but he couldn't imagine how talking about the latest turn of events would help him. Maybe he could find out about his brother's health without revealing anything significant. "I have a question for you, then. If you want to answer it."

"I'm ready." Willie backed away from the edge of the cliff.

Charlie relaxed his shoulders. "When we were there for dinner, Father said you'd been in the institution recently."

"Just for the weekend." He made a sweeping motion with his hand. "But I don't want to go back there. As you know, Father has always paid my way to the institution, and as you also know, he encourages me to go. But he and the director are getting to be closer friends, and that's a little worrisome. I'm well enough to know that I'm

261

not being paranoid when I say this. Father has a need to control everything within his grasp." Willie straightened his hand and laced his fingers together.

"I'm glad you can see it." Charlie had never heard his brother speak so clearly about his situation or their father. Willie was surely getting better. "I have one more question." He paused and then asked, "What do you think made you depressed on and off all those years? What started it?" Charlie felt he knew the answer, but he wanted to hear it in his brother's own words.

Willie picked up another rock and rolled it around in his hand. "Father always claimed that being an artist would cultivate more madness than it would great art. But after all these years I see it now. . . . Art was never the problem. It was Father."

Thank God you can see it now.

"I admit, even when Mom was alive and life was good for us, I got depressed sometimes. But the depression was manageable without being institutionalized." Willie closed his fingers around the rock, making a fist. "But when I defied Father at age seventeen and told him what I intended to do with my life, to be an artist, that's when it really started . . . when I found myself in those black holes I couldn't get out of. He deployed all his influence against me as if he were calling in the troops to some great battle. He manipulated me into a frenzy of confusion. I know now it was his control over me that made my depression unbearable."

Willie looked at Charlie. "I know you tried to tell me, but I never really believed it. My respect for him, my need to please him, blinded me from the truth."

"What made you see it now?"

Willie sighed. "Well, I'm older. I eat better and I run." He smiled.

"That's good news, Willie." Unfortunately, if Father could prove that Willie was a threat to himself and others, he could still coerce his son into the institution against his will. But Charlie would do nothing to force his father's hand. He would keep his brother safe at all costs.

Willie threw the stone into the canyon, and it splashed into the creek below.

"Nice hit. So, you haven't told Father what you've told me?"

"No. He's usually too busy firing his secretary or suing his accountant."

Charlie laughed.

Willie laughed.

And their laughter rang out over the canyon.

"By the way," Willie said, "I'm painting again."

"Really? Tell me about it."

"Watercolors. I'm going to have a show in a few weeks . . . at the same place I've had it before, Live Oaks Gallery."

"You always did well there."

"I should make enough money to move out and be on my own. I'll be a free man. So, I came to tell you all that. Well, and to see how you looked as a farmer."

"We should celebrate, then. To art and farming." Charlie pretended to toast with a glass.

"Yes, we should. Hey, I'm starving. I know it's after lunch, but do you think you could feed me?"

"I'm sure we can." He suddenly realized that he'd been so wrapped up in the quiet of the ridge that he'd forgotten to eat. Forgetting about meals wasn't something that happened every day. Hopefully Franny and Noma had gone ahead and eaten lunch without him.

Willie frowned. "By the way, I forgot to mention it . . . but as I followed Franny's instructions on how to find you, I saw a police car of some kind driving up the lane. More like a sheriff's car. I should have said something right away."

Charlie's thoughts raced through a dozen scenarios—and none of them were good. He wondered if it had something to do with Noma— if someone had come to harass her. "We'd better get home. Now."

CHAPTER FORTY-TWO

Franny's whole constitution relaxed the second she saw Charlie walk through the back door. *Thank God he's here.* Charlie's brother was with him, which was also good, but it was unfortunate that Willie's first visit to the farm would be so unpleasant.

Charlie looked at the two men seated at the kitchen table. "Gentlemen?"

Franny introduced Charlie and Willie to the two "men," if you could call them that. Better descriptions would have been, "Sheriff—the minion. And Dunlap—the murderer!"

Charlie paused when she introduced Payton Dunlap, as if he was conjuring up all of Franny's accusations against the man.

Willie seated himself on a kitchen stool by the sink.

Dunlap pulled a pouch of tobacco and rolling paper out of his shirt pocket.

They were the two most unwelcome Sunday afternoon callers who had ever assembled in her kitchen. "Sorry, we don't keep ashtrays in the house." Franny crossed her arms.

Dunlap shrugged, shuffled his false teeth around in his mouth, and then continued the process of rolling his cigarette. The man looked in the general direction of a person but never *at* him or her. He apparently had an aversion to eye contact.

Franny set her lips in a thin line. It was going to be a rough ride. At least Noma was in the middle of a leisurely hike along the creek. Her friend wouldn't have to know—she wouldn't have to listen to the vicious and ignorant ramblings of the local sheriff and Dunlap—two men who didn't have enough intellect between them to fill the head of a pin and two men who'd already given her a dose of their witless lectures. Both guests looked thirsty, but she refused to waste her good Christmas cider on them. And the sheriff could eye those fresh-out-of-the-oven pies on the counter all he wanted. Neither one of them would get a single bite.

"So, how may we help you?" Charlie's tone was reserved.

"Well, they have a *couple* of reasons for their visit," Franny said. "First, they wanted to—"

"I'll take it from here." The sheriff turned to Charlie, scratched his double chin, and then adjusted his badge, which was attached to his soiled shirt. "We just wanted to make certain that no one took advantage of our Miss Martin out here." The way he said her name, "*Miss Mar–TAN,*" was enough to give Franny the heebie-jeebies. "Our wives were concerned," he went on to say, "about your arrangements out here, since you two aren't married. And since we found out that you are one of the boys from *the* Landau family, well, we thought . . ."

"Yes?" Charlie drummed his fingers on the table. "And what does my being a Landau have to do with your visit or this conversation?"

The sheriff flushed the color of bubbling cherries on the stove. "Well, we know that rich folk are used to getting . . . exactly what they want."

"I assure you that everything we're doing out here is proper," Charlie said. "Franny lives in the house, and I live in the small apartment above the toolshed."

Franny had to consciously unclench her jaw. "Charlie owns the farm now, and I'm helping him until he can manage it on his own." She saw a flicker of pain in Charlie's eyes, and it pierced her through to put it there, but she didn't want to give away too many pearls of personal details, especially to a man like Dunlap who was swine even on a good day. And what she'd spoken was the truth. Even though Charlie had professed love to her, he'd yet to mention anything more permanent.

Franny brought her thoughts back to the matter at hand. She'd only missed a bit of grousing between Dunlap and the sheriff. "Please thank your wives for me. Their genuine concern over my welfare renders me speechless." She nearly lost the contents of her stomach with her last

267

comment, but she decided to offer them blank bullets and save the real ammo for the final clash that was about to erupt.

The sheriff's strained smile made him look as though he might bust right out of his uniform, but considering his rotund frame, he always did bulge like an overstuffed sausage. "I'm sure they'll be relieved to hear the rest of the story."

"Thank you for coming," Franny said.

The sheriff picked up his hat and rose, knocking over the dinette chair. As he righted the chair, he dropped his hat. When Dunlap made no move to leave, the sheriff picked up his hat and plopped back down on his chair. He looked more than a little tired of their meeting. He surely wanted to be home eating more of his wife's lard-laced cooking.

Dunlap paid no attention to the sheriff's social fumbling as he calmly licked the edge of his rolling paper and sealed up the tobacco. "But as you know, we have one more issue to discuss."

Tiny bits of spit flew from Dunlap's mouth when he talked, which made Franny cringe and want to swab the kitchen down with what was left of her grandmother's lye soap.

Franny could hardly look at the man. "Yes, you mentioned something about my dear friend, Noma." She tried to keep her tone civil, but it was getting harder by the minute, especially since she knew why they'd really come—to harass Noma into leaving.

The sheriff wriggled in his chair like a guilty child. "Dunlap, I'm not sure this is the best time to get into—"

"Horsefeathers! The law is the law, Sheriff. People around here are good, honest citizens, and they're just trying to do the right thing. That's all I'm trying to do . . . all I've ever wanted to do."

Charlie balled up his hands and rested them on the table. "Noma Jefferson is our friend. She needed a job, and we gave her one. What can be unlawful about that?"

Dunlap raised his chin. "We've had some complaints about that colored cook of yours."

The sheriff didn't speak up but snapped his suspenders hard enough that he was nearly catapulted right out of his chair.

One could only dream.

"We heard she was in the mercantile buying ice milk," Dunlap went on to say, "*and* she bought a box of *matches* too."

Franny leaned forward, pretending to look deeply concerned. "On those matches, were they pocket-sized, or was it the thrifty full-sized box? Makes a difference, you know." She could hardly believe she was having such a conversation with two grown men.

Dunlap narrowed his eyes.

The sheriff spoke up. "I don't rightly see how that . . . Now, wait just a cotton-pickin' minute.

269

I get your meaning, and there's no need to get all saucy with us, Miss Martin."

"Noma was there because we were all out of ice milk and matches," Franny said. "Are you going to need to document her purchases every time she goes into town? That's going to put a real crimp in your hectic schedule."

Dunlap fiddled with the change in his pockets. "Coloreds aren't allowed in the mercantile at certain times of the day. And they can't go waltzing through the front door. You know that as well as I do."

"And who made up those rules?" Franny asked. "You?"

"You have to understand, we just don't get many colored folk in Hesterville," the sheriff said, "so when one of 'em comes into town, people get jittery. Folks aren't sure what to do."

"What to do? Well, they could start by saying hello." Franny felt like giving somebody a good thrashing. "And then, maybe, merry Christmas."

"Now, you hear me right." Dunlap leaned toward her. "That colored woman touched two dresses while she was in the mercantile. Ones that were new on the rack. And now the Gurneys will have to burn them. Who's going to pay for that? You?"

"And why would the Gurneys feel obligated to burn perfectly good dresses?" Franny asked, knowing full well their insane reasoning.

"Because those dresses are contaminated, and if folks get the idea that the Gurneys are letting coloreds touch and try on their clothes, they'll be out of business in a week."

Franny slapped her hand on the table. "That is the most ungodly and asinine thing I've ever heard. And I know the real reason we don't get many Negros in town—it's because of the signs you keep putting up. And those signs, well, you have to put them up in the dark, don't you? You have an aversion to the light. Yes, it's always the skunks and rats that come out at night."

Dunlap merely cocked his head at her. "And one of these days you're going to regret demolishing my signs, missy." He pinched off the excess tobacco from the ends of his cigarette and let the crumbles fall onto Noma's freshly waxed floor.

"Hmm. Sounds like a murderous threat to me." Franny swallowed the bile rising in her throat. "I guess I'd better watch my back."

"And what's that supposed to mean?" Dunlap's lip curled as he rolled the cigarette around in his hand.

"You know exactly what it means." Franny prayed for calm.

Willie shifted on the stool but said nothing.

Charlie writhed in his chair, and Franny could sense his anger rising. In fact, Charlie appeared ready to launch a few fiery words when Henry lumbered in from another room and settled himself next to him. Henry could sense when people were upset, and he always did his best to calm them down. But there was nothing he could do, since both she and Charlie were beyond calming.

Dunlap looked at Henry. "Hmph. What a useless-looking mongrel."

"This may be a very good time to ask you to leave," Charlie said.

"I came with the sheriff, so I think your language should be a bit more respectful." Dunlap's sneer was falsely cordial. "If you don't mind."

"Then I request that you make your language equally respectful," Charlie replied. "*If* you don't mind."

Henry went over to Dunlap and pushed his nose against the pocket of his trousers, as he sometimes did even with strangers, hoping for a treat. Horrified that the man might harm Henry in some way, she called him back. The dog's brief nudge was just enough, though, to push something from his pocket and make it fall to the floor.

Franny stared at the item—a small toy—just before Dunlap snatched it up. The man had actually stolen one of the toys Uncle George had made for her when she was a child. "What are you doing with that toy? It's mine, and it's precious to me."

"Are you calling me a thief?" Dunlap slapped his hand over his heart.

"Yes, I am." Then Franny remembered the

shadow of something or someone who'd been sneaking around the farm in the twilight. "It was you . . . yesterday. You were the one creeping around the farm, spying and stealing from us."

"You have no proof."

"Yes, I do. Those were one-of-a-kind toys that Uncle George made for me. No one else has anything like that around here."

The sheriff grunted as if in a fit of indigestion. "So, is that true? What Miss Martin said? You been stealing baby toys, Dunlap?" A hint of amusement trickled into his voice, making Franny want to throttle him.

"What of it?" Dunlap asked. "It's just a piece of rubbish."

"It isn't to me. I want it back." Franny put out her hand. "You've been sneaking around this farm, trying to find ways to torment me, just as you did all those years ago."

"I have no idea what you're talking about." Dunlap flung the toy on the table, almost breaking it.

Charlie made his hands into fists. "You were on our property illegally, Dunlap. And you stole from us." He turned to the sheriff. "Aren't you going to do anything?"

The sheriff seemed to think for a moment, which was a feat in itself, and then said, "I don't see much harm done. That is, if you agree not to do it again, Dunlap. Agreed?"

Dunlap released some air, letting his lips flap in a revolting way. "Your old George. I remember him too well. He'd stand by the back door of the co-op office to pick up some papers for your daddy, and, boy howdy, if he wasn't proud, standing there. Just a-bragging away that he'd made some worthless little toys for the Martin girl. And all the while, you know what we were doing? Laughing at him. Yeah, old George sure provided us with some good entertainment in those days. We shoulda told him to dance for us too."

Franny felt ready to burn up in a flare of white-hot fury. His insults were maddeningly casual for a murderer—Uncle George's murderer! But if she accused Dunlap of the crime head-on, they would both laugh at her. She leaned toward him, hoping Dunlap could experience every bit of indignation in her eyes. "Did you steal all the toys out of our storage? Just to harass me because my family hired George? How low can you slither, Dunlap?"

Dunlap stared at his fingernails. "The people 'round here should give me a metal. No, a statue should be erected in my honor in the square, thanking me for all I've done for this town. I've been the watch keeper, the caretaker here, and yet so few know to thank me for my service."

"People don't need to thank you. They need to be protected from you." Franny thought of their house being unlocked at night and realized that

Dunlap would now take away that innocent practice, the freedom they had always taken for granted. Life would never be quite the same again. "And you've been spying on Noma, haven't you?"

Dunlap released a low snarl. "It's a mystery to me. You people. Taking up for these folk. Can't you see? They were meant for a lower order. It's revolting, what you people are doing in this house, making that woman your equal and friend. It's not acceptable. It will *not* be tolerated!" Dunlap's eyes became dark glowering orbs, as if some of the foul stirrings inside him suddenly rose to the surface.

Franny shivered—at the sight of such evil.

"Or you'll do what?" Charlie asked in an ominously quiet timbre.

"Adjustments will have to be made." Dunlap took the toe of his boot and twisted it on the floor as if he were snuffing out something under his foot. "I will prevail."

Charlie rose. "And so modifications must include silencing those who go against your views?" He seemed to ask this as if unaware and needing enlightenment.

"Yes, of course. I am the protector. The appointed one!" Then, like a bolt of red lightning, Dunlap's laughter sliced through the room, demented and raucous.

Charlie took in a sharp breath.

Stunned, Franny squeezed the chair cushion

until her hands ached. *Lord, is this a confession? Is this what I've been waiting for all these years?*

Willie had been sitting in silence, but his expression and posture intensified.

Charlie splayed his fingers on the table and loomed over Dunlap. "So, you admit to silencing someone."

"It had to be done," Dunlap hissed. "That creature, George, was trying to replace her father . . . one of our own," his voice rose to a fevered pitch.

"I finally see it. You made a few things right again," Charlie said smoothly. "You did what no one else could do. You smothered the life out of George Hughes so he wouldn't continue to contaminate this town. Or should I give the credit to someone else?"

"No, you fool! *I* alone deserve the recognition." Dunlap slammed his fist on the table. "I'm the one who righted the wrongs in this town. I'm tired of being the caretaker without any of the praise. All my deeds have been in secret, but *I'm* the one who has a right to the glory."

And you're the one, Dunlap, who has a right to the jail time. Franny felt like giving Charlie a big, slobbery kiss.

The sheriff shrank back from Dunlap, his eyes widening. "We've known each other a good part of our lives, and I've put up with your views . . . but I see now that I shouldn't have. I knew better.

When I was a kid, I used to play with the colored kids over in Lancaster. They were my friends. But ever since I met you, I got away from that thinking. And then while I wasn't paying any mind to you . . . well, you slid right into purgatory." He gave the gun in his holster a timorous touch. "I've stomached a lot of things from you over the years, but I sure didn't think it would come to murder."

The sheriff rose as if attending a funeral, his head lowered and his shoulders hunched in what looked like sorrow. "Payton Dunlap, you're under arrest for the murder of George Hughes. If you come along now without a struggle, I won't use the handcuffs."

Franny had to make a conscious effort to close her mouth, with all the drama. *This is it. And those walls—can you see it, Daddy?—those walls of Jericho did come tumbling down.*

"How can you do this?" Dunlap glared at the sheriff, his face changing into a fierce mask. "All this time, I thought you were my friend, but you've always been a traitor to the cause."

"The law is the law," the sheriff said.

"You *betrayed* me."

"Well, I guess the way I see it, it's the other way around."

"But I did it for the good of the town—for their protection! Why can't you see? To keep things as they were, respectable and safe and . . ."

Dunlap's words faded as his chin fell against his chest. A tiny trail of saliva dribbled out of the corner of his mouth. "The caretakers are never appreciated in their own towns." He opened his mouth again, but only gibberish came out.

The sheriff took a handkerchief from his pocket and looked at Franny. "Guess you were right all those years ago. No one believed you, including me." He dabbed at the perspiration on his face.

Franny knew that would be the best apology she'd ever get out of the sheriff, but considering that justice was now served, it would do just fine.

The sheriff helped the ireful Dunlap out of his chair, a man who seemed to be more angles and shadows than human, as if he were a sinister villain from a Flash comic book.

As the two visitors shambled out of the house, Franny said to Dunlap, "I want you to go away with one more thought besides knowing that my prayers are with you for your redemption."

When Dunlap didn't answer, the sheriff gave him a sharp nudge with his elbow.

Dunlap gave her a murderous glint. "What is that?" he growled.

"Noma isn't just a friend," Franny said. "She's becoming like a mom to me."

CHAPTER FORTY-THREE

When the two guests—the two undesirables—were finally out from under their roof, Franny collapsed onto a kitchen chair. The emotional residue from the scene would last a lifetime, and yet Franny also embraced a sense of peace, knowing that justice had been served for her family's friend. What a blessed Christmas present. And the person who'd helped make all of it possible was her beloved Charlie. He'd been amazing and rather clever in getting Dunlap to dive headlong into an admission of guilt. And Henry, of course, could not be forgotten for his astonishing part in the whole affair.

Willie hopped down from his stool on the sidelines. "Man, oh, man, I've never seen anything like that. You guys were quite the team. Are you sure you two weren't meant to be prosecuting attorneys instead of farmers? You got that odious man to confess to murder!"

Charlie chuckled. "I don't think I ever want to do that again, let alone for a living. Once is plenty." He wiped the sweat from his forehead and then pressed his fingers on his eyelids.

Franny walked over to Charlie and gave him a hug. "I've never been prouder of anyone in my life. You're my champion."

Charlie kissed her forehead. "You were such a noble force that you were unstoppable."

Henry looked up at them both and whimpered, looking neglected.

"And you too, boy." Franny squatted down and gave Henry a good hug.

Charlie scratched him behind the ears. "Not sure if we could have pulled it off without you."

"I think he deserves something special." Franny reached on top of the kitchen cabinet for a rawhide treat and held it out to Henry. "You don't need to work for this one. You deserve it."

Henry accepted the treat and trotted over to his bed by the furnace, wagging his tail and looking more than content. Perhaps he could sense that something good had just happened to them all. And good it was. She'd waited a long time for justice to be served on Dunlap, and finally that day had arrived.

Charlie tugged on Franny's sleeve. "I think I need some fresh air. Willie, would you excuse us for a minute?"

"I think I can handle it." He winked.

Charlie gave her his full attention. "How about a stroll by the hog lot?"

"I would love it."

Willie stood over one of the pumpkin pies and ogled it.

"I'd love for you to have some of that pie," Franny said. "There are plates in the cupboard, forks in the drawer, and milk in the fridge."

"Ahh." Willie tapped his fingers against his chest. "A woman after my own heart."

Franny chuckled. "And when I get back, I'll make sure you both get a real meal. I wish your first visit here hadn't been so grim, Willie."

"It was pretty heavy, but I wouldn't have missed it for anything." Willie took a plate from the cupboard. "I'm sorry I wasn't much help to either of you."

"It worked out fine." Charlie took hold of Franny's hand. "If we all three had been after Dunlap, it would have changed the dynamics. He might not have caved the way he did."

"Good. Now I don't have to feel guilty." Willie lifted out a large slice of pie onto the plate. "You two go have a smooch while I do some serious work on this pastry."

Charlie grinned and then led Franny outside. "I was kidding about the hog lot. Maybe the open porch on the south end of the house would be better."

"It's a good spot." *What could be on his mind?* Perhaps it was about his father. They walked around the side of the house and sat down on the two rocking chairs.

Charlie grasped the arms of his chair and looked over at her. "We need to talk."

Oh no. A sick feeling seeped through her. "Ever since your father was here, well, I've been waiting for you to talk about whatever happened between the two of you. Hoping we could work it out—whatever *it* is."

"I know I've been distant. And I know it hasn't been fair to you. But I just wasn't sure how to tell you. . . ."

"Your father doesn't approve of me, does he? I know I come from a simple country background, and even though I want to please you and your father, he's correct that I'll never be a socialite. I don't think I have it in me. I know I ran off to the city, talking big about living a different kind of life, but that really isn't me. I'm just Franny."

"Most likely, my father wanted me to fall in love with someone who's interested in running a big house and giving dinner parties for his clients. But this isn't about my father. It's about me. I dated enough to know exactly what I want. Thank God. It was the only good thing that came from dating those other women." He looked at her. "You're the one I want. I fell in love with *you*. You called yourself 'just Franny,' but I'll tell you this, she's more than enough woman for me." He grinned. "More than I could have ever dreamed of or hoped for."

Franny smiled at him, but it was weak. His words were reassuring, and yet she still felt the other shoe hadn't quite dropped yet. A breeze stirred the glass-bottle wind chime, but the sound of it seemed more mournful than cheerful.

"What I haven't told you is, when I went outside to say good-bye to my father, he said a few things. A few tragic things that I've not recovered from yet." And then Charlie told Franny his story—all that his father had said to him.

When he finished, Franny just sighed. How heartbreaking, to know that she'd been right about Mr. Landau. His angry scowl from the shadows that night wasn't imagined. He really had disapproved of their relationship. But this . . . His threats against Willie were much more disturbing. "I can hardly believe that your father would do such a thing as threaten to put Willie away. It's horrible. What you've told me can't be legal. Surely not."

"It shouldn't be, but my father has the best attorney in the city, and together they've pulled off some things over the years that would be impossible for most people."

"It's dreadful. It grieves me to know that you and your brother grew up with such cruelty. It breaks my heart." Franny rocked in the chair, wishing she could rock away some of her frustration.

"It wasn't always this way. When Mom was alive, we had some joy. My father stayed at work and Mom stayed at home with us, making our lives good. We knew she loved us. It was in everything she did for us. But when she died, my father removed everything from the house that

283

reminded him of her life with us—photos, clothes, even the little treasures she'd collected over the years. Whatever was a comfort to us became a torture to my father."

Charlie slid his hands back and forth along the wooden arms. "He never treated Mom well through the years. At least, that was my impression as a child. Perhaps this purging of her belongings came out of guilt, I don't know. Willie and I did everything we could to keep her memory alive, but it was hard at times. I have a few photos of her, but she's already faded in my mind."

Franny reached out and touched Charlie's hand. "I'm so sorry. This is all so terrible. Your family should have been able to mourn together, but you and your brother were denied even that." She tried to take it all in. "And now this. I want you to know that I will never ask you to do anything that might make your father follow through with his threat. I could never live with myself if something like that happened. How could we have joy when your brother was being tormented?"

"Thank you, Franny, for saying that."

Another breeze rustled the chime. Franny rocked quietly, thinking, wishing life wasn't the way it was but instead more like heaven. "I really did enjoy meeting your brother. It startled me at first to see him because he looks so much like you, even more than the photo."

"Except I've always been the handsome one, of course." Charlie grinned.

"Yes, so true."

Charlie lost his jesting demeanor as he rocked back and forth in the chair. "When I first saw Willie up on the ridge, I was amazed to see him so well. I couldn't stand for my father to destroy that, but he's placed me in an impossible situation." He looked up into the elms and then back at her. "And yet somehow I believe God will come to our rescue. I'm going to hold on to that hope."

He tugged on her sleeve. "When you told the sheriff that you were just staying out here long enough to teach me how to farm . . . I understand why you said it. You'd already sensed that something had changed between us. Something that wasn't as it should be. But please don't leave me yet. Will you wait with me a little while longer? At least until Christmas?"

"To live so near you and to never be . . ." *To never marry the one I love would be unbearable.* Franny wasn't sure how to answer him, but in the end she nodded. "I do love you, and I will wait. That is, until God tells me it's time to go."

Charlie squeezed her hand.

The sound of her words ripped at her spirit until she could no longer look at him.

CHAPTER FORTY-FOUR

Later that Sunday afternoon Franny stood alone in front of her momma's dressing table, staring at a photograph of her parents on their wedding day. They were so blissful-looking, their eyes telling their story of affection and wistful expectations for the future. She didn't go into her parents' room very often. Sometimes it felt more painful than soothing to be there, so most of the time she just avoided the room altogether.

But suddenly, in the light of what Charlie had said, she felt thankful to have so many things around her that reminded her of her parents. She was grateful that her grieving hadn't been given unnatural restraints. It was right and good to acknowledge all the many facets of her loss—the joy, the angst-filled moments, and the many ways her parents loved their way through life.

Franny opened the top drawer of the dressing table and lifted out her momma's white gloves— the ones she'd always worn to church on Sunday mornings. She brushed the soft fabric against her cheek. The material had gone yellow with age, but the gloves still held the powdery scent that she remembered about her mother. Franny slipped the gloves on and wiggled her fingers. Too big. They always were. She looked at herself in the large, round mirror and touched her reflection. "Momma, how I wish this were your reflection and not mine. I wish I could talk to you about what's happening to me. I miss all our . . ." Her voice faded as her spirit swelled with emotion.

She sighed. "Another Christmas without you both." And Franny missed their many family traditions, especially the caroling. They would bundle up, drive into town, and go from house to house, singing all the most popular carols. People had loved it. Some handed them homemade popcorn balls. Boy, how she'd grown to hate popcorn balls. Franny released a half sob, half laugh. At the time, she'd had no idea how precious those memories would become. *I miss you both so much.*

Franny sat down on the velvet stool and, after returning the gloves to the drawer, went through some of the other keepsakes—a compact, a rhinestonc barrette, a pair of spectacles, a Bulova watch that still worked, and her momma's Bible, which was frayed around the edges . . . probably from looking up verses to deal with a teenager who grew more indcpendent by the day!

She smiled and opened the Bible to Psalms, the book where her mother had tucked away some of the tiny blossoms she'd given her when she was little. The buttercup petals were translucent now, but they were still bright with memory. Franny had loved the way her mother's face lit up when she picked them in the field and handed them to her. She'd acted as if they were the finest of store-bought flowers.

"Momma, I hope I said the important things, everything you wanted to hear from a daughter. I hope that, at least for a little while, I brought you both as much joy as you gave me. And I hope I said 'I love you' enough."

How strange, that after growing up and finally learning the meaning and importance of love, she would come face-to-face with a merciless ultimatum from a man who seemed determined to destroy it.

Franny placed all the family treasures back in the drawer. Her plan had been to give the mementoes to her children someday so they'd know something about their grandparents—how generous and fine they were. How they lived their lives for others and for the pleasure of the Almighty. It would become her life prayer as well, even if it meant giving up the one thing on earth she loved most.

Charlie.

Franny picked up her momma's wedding-ring box, cracked open the velvet container, and fingered the gold band with the tiny diamond perched on top. She would carry her desire for marriage and children the rest of her life—and yet she feared it was now no more than that, a dream. She put the ring back in the box and shut the drawer a little too loudly.

Her mouth was pink from twisting her lips with her fingers. A tear fell without permission, and then a few more came, leaving wet trails down her cheeks. How could joy turn into sorrow so quickly? *Oh, God, this world is as sure and steady as an earthquake. Why does it have to be so unpredictable and frightening?* She plucked at some loose threads on the chair.

The house felt cold and empty. Maybe she should stand over the floor furnace to take off the chill. Or maybe she should think about rekindling some of her old friendships. Or hunt down her dear old Aunt Beatrice. Since she'd farmed all by herself over the years, it had become easy to neglect things—neglect people.

Franny started to hum, since humming warmed her.

Someone in the house stirred. Henry had just eaten and fallen asleep. Charlie was outside feeding the animals, and Willie had gone out to help. Noma must have come in from her hike along the creek. So much had happened while Noma was gone. How would she ever tell her all that had transpired? It was a miracle to have Dunlap behind bars, and yet Noma might see the incident as a reason for deep concern—a reason to leave.

The door eased open, and Noma peered inside. "Didn't mean to trouble you. The house was so quiet I got a little worried, wondering where everybody had gone off to. And then I heard some little mouse noises in here."

"I'm the mouse. It's all right. Come in." Franny waved her inside. "Did you enjoy your walk?"

"I did. I sure do enjoy the outdoors around here. I saw the creek and the woods and spotted that cedar you talked about. That'll make a fine Christmas tree. Should reach all the way to the ceiling." Noma rubbed her arms. "But I should have helped Mr. Charlie feed those animals."

"No, he insisted you take every Sunday off. And I do too."

"You're both awfully good to me." Noma glanced around. "So, this was your momma and daddy's room."

"Yes. I was just in here . . . remembering."

"I hope they was good things."

"Yes, mostly." Franny circled her finger in the dust on the top of the dressing table.

"I have those remembering days too."

Franny looked at Noma's reflection in the mirror. "And what do you remember?"

"Oh, hon, all sorts of things. I've been alive a long time, so I have lots of remembering." She shook her finger in the air. "But I will tell you this tale. You might like it. When I was a little gal, my mamma shared the gospel with me. She said to me on our porch swing, 'Jesus can wash you white as snow if you just let Him.' After I welcomed the Lord as my Redeemer, I found out my mamma was talking about my soul, not my skin." Noma chuckled. "I have to tell ya, I felt a little hood-winked at the time, but I've lived my life for the Lord a long time, and I know I got the better end of the deal." She let her fingers alight onto Franny's shoulders.

"I like that story."

"I do too. It has a happy ending, and *your* story will also. Keep on staying in the faith and resting in His arms. It's a good place to be. Like I've heard you say, 'God is up to something wonderful.' "

Franny reached up and gave her hand a squeeze. "I'm so glad you're here. I don't know what I'd do without you."

"Well, that is something I do need to talk to you about." Noma looked away toward the window.

"What is it?" *Oh no.* Surely Noma hadn't seen the sheriff's car. Wasn't she out the whole time?

"I saw who all was here," Noma said. "I know you didn't want to tell me, 'cause you knew it would be upsettin'." She pressed her hand along her dress, smoothing it. "Those men, they was here because of me. I don't know the whole story, but I don't need to."

The joy drained right out of Franny. "Oh, Noma. Please know—"

"Shh. It's all right now." She gave Franny's shoulder a pat. "But I came to tell you . . . and it's not easy to say it. Not easy at all. But I'm

291

leaving." Noma clasped her hands together and put them to her lips. "I love this place, so full of peace. And being here with you and helping out and all—the little bit of work I've done has been more joy than I've known in a year. But when I went into town, well, I could tell people was staring. I didn't see hate in their eyes, but I did see fear. And if there's anything I've learned, it's that it don't take long for fear to snake itself into hate."

Noma took out the hankie from her belt and dabbed at her eyes. "You've been kind to me, coming to *my* rescue this time. You welcomed me as a friend, and so did the folks at that sweet little church you took me to. I will never forget the way the pastor's wife hugged me and welcomed me into the fold and even gave me some of her home-made Christmas candy. *But* I don't want to be the one who brings trouble down on this farm, on this land. From what little bits of whisperings I heard in town, you've had more than your share of it over the years."

Franny stood then and embraced Noma. "Please don't go. I beg you. I can't bear to see you go. And I know Charlie has said he's glad for you to stay as long as you want. Consider this farm as your home too." She pulled back to look at Noma. "If you go, it will mean they've won, and God doesn't want them to win. He's on our side. I'm not as brave as I want to be, but together, you and me, we can overcome this. We can make a difference."

The clouds outside the window loosened their hold on the sun, letting the light spill through the thin gray curtains—letting it mingle with every color in the room. Franny stood there with Noma, in that silver haze, in that numinous covering, watching all the colors become one.

"So, what do you think?" Franny breathed a prayer. "Can you stay?"

"Yes." Noma smiled. "Home . . . it's a mighty good place to be."

CHAPTER FORTY-FIVE

Charlie glanced over at Willie, who was gathering eggs and placing them ever-so-gingerly into his wire basket. Trying to keep the conversation light, Charlie said to his brother, "Who would have guessed it a few years ago—us, gathering eggs together."

"This might be an amusing pastime if you didn't have to do it every day." Willie reached underneath one of the chickens to retrieve an egg, but the chicken squawked and pecked at his fingers. He yanked his hand back. "Well, maybe I'd rather paint a still life of eggs than gather them." Willie set his basket down. "I guess there's one thing about this work we're used to."

"What's that?"

"We're used to getting pecked at."

Charlie looked at him and sighed. "True."

"Hey, why do you have music playing for the chickens?"

"Oh. Well, Franny seems to think it keeps the chickens happier, and so they produce more eggs."

"Does it work?"

Charlie shrugged. "Haven't been a farmer long enough to find out for myself. But the music keeps *me* happy."

Willie smiled and then kicked at a pan of oyster shells that Franny kept around for the chickens to eat.

When he didn't pick up his egg basket again, Charlie asked, "Something on your mind?"

"There is, actually."

Charlie stopped his work and waited for his brother to continue.

"Your Franny is an amazing woman."

"Yes, she is."

"You wouldn't want to lose her."

"No, I sure wouldn't." Curious conversation. What was Willie trying to say?

Willie crossed his arms. "I noticed that Franny likes to keep a couple of the windows open a bit."

"Yes, she does, when it's not too cold."

"Well, today," Willie said, "it wasn't all that cold."

An uneasy feeling needled Charlie, prickling his flesh. "What do you mean?"

"Well, voices carry on the breeze." Willie rubbed his forehead. "I'm sorry, Chuck, but I was in the front room looking at Franny's family photographs, and I heard enough of your conversation to know what our father intends to do. I know about the threats. I know what you're hiding from me."

Charlie's fingers lost their grip on the handle and the basket fell, spilling eggs all over the floor.

The chickens wasted no time in scuttling over and gobbling up the gooey debris.

Willie looked at the mess. "Sorry. Guess I startled you."

"They're just eggs. But this is your life we're talking about."

Willie picked up the two eggs that hadn't broken and set them on the windowsill. "I know I'm your little brother, but you're going to do this one thing for me."

"I would do anything for you. You know that."

"Good." Willie dusted off his coat and hands. "Then this shouldn't be a problem."

"What is it?"

"Truth?"

"Yeah, truth."

"I want you to marry Franny," Willie said. "She's going to make a great sister. I've always wanted a sister. Oh, and she'll make you a good wife too. And then you're going to buy that music store so I can take piano lessons."

Charlie frowned. "Let's get out of here. These low ceilings are suffocating and all this dusty air makes my head ache." He headed outside, buttoned his coat, and breathed in the coolness of the evening.

Willie followed him outside. "So, are you going to do this for me?"

"I will not let Father follow through with his plan. You know how he is when he wants something." Charlie shook his hands in the air in utter frustration. "He will go to any length. Any expense. All these years he could have used his money to help the poor, but instead he spends a fortune on attorney fees just to get what he wants when he wants it. Just to prove a point that means nothing! Sorry, I didn't mean to shout."

"Well, Father has a way of doing that to us."

"It's just . . . well, I remember the look in your eyes when you first came home from the institution. You were so full of fear, as if you believed no one was watching out for you. Don't you see? If Father can prove you're a danger to yourself, I'm afraid you might not ever come home again. I will not allow—"

"But you no longer have any say in the matter."

Charlie looked back at him. "What do you mean? What do you intend to do?"

"I'm going to confront Father about this tomorrow, and you're not going to stop me. I'm older now. And I'm healthier than I've ever been." He smiled. "I am determined, Chuck. And no amount of debate or argument or negotiation is going to turn me back."

"No turning you back, eh?"

"Nope."

"You absolutely sure?"

"Yes."

Charlie paused to give it some thought. "All right. But you're not going it alone. If we have to do this, we'll do it together. And if we have to, if Father won't be reasonable, I'll hire our own attorney. But don't go sneaking off in the night on me, like you did when we were kids. We'll do this as brothers, together, or not at all. Agreed?"

Willie put his hands up. "All right. All right. Man, you really do take this big brother thing seriously. But it's all right. You're the only family I've got. Well, that is until you marry Franny." He wiggled his eyebrows.

Charlie shook his head, but he let those words, those hope-filled words, sweep over him. Marrying Franny had seemed impossible, and yet with God . . .

Willie climbed up to the top of the fence and sat down. "You know, when you and Franny faced that sheriff and Dunlap character head-on, well, it was like being inside the clouds of an electrical storm. There were so many sparks in the room, I thought the kitchen would catch on fire. I've not recovered. I never will. Such boldness and bravery and integrity. God was with you two, and He will be with us tomorrow."

Charlie smiled. "You *have* grown up."

"It always helps when there's a girl." Willie jumped down from the fence.

"So, you're dating someone? Who is she?"

"Her name is Veronica. Such a peach. She's compassionate and unique. And of course, she loves art and worships me."

Charlie chuckled. "Comes in handy."

"Father would hate her."

"Most likely. But you'll have *my* blessing."

"And that's the one that counts." Willie slapped Charlie on the back. "Funny how women have this way of turning boys into dragon slayers."

Charlie thought about it for a moment. "No truer statement has ever been uttered." He wiped his hands on his overalls.

"What's all over your hands?"

"Around here, you never know." Charlie chuckled.

"And what's that smell in the air?"

"The smell of money. Actually, it's the ripe and aromatic scent of manure. Everything has an odor here. You get used to it. Listen, I need to check on the cattle. Want to go with me?"

"Sure." Willie straddled an old bicycle that had been leaning against an elm tree and rode it in circles around him like he had when they were kids. "One last thing."

"Yeah?"

"As you know, these threats from our father . . . they're not new. They've just never been this dramatic. Remember when we were kids, when he told us one day he would give that infernal spyglass to the son who pleased him the most?" Willie stopped riding. "I mean, what kind of a father would *do* that? Pit us against each other to compete for his love. Thank God we were both smart enough to love each other more than a trinket or play his heartless game. In the end he never did give either one of us the stupid thing, which is the only blessing in all this. The spyglass is still sitting on his desk, covered in dust. Just where it belongs."

Charlie looked at his brother. "Yeah, I remember. I tried to forget about it but never did, totally. And he wanted it that way. Always haunting us. He must have thought that if he could drive a wedge between us, then he would gain even more control. Thank God that part of his plan didn't work."

"We should have talked more over the years. Too much was left unsaid. Things *I* should have said. It was my responsibility as the oldest to protect you. To make sure Father didn't get the upper—"

"No reason for any guilt, man. Father gave us enough to last a lifetime. Hey, why don't we go inside and eat? Is Franny going to offer us some of those biscuits I saw on the counter? They'd be pretty groovy with some homemade jam. Right?"

Charlie laughed. "Maybe. If you wipe your feet. But we still have to check on the cattle."

"Man, this farm thing is relentless, isn't it?"

"Yeah, pretty relentless."

"Surely you'll get Christmas day off, right?" Willie asked.

"Not the whole day. Unfortunately, animals aren't like a product you can store on a shelf . . . they like to eat every day, just like we do."

Willie grinned, but his attention seemed to be pulled elsewhere.

"What's the matter?"

"Look over there." Willie pointed to one of the hog pens. "My guess is that those pigs over there aren't supposed to be having a party *outside* the fence."

CHAPTER FORTY-SIX

The next morning, after a strenuous evening of convincing a herd of pigs that they would be happier *inside* the pen, Franny felt bleary-eyed and spent. She put the last of the breakfast dishes away while Noma hung the clothes out on the line.

Franny knew the real reason she felt drained— it was knowing that Charlie and Willie were minutes away from leaving the farm to meet with their father, a meeting that could end in great joy or great sorrow. She'd given Charlie her full support when he told her about the decision they'd made to confront Mr. Landau, and yet there was an equal amount of fear for what might happen to Charlie's brother after such a verbal skirmish. The whole affair might end badly. The two young men might sever their ties with their father. To lose one's family was always a distressing thing, even if the family member wasn't acting like family.

Franny closed the cabinets and hung the tea towel over the sink. Amid the doubts of the day, though, was the prospect that Charlie might finally be free from his father's tyrannical controls, which also meant he would be free to marry.

Charlie stepped into the kitchen all dressed up and ready to drive to the city. "It's time, Franny. We're leaving now. Willie is already in the car waiting. He's anxious to see this through. By the way, if it doesn't go well, Willie might need to stay here for a while. He can continue to sleep in the extra rollaway in the apartment, but I wanted to ask you first."

"Willie is always welcome here. It's *your* farm."

Charlie walked over to her and took her hands in his. "It is for now, but I'm hoping everything will change today."

"I hope your father will see the error of his

ways, but I also hope God will somehow keep your family from breaking into pieces."

He lifted her hands to his lips and kissed them.

"Are you sure you don't want me to go with you? I could be your silent cheerleader."

Charlie grinned.

"You're right." Franny nodded and smiled. "There's no way I can be a *silent* cheerleader."

"I don't want you to change a thing about yourself, Franny, but this is one battle I have to fight alone. Or at least by my brother's side. I'm sure you understand."

"I do."

"But I'm glad you'll be waiting for me when I get back tonight." Charlie gave her a lingering kiss.

When they came up for air, she smiled, wishing they were already married. "I'll walk you to the car." She took off her apron, slipped on a jacket, and followed him outside.

They said their good-byes, which included a brief but promising kiss.

Willie was hunkered down in the passenger seat of Charlie's Rolls, looking more serious than she'd seen him since he arrived. Franny's heart went out to him, to them both. How could a father do this, force such a dreadful day on his own flesh and blood?

Noma came over from the clothesline and waved. "You two be careful. We'll be praying."

"Thanks, Noma."

Just as Charlie eased into the driver's seat, Franny's attention got redirected. A car motored up the road, and the vehicle looked a lot like Mr. Landau's Bentley.

Franny's stomach took a dive as if she were on one of the rollercoaster rides at the state fair. "Charlie, I think your father's coming up the road." *Oh dear.* She would get tangled in the conflict after all, but perhaps he still wanted to fight this one alone. She stood there in a fit of indecision, not knowing whether to stay or to go.

Charlie got out of the car. "It *is* Father. I wonder why he came back. Must have noticed that Willie was gone."

"Surely he's not here." Willie stumbled out of the car and then looked toward the lane. His hands twisted as if he were in physical pain. "Guess he came to check up on me. What do you bet he's not in a good mood?" He tried to laugh, but it came out as a cough.

Franny joined Noma and circled her arm through hers. When Charlie glanced back at her, he nodded, which seemed to welcome their presence. They would both stay, then. Franny just wished she'd worn better clothes, instead of a faded housedress.

The Bentley pulled up in front of them and stopped. Mr. Landau seemed surprised as he stared at the crowd, who must have looked as though they'd gathered to welcome him. Little did he know.

Charlie opened the car door. "Father?"

"Charles." Mr. Landau got out, made a frowning nod toward Franny and Noma, and then turned his attention to his other son. "William, what are you doing here?"

"I'm a guest here . . . a *welcomed* one." Willie shifted back and forth on his feet. "How did you know I was here?"

"The maid told me."

"Matilda never could keep a secret," Willie murmured.

"Never mind about Matilda. She was just helping me since I got worried about you."

"Worried, Father?"

"Yes, of course I was worried."

"It's good that you've come, actually," Charlie said. "We were about to drive into the city to talk to you. We have something important we need to discuss."

"Perhaps we should talk in private." Mr. Landau pointed to the house.

"No." Charlie crossed his arms. "Right here. Now." He glanced around him. "Everybody, please stay."

Franny could feel her heartbeat wanting to pound itself right out of her chest. Noma bowed her head.

"Let's get right to it," Charlie said. "Willie knows about your ultimatum."

"What? You told him?" Mr. Landau asked.

"No," Charlie said. "He accidentally overheard me talking to Franny."

"You fool." His father shook his head as if in disgust.

"How can that be, Father? I'm not the one who's making coldhearted threats against one of his own sons. Dogs treat their offspring better than you do."

Willie coughed and held his stomach as if he might be ill.

Even from a distance Franny could see the red mark on Mr. Landau's face deepen into bright scarlet.

"Charles, I will not be spoken to in such a manner. Do you hear me?"

"I don't want to speak to you this way. I've never wanted to. It feels disrespectful." He glanced at Willie. "You've left us no choice. All we've ever wanted to do was please you. And it's nearly destroyed us. Instead of raising self-sufficient men, you've kept us as schoolboys who cower in your presence. We've been reduced to begging for crumbs at your table, waiting for you to toss us a kind word. Not love, of course; we gave up on that long ago when Mom died. But I know—"

"Do *not* bring your mother into this discussion!"

305

Franny startled at Mr. Landau's sharp tone.

"Why not?" Charlie asked his father. "We loved her, and she loved us. When she was alive, there was kindness and affection in our house. She made it a real home. And there was understanding and enthusiasm for our dreams. That is, what God called us to do. What He created us to do. Don't you remember how things were? Even a little?"

"Not anymore." Mr. Landau pulled on the ends of his vest. "Her memory is gone from me, and no amount of pining is going to bring her back. So, like any smart businessman, I cut my losses and moved on."

Charlie's hands shot upward. "She was your wife, not an investment!"

Franny moved her fingers over her lips as a reminder to remain silent. *Oh, God, please keep everyone safe, and help me to stay in the shadows of this quarrel.*

Mr. Landau pointed his finger in the air. "How dare you—"

"All these years I've said very little," Charlie said, "but I know the truth about what happened to Mom."

"What are you talking about?"

"I knew why she died. She got trampled by the verbal beatings and the petty demands. She could no longer take the abuse. She died of a broken heart, because she could no longer withstand living in such oppression."

"That's a lie! You're accusing me of scandalous things. Your mother had a weak heart, and you know it."

"Yes, she had that too," Charlie said. "But she also had a big heart. And a lot of love for her whole family . . . including you."

"Love is a precarious word." Mr. Landau glanced at Franny and then back at Charlie. "I refuse to toss out that word like the younger generation does. People say it, but most of the time I don't think they really mean it. One minute they'll smother you with their maudlin affections, and the next minute they'll be cackling behind your back. You can't—"

"Better to try and fail at love than to spend your life forever holding back. And that's what you've done." Charlie took in a deep breath as if to calm himself.

"Charlie and I must mean nothing to you," Willie said quietly, as if to himself.

"Another lie. I just don't express my feelings as your mother did. But my ways of caring are shown best in things that are tangible, quantifiable . . . concrete. That's what I've created for you both. And what you both have thrown back in my face."

Charlie looked toward the heavens and then at his father. "We do appreciate your hard work. We've always admired it, in fact. To the point that we've come close to sacrificing our

307

ambitions for it. But we can't live your life. God didn't set it up that way. We love you, Dad, but you have to let us go."

Mr. Landau stepped backward as if he'd lost his balance. "You've never once called me by that name. Why would you use the term now?"

CHAPTER FORTY-SEVEN

"I don't know." Charlie wasn't sure why he'd called his father by such an intimate word. It felt out of place during such a heated discussion. He'd never even called his father by that affectionate name when they were being civil . . . but somewhere in his father's wild-eyed declarations he was reminded of Dunlap, and he couldn't endure watching his own father's spitefulness spiral into evil. "I'm not sure why I called you *Dad*. Maybe I thought you needed to hear it today." He glanced over at Franny, who was still standing with Noma and still lifting him up in love.

"My father never allowed me to call him that, even though I asked . . . even though I begged," he murmured. As he settled a bit—or perhaps reloaded for another round—his father's gaze swept across each of them as if he were in the midst of an awakening, as if what he saw reflected in their eyes seemed terribly disturbing to him.

"Why are you all looking at me that way?" He scraped his fingers back and forth across his beard. "Why?"

For the first time, Charlie saw a glimmer in his father's eyes, of recognition, perhaps, of all that he'd become—a lost and bitter man.

After a moment or two, which felt more like an eternity, his father eased himself downward and sat in the dirt.

"Are you all right?" It had to be one of the most extraordinary things Charlie had ever seen. His father had always been meticulous with his clothes, and he hated anything soiled. Charlie glanced at Willie, who appeared to be as bewildered as he felt.

"Sir?" Willie just stared at their father, looking unnerved.

"I haven't been all right in a long time." He leaned against the car from his place on the ground and donned a vacant expression. "I have a story to tell if anyone wants to hear it."

Slowly everyone moved closer to him.

His father wrapped his hands around his knees, his fine shoes and pants now covered with fine red dust. He didn't seem to notice or care about the mess. After a few moments, he said, "I was eighteen and a violinist. My father, *your* grandfather Landau, hated the fact that I'd become a musician. He demanded I quit. But I had a teacher at school who knew of my situation. His name was Nelson Wimberley. Haven't thought of his name in ages. Anyway, Wimberley knew how much I loved the violin, and so against my father's wishes, he continued with my lessons at no charge."

"What happened?" Willie asked.

His father patted his hands against the dust. "Well, one day my father heard me playing in the conservatory. By then I had greatly improved. He seemed proud of me and even asked me to play for a function at his country club. So, fool that I was and eager to please my father, I agreed to it." He released a mirthless chuckle. "At the time, it felt like the happiest moment of my life, to think that my father wanted me to play for his friends."

For a brief moment his father cocked his head and positioned his hands as if holding a violin under his chin. "But when I attended my father's event and walked across the stage, I tripped on a loose board. I was overweight at the time, and when I fell on my violin . . . well, it broke. So easily. *Too* easily. And then my father did something that became impossible to forgive. He laughed. He laughed so loudly, in fact, that everyone could hear him. Then his laughter seemed to open the floodgates, giving everyone permission to laugh. And they did. I pretended not to care. I even chuckled along with them. But inside . . . I died."

He picked up a loose nail in the dirt and brushed

his thumb against its rusty point. "I never played the violin again. I felt so mortified, so disgraced, that I decided I would pursue a profession that would garner only respect. I made a promise to myself that no one would ever laugh at me again. And no one would laugh at my children—even if I had to force them into professions against their wills for their own good. I knew someday you both would be grateful. Because to be uneasy in one's profession can be tolerated, but to be laughed at is unendurable."

His father dropped the nail into the dust. "And since you know the truth about that, you should also know . . . this mark on my face isn't a birthmark." He touched the red stain on his cheek. "I've lied about it all these years. It's really a scar, and it came from injuring myself when I fell on the violin. This wound . . . it's all I have left of my music." No tears came, but his father took on a desolate look, his eyes hollow with regret and sorrow. "I'm sorry . . . for everything."

Without even looking at each other or giving a sign of what to do, Charlie and Willie went over to their father and sat on either side of him there on the ground. The three of them said nothing more. It was enough to be together, to let the miracle of understanding and forgiveness wash over them all.

Charlie looked toward Franny. Smiling, she and Noma walked back toward the house.

His father tapped his finger against his lips. "I think it was Victor de LaPrade who once said, 'It is incontestable that music induces in us a sense of the infinite and the contemplation of the invisible.' " He looked up. "In my revenge, I'd forgotten not only the music, but I'd left God behind as well. Music was a good friend to me in spite of my father. And God was always a good friend to me even though I abandoned Him."

Charlie gazed across his father over at Willie, who nodded, tears filling his eyes. He could tell that his brother was moved and profoundly grateful for the reunion, but perhaps he was also a little embarrassed that he hadn't participated in the discussion. Someday he would tell Willie that he'd needed an opportunity to do right by his brother. And God had given him the chance.

Charlie sighed, a soul-relieving kind of sigh. The three of them remained sitting there, quietly resting against the car, while Charlie processed his father's revelations. He'd never imagined that his father had been hiding such a traumatic story from his youth.

But Franny had been right. She had gotten close to guessing the problem when he'd been blinded to it. His father had said little about their deceased grandfather Landau over the years. They'd not known of his cruelty toward their own father. It would have been hard, no doubt, to grow up that way, to break free from such a vicious generational pattern. Right then Charlie made a promise to himself and to God that even if the temptation ever presented itself to fall back on his father's manner of child rearing, he would not give in. No more would their family's history be to inflict emotional wounds on their beloved. He would raise his children to know the Lord and to know that they were valued and loved. And they'd be free to become whatever God created them to be.

Charlie draped his arms around his knees, still thinking how amazing it must appear for the presumed pillars of the Oklahoma City community to be sitting together in the dirt. The newspapers would love every speck of it, and the photographs would be a sensation. But if someone asked him about it, he'd tell them how wonderful it felt.

His father looked at Willie. "I guess I should confess something else while I'm at it. I wasn't really going to put you in that institution for good. It was just leverage, but now, well, I see it for what it was."

After a moment, Willie said, "I forgive you."

Must have been hard for his brother to say those three words, considering what he'd been through, but it was the right thing to do. And it was pure relief to Charlie to hear his father admit that it wasn't in his heart to be so cruel.

In the distance, the roar of a bulldozer snatched his attention. Hmm. Guess the insurance company had finally followed through with their promise.

313

Soon the huge machine roared past them like a hungry beast and pulled up in front of what was left of the barn.

When his father struggled a bit to get to his feet, Charlie and his brother helped him up.

"So, you're going to get that new barn." His dad smiled, and Charlie couldn't help but think how well he wore the expression.

Hope flowed through Charlie as he dusted himself off. Their first step at a reunion carried a weight—not of anguish but of glory. The moment held an almost prophetic revelation, because Charlie knew their time of reconciliation, their miracle, would have a ripple effect that would not only alter his life but influence the next generations. And in the here and now, he thought of Franny, his Franny, and when the right time might be to propose.

But in the meantime, on the other side of the farmyard, a man cut the engine on the bulldozer, hopped down from his machine, and stared in their direction, looking eager to sweep away all that was old and damaged. Charlie took in a deep breath. A new season had arrived in the Landau family, and it had the feel of Christmas all over it.

His father placed a hand on each of their shoulders and gave them a squeeze. The two brothers embraced their father, and deep inside Charlie's heart, he also embraced healing.

His father took off his jacket and rolled up his

sleeves. "Well, now, guess we'd better go over there and make sure this idiot does a good job," his father said, laughing.

Charlie and his brother laughed along with him. Guess not all of his father's rough edges were worked out—but as they all three headed toward the bulldozer, somewhere in their walk across the farmyard Charlie's father became his dad.

CHAPTER FORTY-EIGHT

On the eve of Christmas, Franny stood at the ridge next to Charlie. They looked out over the canyon together as she pondered the miracles that had brought them there. In fact, Charlie's father had become so merry in spirit and wanted so much to be a part of their lives, it was like living inside the last pages of Dickens's *A Christmas Carol*. Not a bad place to be.

She looked up toward the heavens in grateful response. Yes, God really *was* up to something wonderful.

And Charlie had that look in his eyes—as if he just might propose. If not, she could always pop the question. Women did that sort of thing these days. And yet, if she had her druthers, she really did want to be asked.

Charlie turned toward her. "I guess you know why we're here."

Franny put on her most innocent face. "We're here to celebrate Christmas?"

"Yes, but a bit more than that." He grinned. "You said that your family brought every important event to the ridge."

"Yes, they did. Hey, that would make an interesting song . . . taking it to the ridge."

"I like it." Charlie made a blusterous sound and tightened the woolen scarf around his neck. "Here, allow me." He buttoned Franny's coat. "It's getting colder by the minute out here."

The clouds had darkened and the air had indeed turned chilly, but it was far from what Franny felt inside. She fluffed her hair, but it did no good at all since the wind just whipped it wild again. It was a moment she'd dreamed of since she was a little girl, and she wanted to look just right—and for once, just once, she didn't want to look any-thing like a farmer—and yet here she stood. Just Franny.

"Why do you keep fidgeting with your hair?"

"I want to look right for this moment, but I still look like a farmer. I couldn't even get the dirt out from under my fingernails." Franny blew her bangs off her forehead.

Charlie took her hands into his, glanced at her nails, and then kissed her hands. "I don't care about the dirt."

"You don't?"

"Nope. We're going to have dirt under our fingernails for a lifetime."

"And music in our hearts?"

Charlie nodded. "That's right."

"Then I'm ready whenever you are."

"I've been ready since the day I met you, ever since that day I let you fall into the mud."

"And you so gallantly rescued my radio," Franny said with a deep Southern drawl.

Charlie touched her chin with the tip of his finger, and she went quiet.

"Franny girl?"

"Yes, Charlie boy?"

"Will you be my wife?"

Franny whispered in his ear, "I think that can be arranged."

Charlie leaned in for what Franny knew would be a very good kiss, but just before their lips met, he asked, "Most women want a big wedding. What do you want?"

"How about an intimate ceremony and we say 'I do' right here? Just family and a few friends. If that's okay." And Franny certainly wouldn't forget to invite Aunt Bee. What a joy it had been to find her still living in the city only a few blocks away from her old house.

"Then I shall build you a big gazebo, right here, just for the wedding."

"You'll build me a gazebo? Really?" Franny bounced on her toes.

"Well, I'll hire someone to do it."

"Have I told you lately that you're my hero?"

"Yes." Charlie smiled. "But you're more than welcome to say it again."

Franny gave Charlie a shove . . . but only a petite one.

And then, as if someone had signaled the realms of glory for a little ambiance, one by one snowflakes fell from the sky. "Snow." She leaned into his arms as he closed them around her. "Merry Christmas, Charlie."

"Merry Christmas, Franny."

The confetti flurries soon became a cascade, surrounding them in light. There in his arms, she could imagine their lives through the years—sitting on the back porch, holding hands, growing old together. And during the holidays—especially when "Have Yourself a Merry Little Christmas" was playing on the radio—Franny would remember the day when God brought a city boy named Charlie out to meet his farmer gal—so they could sing out their lives together. Maybe not always in perfect harmony, but always in love.

Guideposts magazine and the devotional book
Daily Guideposts are available in large print
editions by contacting:

Guideposts
Attn: Customer Service
P.O. Box 5815
Harlan, Iowa 51593

(800) 932-2145
or
Guideposts.org

Center Point Large Print
600 Brooks Road / PO Box 1
Thorndike, ME 04986-0001 USA

(207) 568-3717

US & Canada:
1 800 929-9108
www.centerpointlargeprint.com